Bob and Brigit, a Canadian couple, have managed to screw up their previously successful lives when a wild investment in GoldRush, a mining company, lands the family in deep debt. Brigit is a heroine through it all, we might say a heroine-martyr. The debt paid off. Church-going Brigit persuades Bob they need to hike the Camino de Santiago, the ancient pilgrim trail through northern Spain. Bob is all up for some European sophistication and good times. Grand idea, but life and the Camino seem to have other plans and adventures for them. Adding to the sleepless nights in hostels, blisters and a disappearing backpack, old and new secrets come to light.

There is energy and humour, and lessons learnt, often in unexpected ways, from other pilgrims, local people, hostel volunteers, monks, nuns and history. Pardon my Camino is a thoughtful and humorous, better-late-than-never coming-of-age story. This tale will keep you laughing, concerned, engaged, entertained and carry you off on an adventure in Spain to follow the trail.

PARDON MY CAMINO

A Tale of All That Can Go Right and Astray on the
Camino de Santiago de Compostela

A Novel by Julia Sargeaunt

PARDON MY CAMINO

Table of Contents

1. The Teacher's Tale

Brigit dismissed a twinge of guilt at the idea that she was hacking into her husband's airline rewards account. True, with his work travel it was in his name, but really, they shared it. *B&BgoWest.* "Yes! That was the password". She tossed back her hair and squared her shoulders. It was no big deal; she just had to check their points. "Well, look at that: enough for tickets to Spain."

She needed all her ducks in a row for this project—first step: get Bob on board. It was a perfect plan for both of them. Brigit thought back on all the travel they used to do: camping with the kids in Canada and the States, adventures in Europe with their French friends. All this had changed five years ago—with a crash when they had landed in deep money trouble with a large debt.

Brigit taught at a suburban high school and most evenings she was home before Bob. It was time to get going and into the kitchen. Her dear kitchen, maybe looking somewhat staid, no stainless-steel appliances or marble countertops. It had been touch and go with the money mess; however, they had managed to keep their house—and her kitchen.

"I see you put the car away. You are home this evening? That's a nice change!" Bob said as he came into the kitchen.

'Oh shit,' thought Brigit. 'Not such a good start.' But she took the high road, and gave him a welcome-home kiss, which he had the grace to return. "It's Friday. They don't usually have school events scheduled." It was a weak explanation, but it would do to let them start again for their evening at home.

"What's a-cookin'? Smells good."

"Lasagne. Your favourite."

Bob inspected the collection of bowls and the casserole dish on the kitchen counter. "And you're following the recipe!"

Brigit found it a pain getting all those layers in the right order.

"Yes, so go and change and let me concentrate. Then I can put it in the oven."

Out of his suit and into jeans and a flannel shirt, he was back in the kitchen. "Don out this evening? Just the two of us? I'll set the table." Don was the youngest of their three children.

"Yes, Friday night, out with his chums. I have the table ready in the dining room."

"Oh, we have guests?" Bob asked.

"No, I just thought it would be nice."

"I'll choose a suitable wine then."

"How about that red Spanish one?" Brigit suggested.

Chapter 1

"The Rioja? I thought you might like something Italian. Not like you to want to choose the wine. But the Rioja's good."

Brigit was well aware that her approach was not very subtle: the lasagne, candles, the best wine glasses, but this was the moment to convince Bob about Spain.

"This is lovely, darling. Something special on your mind?" Bob liked to be proactive when it came to surprises.

"I hope it's what WE will be planning."

"Okay…and?"

Brigit set down her wine glass and shifted to face Bob. "It's Spain, the Camino, the pilgrim trail. You know how we keep hearing all about it: that documentary and the article in the travel section in the *Citizen*."

"Guess you discuss it at church. What about it?"

"I think we should do it."

"Together? It's a pilgrimage? Religion is more your department," said Bob.

"That's the great thing about it. I can do it as a pilgrimage, and you can do it as a hike; we can both do it as travellers to Spain. Not tourists, it's more than that. More like being a local."

"Why don't you do it with some church friends? You would enjoy that."

"No, darling. It's really important that we do this together."

"Why all of a sudden? Where did this come from?" Bob asked

"It's fascinating, don't you think? And we both need to get away, have a real break. We haven't been able to do that for years."

Bob sat back. "You can't say that. Our trips out west have been great. Are you saying the Rockies haven't been a good time? And here in the city, weekends we go out to Liz at the farm."

She felt the wave of claustrophobia hemming her in again. Of course she loved her family and spending time with them. But now it was urgent to break out, to breathe, to see new horizons. She took a deep breath. "Bob, we can do it now. We have been working so hard and had no holiday abroad for such ages. We are in our fifties, and we have to seriously get back to living."

Bob looked at her with horror. "Really! Then, let's hear your idea. I'm always up for a trip to Europe, but Brigit, why would we do this? If you think we can manage a trip to Europe, which I don't, let's do something worthwhile, like visit Berlin or Prague. We can have a great time in those cities and with two weeks, we could see so much. Your pilgrimage idea will take months away. I'm not going to do that. And where do you think the money is going to come from?"

"That's the beauty of this. We can afford it. Just imagine for a moment. We can walk the Spanish bit of the Camino. It's a big chunk—eight hundred kilometres right across northern Spain to the city of Santiago de Compostela, the historic and important pilgrimage site, with the cathedral and the tomb of St. James. There are hostels along the way

4

where we can stay for just a few Euro. The local restaurants do simple meals for pilgrims. It's really reasonable cost-wise. And we're walking, so there's no transportation to pay for."

"We still need equipment and airfare," said Bob.

"Yes, and of course we need time to get organized, the money, a bit of extra time off work. But we have our boots, and we do need to find the right backpacks. As for the airfare, we can use points."

"Points! We save those to go to Alberta."

"No. That's what we have been forced to use them for because it's a cheap holiday going to your family in Calgary. We've just been stuck not going anywhere else."

"How can you say that? That's ungrateful when we have been welcomed by my family and had good times in the mountains. You say family ties are important."

"This isn't about gratitude or not appreciating family. This is different. It's for you and me. Those family times will still be there. Please, you know we can do more, go further, have loving fun again."

Bob took her hand. "Brigit, let's just focus on getting back to life as it was before, before the money upset. You're in a great rush here. I don't think you have thought this through."

Brigit snatched her hand away. "I have so thought this through. You're the one who needs to think it through. You used to be up for new ideas and adventures. That was the man I married. What has happened to him? I'm telling you we have to do this. Otherwise what's the point of being together?"

"Whoa, I don't think you mean that. How can you talk like that?"

As Brigit sat alone at the table, she thought how grim these last years had been, paying back the money. But they had, and there had been forgiveness. She had been heroic about it all, putting in extra work, and so had the rest of the family.

Later, Brigit found Bob stretched out on the sofa in the living room reading. He didn't move to make room for her, so she sat on the armrest. "I know this seems sudden for you, but I have thought about it a lot. And we wouldn't be away for months. Seven weeks would be enough. And you would love it: all that history, the buildings, the ancient trail, and the other pilgrims from all over, especially Europe." Bob sat up and she moved down next to him. "Please think about it," she said.

****

When Brigit got back from church on Sunday, Bob was checking the pressure on their bike tires. "Ready for a ride?" he asked. They took the trail along the Ottawa River. At a lookout point, they stopped and leant on the rail to watch the water breaking into constant waves over the shallows.

"Have you thought any more about my trip idea?" asked Brigit.

Bob turned to face her. "I still don't see why we need to do this. Why the Camino? Is it a religious thing for you? You could go on another retreat. You don't need me along for that."

"But I want you along," said Brigit. "You know how important my faith is for me. You always support me, but you don't share it. I have never expected you to. But this would let us both experience this—the endeavour, the joy, the love, in our different ways and together."

"Does it need to be the Camino?" Bob asked.

"It would give us distance, and the space and time. And with all we've been through with the debt and working to pay it back, we need to take care of our relationship. Do a reset."

"What does that mean, a reset? Look how strong our relationship is. How we have weathered these last years," said Bob.

"It would give us time to get to know ourselves and each other better."

Bob gave a laugh. "If there's one thing we are good at after all these years of marriage, it's knowing each other."

"I don't think we've been keeping up with each other very well. I don't see our relationship strong like it used to be. I've got my part in that too. I haven't been very caring, and I've been distant with you this last while, spending time away from the house. I don't like that version of me."

Bob met her eyes and took her hand. "Do you really feel that? Like we're in trouble."

"I do. It scares me. Please, Bob. Do this for me."

He put his arms around her. "Okay. Now you're scaring *me*. If that's how you really feel, let's see if we could make this Camino thing happen."

****

Bob rarely left the office before six-thirty, so in late February it was already dark as he took off for home striding along the path by the Rideau Canal. He headed up a major division in his government ministry that dealt with international trade. He found the work exhilarating: negotiating treaties that took years of meticulous detail and diplomacy, then in contrast, the urgent pressure to deal with sudden trade sanctions and tariff barriers. As international trade was a tool of modern warfare, these came with scant warning. It was all political, but Bob was very aware of how these sanctions could ambush the lives of many people trying to earn a living and businesses trying to survive.

He glanced at the skaters on the frozen canal picking one to pace himself against as he walked. This walking home was a recent routine, part of his training for the Camino. Once the two of them had made the decision, Bob got deep into the project. The preparations had been a whole enterprise: meetings of the Ottawa pilgrims' group, Sunday afternoons devoted to hikes with their packs, research on what gear to take, Spanish language evening classes, and planning the route.

Chapter 1

"Bob, we don't need every day and every night all decided ahead of time. We will just walk along and see where we are. That's the spirit of the Camino."

"We only have the seven weeks, so let's make sure we get it all scheduled."

****

"Door bell!" Bob called out. "Can you get it?"

"On my way." Brigit went to the door. A young woman was holding an overflowing arrangement of large blooms and greenery in a vase, the whole edifice shrouded in cellophane with a bow and a card.

"What is this? I think you have the wrong address."

The delivery woman looked at her phone: "Mrs. Brigit Matthews?"

Brigit gazed in fascination at this flashy mass of extravagance.

"They can't be for me. We are due at the airport this afternoon for a plane to Europe." Brigit had a vision of arriving at airport security holding this forest of vegetation. "They can't possibly be for me!" She gave a nervous giggle.

The delivery woman was pushing the whole assemblage at her. "Well, it's yours. Better not miss your plane!"

Brigit mechanically took the flowers, almost dropping them under the awkward weight. She wanted to refuse them. Could she pretend she was someone else? She had a horrible idea of what this could be about. The 'Bon Voyage'

card confirmed it: *To Bob and Brigit. Have a fantastic trip. Earl.*
Was this a loving gift or a prank? Bob must not see them. She
was not about to start explaining this whole thing to him
now. She needed to get rid of them— just so wasteful and
wanton, but there was no choice; she had to get them out of
sight and fast.

"What is it, darling? Who was it?" Bob called from
upstairs.

"Yes, all okay. Just the wrong house."

'Come on. Think!' She scooped it up, the cellophane
screaming in protest and headed for the back door, the
towering mass blocking her as she struggled to reach the
handle to get out to the garbage bins. "Oh give me a break!"
The vase was recyclable; the whole thing could get rejected
if she put it in with the vegetation. She opened the compost
bin, tipped the flowers in, upside down, wrenched off the
cellophane, hauled the glass vase out and stuffed them in the
blue bin. The flowers stalks reared up; she rammed them
down.

"Brigit, what are you doing?" Bob was at the back door.

"Just a bit of last minute clearing up and garbage."

"I'll get the rest."

"It's fine. I've got it! You check the thermostat settings.
'Just keep Bob away from the garbage bins.'

Chapter 1

****

It was the end of April and six months since Brigit had put forward the Camino idea. As they left Ottawa, the Canadian winter was ending in a messy, melting pile of grey snow. Brigit finally began to feel a lightness; she was into the great blue sky over the Atlantic Ocean. She gave a little prayer: "thank you that it has all worked out and we are on our way." And this took her back to thinking of the last years—her anger and bitterness over the money, anger with Bob for that, and how it had brought out a new side of her that left her unsettled and disconcerted. Doing this pilgrimage would put all that behind them. They would atone for their sins and bad behaviour.

2. She'll Be Coming 'Round the Mountain

"What a crowd," said Brigit, "I had imagined just a few locals with their market shopping." As Bob looked out the window, he could see the mountains coming into view. They were on a local train with other pilgrims and on their way to St-Jean-Pied-de-Port, a small town right on the French side of the border with Spain in the Pyrenees Mountains. A cavalcade of boots and poles clicked along the platform as they got off the train in St-Jean.

"Just as well we booked our hostel," said Brigit. "But we are actually here!" They stopped and looked around at the mountains, the little town, and the old stone buildings. They found their way up the steep cobblestone streets to the hostel. One of the owners welcomed them and pointed to their reserved bunks in the roomy dormitory. "We eat at seven. Listen for the bell."

"I love this place! Such a relief to be here," said Brigit taking in the pleasant room.

"Good choice of hostel," Bob agreed.

Supper was served at a long table in the narrow backyard. There were about twenty of them from various countries: Germany, a guy from the US, someone from England, two from Sweden. Bob and Brigit sat at one end with a Dutch couple. Most were starting their pilgrimage the next day, but a few had already been walking the trail for several weeks through France. Opinions and advice flowed around the table as people lingered in the cooling evening air.

"Hallo. Your name is Bob, yes? I am Sven. I was at the other end of the table. Is this your first Camino?"

"Nice to meet you Sven. Yes, the first. Do people walk the Camino more than once?"

"They do. For some, they come back many times."

"And you?"

"This will be my third time; I have a friend, Astrid, with me. She wants to take her time and that suits me too."

Bob looked at Sven, quite a hippy: tall, blond, long hair, an earring, early forties, and a warm smile. He wondered what would motivate this man to go on a third pilgrimage.

"I am from Sweden, and you Bob—you are with your woman?"

"From Canada, yes with my wife. Are you starting from here?

"Here, yes. Why are you doing the Camino?"

"My wife is religious so she wants to do it. I'm keeping her company and I love the idea of the hike and seeing Spain this way."

"You look fit, Bob. You are ready for the Camino?"

"Absolutely. We are prepared. We've got our training and equipment."

"The Camino has surprises and tricks; it has an energy beyond the walking. But you will see. Already you see it is a path with one destination but many starting points. Buen Camino. I will see you on the trail. Sleep well, my friend."

****

Bob found Brigit sitting on her bunk. She had retreated up to the dormitory right after supper.

"How's it going, Bridgy?"

"Trying to find yet another brilliant way to organize my pack." She gave Bob a crooked smile.

"Are you okay, darling? You seem a bit edgy. Here— make some room for me." Bob moved her pack so he could sit next to her.

"It's all strange."

Bob put his arm around her shoulders. "Tell me."

"Don't know really. Worried about setting out and tomorrow we walk from France over a mountain into Spain, and that's just the start. We have eight hundred kilometres to go. How crazy is that! And what if we get hurt or sick?"

"You know we are up to this. It's not as though we are in the wilderness. We have our plan, how far to walk and where to stay each night; we can just relax and enjoy it." Bob gave her a warm hug. "I love you. This is going to be a great time together."

"I know, and I love you darling." She smiled at him and put her hand on his chest. "Sounds crazy, but I think I would feel better if we got going, straight away." She laughed.

"No no, there's a mountain or two to climb and it's getting dark. Talking about the unknown, I had a strange conversation with a Swedish guy. It started off with the usual—where we're from—then he asked if I was prepared as the Camino had tricks and energy beyond the walking."

"Did he explain?"

"No. He said I would see, and then floated off like some spirit from the northern forest."

"Excuse me, you two. I'm Al. I'm in the bunk opposite you."

"Hi Al. I'm Brigit and this is Bob. I saw you at supper. Are you starting from here?"

"Yes, I am. I'm a bit stressed. I'm not in shape. I had no time to train."

"I'm finding it all a bit daunting too. Where are you from? We're from Canada."

"From the States" Florida. Actually, I came over to warn you, I snore." And he held out a clear plastic drum of florescent orange ear-plugs. "This is my spiel: 'Hi, I'm Al, and I snore. Please have some ear-plugs!' You're my first candidates. Sorry to use you as guinea-pigs."

Despite Brigit's plan for a good night's sleep, she lay awake worried about the path and where it would actually lead her. She turned on her side trying for sleep. Maybe a prayer would calm her: "Bless Bob and me on this adventure and everyone else walking, following the footsteps of all those holy people who have walked this way before us. And bless Al. Forgive me, help me to be a better person than I have been these last few years."

****

Next morning, with a stream of other pilgrims, Bob and Brigit found their way under a clock tower, over a bridge, to a narrow mountain road. The town fell away behind them. The climb was unrelenting and steep, rough stone walls on either side, past meadows with cream-coloured cows, the fresh sweet grass a vivid green.

"How does she manage?" Brigit said as they heard a crisp, "Bonjour" and were overtaken by a trim French woman with a day-pack. "I guess you really can travel light when you start from your own country."

"All these people. Half of Europe is along for the walk," Bob grumbled. It was the May first weekend: a European holiday. Brigit glanced at Bob: his tall compact body, and his face that was already quite tanned. His short hair, though liberally streaked with grey, was still thick. She usually found his characteristic fluid stride enchanting but as she struggled up this mountain, he got on her nerves.

"Okay, Bridgy? You're doing great."

"No. This mountain just keeps going, and you're going too fast. I'm stopping for a break."

16

"All right, if you need to. Just look at that view." The valley, now far below, was woven with white roads and tracks connecting small villages and farms and beyond that, mountain slopes covered with dark woodlands. Brigit took off her pack and sat on the grass by the side of the road. She knew this first day was demanding; she was confident she could make it to Santiago. She had the grit and strength and had followed that voice that had said to her: "Brigit. Walk the Camino!" She was inspired by St. Francis of Assisi who had come this way in the Middle Ages, and then she had followed the hype created by the American film star Shirley MacLaine who had not only hiked the Camino but then wrote a bestseller about her journey.

"Still got a ways to go today."

"I know, Bob." Brigit rocked her shoulders to see if that would make her backpack feel any lighter, flicking back her hair. Onward and upward!

****

As Bob stopped to let Brigit catch up, he looked at her with pride—trim in her new gear: green sun-block shirt, hi-tech hiking pants and a rimmed hat for rain or sun. As she got closer, he had a memory flash of their lovemaking: her strong legs around him, sharing her eagerness for his body.

Gradually the land grew bleak, the grass cropped short by the sheep, the wind sharper. Here was what they had

17

been looking out for: the wayside shrine draped with ribbons and flags, walking sticks and crosses—pilgrim memorabilia. A yellow arrow marked the sharp turn off the road and up a track over the first pass.

"It would be wicked up here in a storm. They do get them and dense fog too," said Bob. "That's the mountain refuge, in case you get stranded." He pointed to a stone shelter crouching into the side of the slope.

"A pile of rocks with a door: very Hobbit," said Brigit.

Now it felt as though everyone had overtaken them and they had the mountain to themselves. Behind them France, Spain before them. Brigit stretched out her arms to the landscape. "Amazing to think that Napoleon brought his troops back and forth over this pass, and the Romans too."

The chill air felt thin. Out with the jackets.

****

"Is this it?" said Brigit catching her breath as they stood by a cattle grid that marked the frontier along with a stone marker. "No one to check our passports or ask what we're doing here." They filled their bottles at a spring. "Can't believe we've got more uphill. It should be down now that we're in Spain. Bob, can we take a proper rest? My legs and shoulders are really aching."

"Let's find a more sheltered spot. We've still got a sandwich left." The hostel had sent them off with a packed lunch. Seemed to Brigit like an age ago.

"I'm a bit worried." said Bob. "It's four o'clock, and I read that you need to book supper by six in Roncesvalles. Let's get going."

Finally it was downhill, through beach trees with young leaves so green they were shocking.

"This valley," said Brigit. "Roncesvalles is where Emperor Charlemagne and his nephew Roland fought a battle to save Christendom against the infidels."

Despite her aching pain, Brigit was awed by the beauty and the history around her. Of a time when the sound of a horn gave battle orders, and swords, with mythical names like Durendal, made history. But now Bob was almost running down the slope in front of her.

"Bob, wait! — Why don't you go ahead and book things and I will make my way down."

"Do you think that's a good idea? You could get lost."

"It's just downhill now isn't it?"

"All right. If you think you'll be okay, I'll go and sort things out." And Bob took off.

****

"There's no discouragement shall make him once relent, His first avowed intent to be a pilgrim." Brigit sang the old hymn, going carefully now on the steep downhill. At one point she caught a glimpse of roof tops, still far below. It was peaceful not to have to worry about keeping up with Bob.

19

By the time Brigit made it to the monastery complex of Roncesvalles, Bob had supper organized and beds at the albergue: the pilgrims' hostel. "When I got here, it was after six. It didn't seem to matter. I'd been rehearsing my Spanish. At the hotel I asked about supper, and he just said to pay now. But I'm disappointed; we can't get beds in the main dorm. We're in the overflow."

In fact they were in the second overflow dormitory which was decidedly cramped compared to the converted chapel that could sleep a hundred and fifty pilgrims. They registered with their pilgrim 'credencial' or passport—the booklet they needed for access to the hostels along the way. At each stop they would get an ink stamp; here it was a lozenge shape with a cross and a bishop's crosier on top.

"Brigit, did you want a scallop shell for your pack? They have them painted with a sword. Well, maybe it's a cross."

They were shown to one of the round tables for eight set aside for pilgrims. The first course was promptly served into their large soup plates— spaghetti with tomato sauce. Bob asked the server for the wine list. "Vino?"

"Si, si," she replied and came back with two open bottles of red wine with no labels and put them in the centre of the table. Wine came with the meal; like the spaghetti for first course, there was no choice. Bob asked the server for wine glasses to replace the juice style glasses they all had at their places.

"For pity's sake," Brigit hissed at Bob. "We're not at the Ritz."

The waitress flashed a smile at Bob, "Si, si, vaso de vino," and waved at the glasses on the table as she sailed away. Brigit caught herself up sternly — 'we have a long way to go and I had better be supportive and not send out negative vibes about Bob being a pain and a snob.' In the meantime, François, a Frenchman at the table, was filling up the glasses and he now proposed a toast to the Camino and their success on having crossed over the mountains that day. Brigit settled back and prepared to enjoy the company, swapping stories of the gruelling day. It was some consolation to hear that they weren't actually the last to arrive and some latecomers would have to sleep in the entrance hallway of the monastery building. A piece of fried fish had now been deposited on their plate and when another bottle of wine was brought to the table, she happily nodded at François when he waved it in her direction.

Later that night Brigit had plenty of time to think of how, if she had been a bit more restrained with the wine, she might not now be lying awake in her bunk. 'I really don't feel very safe up here,' she thought. 'So narrow and no sides.' She threaded one arm through the metal hoop of the headboard. Bob had offered to take the upper bunk, but she had made a bit of a fuss about having the lower bunk the night before and they had agreed to alternate. Last night's bed had a ladder and safety bars on the upper bunk. She cautiously turned over and then heard the sound of falling as her watch dislodged from under the pillow. "Shit, shit, oh please God don't let anyone step on it." She lay there, stiff shoulders, leg muscles aching, eyes gritty and she could hear snoring. Well that was one expectation of the Camino fulfilled—snoring pilgrims!

3. "Will You Walk a Little Faster?" Said the Whiting to the Snail

(As heard by Alice when in Wonderland)

Brigit had got up at six-thirty, dangling out of her bunk in the dark room, managing not to land on Bob or her watch. She felt gritty, but a shower helped. She wondered if there was a church service, but Mass had been the evening before and now her fellow pilgrims seemed only interested in getting their packs together, anxious to get going. There was no breakfast to be had for pilgrims in Roncesvalles, but there were promises of food in the next village according to the ancient attendant who was there to see them off.

A small crowd buzzed around the café door in the main square; otherwise the village of Burguete appeared asleep. Bob jostled with the customers at the long zinc bar to get served. Tables and chairs— the white plastic universal variety— were set up in the square. He came out with coffee, juice, and ham sandwiches on crispy bread. Al of the ear plugs arrived at their table. "Yesterday I took the valley road. I knew that over-the-top way would be too much for me," he explained to Bob.

"How did it go? I think it's quite a hike anyway,"

"I joined up with Sven and Astrid from the hostel. Sven seems to know his way around. There's an eleven-kilometre stretch along the highway through the narrow valley, so we took a taxi for that part. We arrived in time to get beds in the old chapel."

"That was smart. The last thing you want to do is injure yourself on day one." As soon as he had finished, Bob jumped up and brushed off the bread crumbs. "Eat up Brigit!" he said, and swung on his pack. He said goodbye to the others. "I know we will see you as we go along."

Out of Burguete the path went through a farm yard and they could see into the open sheds where cows were being milked. The landscape ahead of them was rolling hills. Behind them there was snow on the mountaintops. They crossed a stream with stepping stones; Brigit was enchanted and stopped to take photos. Now Bob was ahead again, but she would catch up when he took a break. 'He rushed me over breakfast; he didn't have to do that.'

"Bonjour Brigitte." It was François from supper along with four others from the table.

"Bonjour, François. Comment ça va aujourd'hui?" He was fine this morning, and asked how she spoke such good French. She explained she was Canadian and with a wave of her hand instantly turned all Canadians into perfect bilinguals.

"Ah! Une cousine canadienne," said François. As she and Bob lived in Ottawa, the capital, they were surrounded by more bilingual people than the national average; she did not seek to disillusion her cousin français. François waved to the land around them. "Scholars now think that this could be where Charlemagne fought his battle against the Saracens. Roland was in the vanguard. He sounded his horn Oliphant for help and Charlemagne took it for victory and didn't come to help him. It was tragic as Roland died."

They walked together for a while. François was leading a group from his church in Grenoble, a city in the French Alps. "So we are used to mountains," he explained as he waved goodbye and the group pulled ahead. Around the next bend Bob was waiting for her.

"I think it's important that we stay together and you keep up. When we get to the next town, you can take a break and I'll buy us lunch fixings."

"Don't rush me!"

****

It had been a shock for Bob to realize that beds at hostels could be at a premium. Zubiri was the next hostel on their list. That would be a twenty-kilometre walk that day, but he felt they were making good time and could easily reach the next one. It was only a further six kilometres and the guide book said it offered a warm Camino welcome. In Espinal Bob found a supermercardo, not very super size-wise but good enough for lunch supplies. Brigit sat on a bench outside with two young English women, Jessie and Jenny.

"It's just brilliant. We left London; it was dark and raining and a few hours later, here we are on the Camino," said Jenny."

The yellow Camino markers pointed Bob and Brigit out of the valley up a road with farm houses and high hedges around meadows dense with grazing sheep, the breed with black faces and shaggy thick wool. As they came around a bend, there in the middle of the road was a large black ram gazing at them, with curly horns, big ears, and legs like spindles below his thick woolly body. They both burst out laughing.

"The king of the Camino," Brigit said.

"The proverbial black sheep," Bob laughed, "and look at the attitude." After that they took time to look around, photograph flowers, and eat their lunch. "Orchids—they survive the pilgrims and the sheep," said Bob.

More climbing, now through a plantation of beech and hazels trees. They could see far below the highway snaking along through the valley. Brigit stopped. "It's getting hot, my legs are starting to ache. Here we go down again, which means there will be another hill to climb."

"All these streams flow down from the hills and mountains," said Bob. "And here's the ford." A row of tall upright white cement blocks made for modern stepping stones.

"This is a perilous crossing." Brigit managed to keep her balance. A cyclist splashed through the stream to their left.

Chapter 3

"Hallo Brigit! You are well?" It was Romeo from Brazil. He had been in the bunk across from them the night before. He was wearing a bright yellow cycle jersey and looked very fit.

"This is only our second day and we have all these new friends," said Brigit. "I guess we won't see Romeo again. He said he averages at least sixty kilometres a day."

"We should phone Liz this evening. It will be morning for her," said Bob.

Uphill and two villages later they followed a wooded hilltop and after a short steep downhill they came to a memorial for a person from Japan. It was draped with ribbons that people had woven in memory of this fellow pilgrim who had died on the trail.

"Rest in peace," said Brigit. At that moment, a lone church bell rang from a village far below.

"Come on. Let's keep going," said Bob.

"So Zubiri is our hostel for tonight."

"Let's go on to Larrasoaña. It sounds really nice there."

"What's the rush? We had planned on Zubiri."

"Yes, but you look fine. And I heard that Zubiri is a bit grim and that Larrasoana is charming," said Bob.

"I'm tired and my shoulders hurt. There's no way I want to go on. Let's just concentrate on getting to Zubiri."

"You haven't even tried. You'll get a second wind."

"I'm on my second wind."

"At home you were managing twenty-five K with the pack, no problem, and now you're giving up after twenty klicks. You're going all wimpy."

"I'm not going to be rushed and I'm tired. I don't want to go any further than Zubiri."

"I thought this was supposed to be a team effort."

"Don't you talk about team effort—you think that just means having your own way!"

Zubiri and its hostel fulfilled all of Bob's expectations: utilitarian and soulless. They walked along a street with beige apartment blocks on each side until they reached a grey building surrounded by a chain-link fence: the hostel. Already the main dormitory was full so they were shown to a building next door. It was the indoor pelota court, a large cavernous cement space with a high wall at one end. There was a pile of foam mattresses. Brigit washed her undies and socks and hung them on the washing lines strung along the fence. She met Jenny and Jessie sitting on the steps enjoying the afternoon sun. "Our dormitory is quite crowded. You may be better off in your pelota court, as long as Thursday is not their practice night."

They sat and chatted and had a laugh as they watched some of the men constantly feeling their washing to see if it had dried yet. "There's a restaurant that does a pilgrims' supper. Are you and Bob interested?"

"Let's call Liz," said Bob. "You've got the phone."

She went through the pockets of her bag. Not there. Must be in the bottom of the pack. More digging. Nothing.

"Here, let me," and Bob took over the search. No.

"Have a look in your pack." No luck.

"Let's think back. When did we have it last?" Bob asked.

"I know I had it in St-Jean. I charged it to be sure we had a full battery."

"Where did you plug it in?"

"There was an outlet right by my bunk. That's what gave me the idea." Brigit gasped and put her hand to her mouth. "I think I left it plugged in. I was so stressed to get going."

"You should've told me. I would have reminded you in the morning."

"I am so annoyed with myself. I'm sorry."

"Don't make a big deal of it. It's a pain, but not the end of the world. There seem to be plenty of public phones around. It was only for emergencies anyway. We can phone the hostel in St-Jean. We must get it back. You remember you can have items mailed to the Post Office in Santiago."

"Let's ask them in the office to help us," said Brigit.

The crowd at supper was a relief. There was fish soup which sounded promising but seemed to have been made from canned tuna, and then lamb, but more like mutton stew. But with the French style bread to mop up the gravy, all was tasty.

Despite their stark surroundings, the night was peaceful: lots of space and no upper bunks. Next morning they were shocked to see they had slept till eight and were the last to leave. There was a bit of food left over from their lunch supplies so with a skimpy breakfast, they packed, put their mattresses back on the pile, and set off.

4. Beauty and the Camino Beast

The only good thing for Bob about Zubiri was the ancient bridge. There it was, still hanging on to its beauty. He climbed the rough paved surface to the high arch and looked down at the willow branches sweeping the twisting waters of the Rio Arga.

He walked, the sun slapping on his back. The ground was grey and dusty and to his left, was a square block building. A giant pipe snaked along by the path, distorting his shadow.

'A factory. How could they build a factory over this ancient pilgrim trail?' he thought. 'And Brigit, what was up with her? This was to be her adventure and their relationship mend. Now she's just argumentative and won't cooperate. Am I supposed to do all the heavy lifting? Day three and it's falling apart. Great!'

Usually Bob's self-grumbling made him feel better but not this morning. 'What am I doing here? We could just chuck the whole thing in.' Visions of the Guggenheim Museum in Bilbao shimmered before his eyes. It would all be so simple, just hop a bus. But no, they were stuck on this path dragging them along this winding strip of earth. Just beyond there was a country full of culture to explore. Bob felt like a prisoner who could go forward or backward but was unable to break away. He trudged on letting his resentment build up and roar inside him, recasting his enthusiasm for the Camino of the past winter month to the burden of his support for Brigit and her fantasy.

****

Brigit saw her long shadow and moved so it cast a clear elongated shape with her pack and hat and took photos of this surreal pilgrim. Bob was ahead again. The clash of words of the day before hung in the air between them, unresolved and not mentioned. With the dormitory and supper crowd, they had had no opportunity or need, to deal with it.

She had fallen in love with the idea of a pilgrimage when she was a girl and her Sunday school group all walked from the suburbs, out into the country to a small village church for a Harvest Thanksgiving service. They had returned in cars, but she cherished the memory of that walk in the perfect October weather. There had been other trips. Her father was an Anglican minister, so they often visited churches and she always called it a pilgrimage. Her sister and brothers teased her about it but somehow the term stuck to those family outings. But this was wilder. They were not part of a group, just the two of them. She looked up as she reached the side of the road. The Camino arrows pointed across the road to a dirt track heading up through woodlands.

****

Bob was going to wait for Brigit but as he crossed the road to be in the shade he saw Colin coming up from the main road. Colin was an Australian who had been part of the supper group the night before.

"I tried a different route to avoid the factory. I went round by the N-135. Not great, a lot of traffic. How was the path?" As Bob told him of the ugly, but quieter way, they started walking together.

"Hey, have you tried walking poles? Try mine. I find they really help with my stride. Go on; try them." Colin showed Bob how to include his arms in the walking movement. From poles they got talking about equipment and then to their professional lives. Colin was in his mid-thirties, from Sydney where he worked in the Emergency Department of a hospital. "In Emergency, it's all shift work, so I often get time off during the day. For me it's about the outdoors —love it all—cycling, swimming, rock climbing, sailing, I'm there!"

Bob found himself getting into a strong walking rhythm with the poles and it felt good to have a regular chat with another guy. "Brigit – oh hell, I've just been striding ahead".

"Don't worry mate. She'll be fine. The great thing about the Camino is you can't get lost. We all walk the same path.

She's probably enjoying a break from you anyway. So what about Canada? You've got some great outdoors going on there?"

Bob told Colin about his trips back to Alberta to canoe with his brother and father. "We do some white water on rivers in Alberta and over to British Columbia for some longer lake trips. That's easier on my father now that he's older. In the winter I ski, whenever I can, in Quebec, The Rockies, even around Ottawa. I'm a volunteer coach for kids' ski racing. You know from Calgary it's just a couple of hours to the mountains. I grew up there and my parents are still there."

"How come you left?" Colin asked.

"I needed to get away. I was eighteen and I couldn't stand how narrow and red-neck it all was at the time. Alberta's in western Canada and it has a tradition of being independent—the Canadian wild west. For years it struggled financially and then they hit oil and prosperity, but they still saw themselves as the brave-martyr mavericks. The attitude got to me: the constant 'we are victims in the West' thing. And then the anti-French thing. There they were, Calgary, a wealthy city and they could not even see the advantages of another culture and another language. Anyway, that's how I saw it at the time with my parent's social and business crowd. I guess I was an angry teenager. It's different now, more cosmopolitan. I left and studied at McGill University in Montreal. You'd think that my independent spirit would please my parents. But for Dad and his oil patch crowd it was like a major betrayal or that I was out my mind! Then I studied French and Political Science. So what's wrong with becoming an engineer? We are way beyond that now. They love the kids and Brigit. Kids, the great agents of reconciliation, wish we could put that in a bottle and market it for world peace."

By this time they could see the small town of Larrasoaña on the other side of the river. "This looks like breakfast to me," said Colin.

****

Brigit came down from the woodlands and was now walking by the river, through hamlets and beside meadows where horses grazed. In each group one horse had a bell around its neck that tinkled brightly. She stopped to watch a butterfly in the hedge then crossed the river into Larrasoana. Bob was waiting for her by the bridge.

"Let's find a café," he said.

"Thanks for waiting." she said.

They joined Colin in the courtyard of a little restaurant along with a pilgrim family— an American woman with her two college-age daughters. Bantam chickens were hiding out under the bushes in the courtyard and would scoot under their table. After breakfast Bob and Brigit set out while Colin stayed talking to the American family.

"So what are we going to do, Brigit? I suppose that shot yesterday about team work was the money-debt thing. Well, let's talk about it."

Brigit stayed silent. Bob continued. "We've been over this. Yes it was my fault. I should not have made those investments. That happened six years ago, we have paid off the debt, the kids are fine, a big part of that, thanks to you I know. We stayed together. I know I said I would come with you but not if you are just going to be the martyr about it all and just amble along. And what happened to the love and joy you talked about?"

Brigit could feel her throat tightening and tears welling up in her eyes. Much of what Bob was saying was true. But she still felt he had not really understood how devastating it was for her when he took out a loan to buy shares in that exploration company. "You know Bob," Brigit's voice was shaking. "I do feel resentment because I feel you never really realized how serious it was for me. You have always seemed almost casual about it."

"Bloody Hell!" Bob exploded. "What did you want me to do? I told you how sorry I was. If you don't choose to believe me, I don't know what else I can do. Don't you think it hurt me too? It was worse for me because it was my fault. How do you think it felt for me as a husband and father doing that to our lives? But these things happen and we made it through. You and I together, but now you don't seem to want to accept that!"

For Brigit it was a vicious circle that went on around and around in her mind and her heart. It seemed so simple for Bob and now all was right again.

"There were so many times when you could have helped me. Sometimes I felt that it was all on my shoulders." Brigit's voice was harsh, it was the only way she could keep talking without crying.

"Like when?"

"Like when I came back late and tired from work and you hadn't even thought to put out the garbage," she said.

"Oh God Brigit! I can't believe this is about me not putting out the garbage! You know I tried to help as much as possible and I did. I don't think you realized all that I did. And just because I screwed up didn't mean I turned into some model husband who all of a sudden realized all the stuff that needed to be done. Anyway, you know you pride yourself on running the house."

"Shit Bob, I don't have a monopoly on house work. Join in any time! Sometimes I came home so tired"

"I know you did Brigit. And you seemed to almost enjoy the whole self-sacrifice thing. And now that has been taken away from you, you're lost".

Brigit turned to him in disbelief. "You son of a bitch! I hate you."

They gazed at each other in horror. There had never been so much anger and fury expressed between them. Their arguments in the past had always been rather controlled.

Maybe too much so. Bereft, they started walking again. The scenery passed by unnoticed.

"I didn't mean that Bob, about hating you. I'm sorry about that".

"I know, but we're still in a big fix here Brigit. I was too harsh the way I said things. I apologize. But listen. I think you got into the habit of being brave and managing, and you did, but now you've got to get beyond that. It was tough, but lots of other people land in big money problems. We are lucky because we got out of it. And we didn't have to ask for help from my parents, or sell the house. We could have done that but you didn't want to. So we worked really hard and now we can start being normal again, like we were before. Can you accept that? Do you know how to do that?"

"You always make things sound so simple," Brigit replied.

"That's no answer. I'm not going to go on living as the bad guilty one and you as the heroic Brigit. It's time to get over it. And here we are on this trip. We can do this. You can do this, Brigit. You kept saying, 'let's see what the Camino will teach us'—well maybe this is it."

"Don't take over my Camino," choked Brigit.

"I thought you were supposed to be the Christian," said Bob. "What happened to forgiveness?"

5. So Many Rivers to Cross

The bridge would bring them to their stop for the night, the parish hostel of the Trinidad de Arre. They had only covered twenty kilometres that day but the emotion of their fight left them drained and silent. In the porch, a sign with a large Stop symbol warned that only pilgrims with a credencial could stay. The dormitory was white-washed with heavy wooden beams crossing the ceiling. Colin was already there, having a snooze; he had overtaken them on one of the steep uphills. Brigit checked out the facilities and found a walled garden. She felt she could find some peace there. She washed her hiking pants as well as her usual undies and socks. She went through these timeless chores: washing and rinsing, watching the rings in the water as it circled down the drain.

With her lightweight copy of the New Testament Bible, she went outside. She had resolved to read The Letter of James during the Camino—who was that James anyway? Probably not the St. James of the Camino, the Iago of Santiago. He was the apostle, the son of Zebedee. He and his brother John were fishermen by the Sea of Galilee when they were called by Jesus to become "fishers of men." They had the nickname "Sons of Thunder" and a reputation as hot-headed and quick to use their fists. Had that James written this letter to all the Christians world-wide at that time? It was plain talking; maybe it did come from the feisty fisherman: "Count it all joy when you fall into various trials."

'Joy,' thought Brigit, 'joy when the going gets tough and messy.' Yes, she knew that was the teaching and it was easy to pay lip-service to it. But to live it? Brigit sighed and went on reading: "...knowing that the testing of your faith produces patience. But let patience have its perfect work, that you may be perfect and complete, lacking nothing." She gazed at a cherry tree in bloom. "God help me have patience with myself and to find my way, your way. I need your help; I can't do this by myself. You've got to help me."

Brigit found Bob, Colin, Jenny, and Jessie in the albergue kitchen drinking Kalimocho.

"Have a glass Brigit. This is a whole new experience," said Bob.

Brigit managed a smile. 'Is he trying to make amends, or has he just drunk a lot of Kalimocho, whatever it is?'

"Well I'm all for trying something new, but what is it?"

"Red wine, cheap is best, and cola," said Bob.

'Really!' She thought. 'How long was it since Bob had been all snobby about having to drink his wine out of a stubby juice glass? Two nights ago. Well, maybe the Camino does change us.'

"Here. Try it," said Colin mixing her a glass, half cola half red wine.

"It's amazing what tastes good after a day in the fresh air," she said.

"Don't be a snob, Brigit!" Bob said.

'So I'm being the snob now. At least we're talking—sort of.'

"Any dinner plans?" Someone had checked out the area and found a restaurant that did a pilgrim's supper.

Supper was fine and she and Bob were able to keep to safe topics such as what they hoped to see in Pamplona the next day: the cathedral, and the square where the festival of the running of the bulls was held. Once again the collective life in the albergue prevented them, or protected them, from any real conversation as to how they would sort out their future.

****

It had rained in the night and was still overcast, but for Brigit it felt like a better time. She and Bob walked into the city of Pamplona through elegant streets with stores and businesses on the ground floor of the apartment buildings. They passed a garden centre store displaying a collection of cement statues: frogs the size of beavers, urns that could have been in the grounds of a Roman villa, dogs with snarling faces. They were overtaken by a group of runners weaving along the sidewalk between the pedestrians. Nobody took any notice of them with their hiking boots and backpacks. "Pilgrims have been walking through their city for over a thousand years. We are just part of the landscape," Brigit realized. They scanned the sidewalk for the Camino path markers. If they took the wrong turn they could find themselves kilometres away from the Camino. Then they saw that they needed to look up to find the stylized yellow scallop shell on a lamp pole or part of a street sign.

"This must be the Magdalena area, outside the old city gates." said Bob, as they passed through a narrow street.

"Look at the decorations," exclaimed Brigit. The front of many of the houses had a mosaic of pebbles and shells: ancient coats of arms, crosses and the scallop shell of St. James—Santiago, the patron saint of Spain.

Crossing the river on the Magdalena bridge they could see the ramparts and fortifications of the long city walls which surrounded the historical centre of Pamplona. The Camino followed the wall, over the moat, through the Puerto Frances, and into the city itself where the road was steep and paved with uneven cobble stones.

"Bob, keep an eye out for a public toilet." But as they walked further up the hill and into the city they saw that this part of town was all apartment buildings. They got to a cross-street that made a space wide enough for an ornate fountain with an old animal drinking trough. The door of a restaurant was propped open. "I'm going to try here," shouted Brigit as she dove under the outdoor canopy. She really did not want to wait any longer. As her eyes adjusted to the dark, she saw a server wiping down tables.

"¡Cierto, cierto!" Closed, she shouted out to Brigit.

"Quiero servicios" Brigit replied. The woman pointed across the street to a bar. 'Hell's Bells! Here I go, delaying Bob again.' She made her way across the tiny square and through construction going on in front of one of the apartment buildings. "They said to try the bar," she called out to Bob on her way past and down the steps to the door below street level. Inside the long and narrow zinc bar was filled with men—the construction workers on their break. Brigit felt embarrassed, but the barman, working the Espresso machine, just jerked his head to the back corner. 'Thank goodness,' she thought. 'Bless these people. They are all pilgrim-proofed!'

When Brigit left the bar, the construction workers were back on site, hoisting an ornate wrought-iron balcony railing up the outside of the apartment building. 'Where is Bob?' He must have walked on, she reasoned. She gave another quick look around and set off up the street. She soon arrived at a square with a palace at one end. She sat on a bench where she had a good view and where Bob would be able to see her. He's probably having a look around. She got out an apple and her water bottle. Brigit could see on the city plan that the cathedral was just a bit further along. The map showed the Camino snaking through the city, over another bridge and out of town. Still no sign of Bob. She decided to walk on to the cathedral—that's where he'd likely be.

Brigit was surprised at how light it was in the cathedral. She looked around for Bob: not there. She went back out and stood on the steps. She saw two pilgrims who had joined the supper group the night before: Mireille, from Montreal and Luigi, an Italian. "Buenos dias" they greeted her with smiles.

"Where's Bob?" asked Mireille. Brigit explained that they had got separated, but she expected to meet him around the centre of town. "If you see him, tell him I'll come back here to the Cathedral steps in about an hour. I'm going to look around and do a bit of shopping."

"No problem," said Mireille—she and Luigi were looking for a café and would be staying around this area.

****

Bob looked at his watch and was shocked to see he had been waiting thirty minutes; engrossed in his guide book, he had not realized how time had passed. 'Where was Brigit?' He went down the steps to the bar—"have you seen my wife who had come in earlier?" The barman asked if she was wearing a hat and a pack? "She went away a long time ago."

'Where could she be? Could something have happened to her; could she be in trouble? I was right here. Did she not see me and just kept going? The way she is at the moment she could do just that.' He set out for the city centre. He met some other pilgrims but no one had seen Brigit. He decided to check out the cathedral. If Brigit was not there, he would walk the Camino path slowly through the city: he was bound to meet up with her. Failing that, he would go to the hostel just out of town where she would wait for him. He came to the cathedral and went in. A look around, no Brigit. He hung around the cathedral steps for a few minutes then set off down a wide tree-lined avenue. He stopped at a deli and bought some sliced meat and cheese, at a baker, a crusty loaf. He passed a group of school girls in their uniform of pleated plaid skirts. Next to a park there was a sign inviting pilgrims to visit the university campus. He cut through the park. Brigit might be there. She would have seen the sign; anyway he would like to see the university. The commissioner at the desk was gracious and asked Bob for his pilgrims' passport as the university had a stamp. Bob sat in the marble hall on a high backed wooden bench and watched the university bustle.

"Buen Camino," a voice greeted Bob. It turned out to be a professor of industrial design and he wanted to know where Bob was from. Then the professor turned and presented him to some people who were visiting— a French consul and an Italian diplomat. Bob felt right at home, though he realized that he was being shown off as Exhibit A—a sample pilgrim. It was the best moment of his time in the city.

Once out of Pamplona, he climbed up the river valley to the old village of Cizur Menor. The hostel was not yet open and the outer gates were locked. There was a bench just where the Camino came into the village and he sat and had his lunch. From here he could keep a sharp eye out for Brigit. As he ate his lunch, he could see the church: so much pilgrim history here. The cloisters were gone but the church had been restored. The Order of the Hospitallers had set up shop here with a hospice in the twelfth century, looking after pilgrims and the sick and fighting the infidels to keep the Camino safe for pilgrims. Only the church tower showed an echo of its fortress past. But still no sign of Brigit. 'Where the hell is she? Did she get here, find it closed, and just keep going? She could have reached here at least an hour ago.'

After another hour and still no sign of Brigit, Bob made the decision to keep going, past the village, down through large fields of fresh green wheat, and over the battle ground where Charlemagne had fought Aigolando, the Muslim leader. The two armies had met here, one on each side of the Santiago road. That was a battle that Charlemagne had won.

****

Brigit was back at the cathedral, but no sign of Bob. François and his group came along. She told him she was looking for Bob. "Have you seen him?" No, but they had been slow getting going today. "Bonne chance!" Not very helpful. She sat down on the steps and got out her Camino guide. They had talked about going to the hostel at Cizur Menor, but nothing had been finalized. They had agreed to take time for some sightseeing; surely he'll come back here— to the cathedral. Brigit waited another hour on the steps, now seriously worried. It was coming up to noon which meant it was well over two hours since they separated. She realized they had no back-up plan, no cell phone, in fact no way of reaching each other. Could he have gone back to the bar to look for her?

She heaved on her backpack and retraced her steps. She saw other pilgrims, strangers. All her fellow walkers must be out of town by now. At the bar there was no sign of Bob. She could now see that the door was completely hidden by the construction machinery. Had she missed Bob? What to do? Back to the cathedral, maybe he would come there after all.

Inside she took off her pack and sat in a pew in a side aisle. All was still, some people praying, a couple lighting candles at a shrine. "Dear Lord be with me. Please be with me…." Brigit found words coming up in prayer. She sat there, remembering. A great sadness was in her heart and as tears started down her face, the sadness became deeper. "Oh God, how could I be so stupid? Forgive me, forgive me." Brigit sat huddled, engulfed in tears and prayer.

At some point there was movement near the high altar, signs of preparing for a service and Brigit saw that the pews at the front were now filled up. A priest came and began to read from a missal and started the mass. Brigit listened for a few moments but did not connect with the reading—external words. She got up with an effort; her knees and shoulders were stiff and her whole body was weary. She picked up her pack and went, as quietly as she could, out into the street. She was surprised to see that the sun was still shining. It was only three o'clock. She felt calm but weary and still engulfed in sadness. She walked through the city, past a park, past more fortifications, over a bridge, a modern one this time with a road that led uphill to Cizur Menor and the hostel.

****

As he climbed the steep winding path to the ridge of the hill, the Alto del Perdon, Bob could hear the high hum from a row of windmills. Cresting the hill, he saw a camper-caravan parked next to a track. A group of people were there talking, some sitting. On the camper was a sign: St. John of the Camino. St. John turned out to be an Englishman who explained to Bob that he spent many months here each year looking after pilgrims.

"Would you like coffee or a soft drink?" Bob said yes to coffee and soon he was handed an instant coffee and some cookies. "People give a donation if they can. Otherwise that's just fine. How are your feet? I have foot-care supplies here and I can do some patching up if you need." Bob said his feet were fine.

"I wonder if you can help me. I've become separated from my wife. Would you have seen her? She's five foot six, dark blonde shoulder-length hair, slim, green jacket and blue backpack, dark blue hat—does that ring a bell?

"Sorry and nobody has asked me about you today. When this happens, I tell people to write a note and I tape it to the table here. That way they see it as they arrive." He supplied Bob with paper, a marker and tape. "I will be at the hostel in Puente la Reina. I will wait for you there," wrote

Bob. At least with the note and John, if Brigit was still behind him, she would get the news. He stood at the top of the ridge looking at the view ahead: a broad lush area of farm and woodland was spread out below and in the distance, and on every side, blue hills making a far-off ring around this fertile basin.

"Pas mal, eh!"

Bob whipped around. He knew that voice. "Charles-Michel! Qu'est-ce que tu fais ici? What are you doing here?"

"I'm looking at the view, like you, mon vieux," and he reached out and gave Bob a hug, then taking off Bob's hat: "Well it's really you, and you still have all your hair!" He reached up and tousled Bob's hair. "A bit of grey but not bad for a guy in his fifties." Bob felt his cheeks flush as the blood rushed to his face.

6. All Souls Camino

"I'm not a ghost. You needn't look at me like that," said Charles-Michel.

"The phantom of the Camino. That might suit you." Bob managed a smile. He grabbed back his hat, trying to keep his voice steady. Bob knew this was no ghost, but it was astounding to meet him here, now. Charles-Michel had been a close friend but it was a complicated relationship. "Where did you start walking?" Bob asked, keeping on safe ground with a standard pilgrim question.

"From Le Puy-en-Velay, in France. I've been walking for a month now. How about you? Where did you start? Are you alone?" Bob explained that he was walking with Brigit. Charles-Michel had been a teaching assistant for Bob's French language class at university and a friendship had grown from this. He was a couple of years older than Bob. He had introduced him to his friends, to the music, art, and the political scene, so much that made Montreal an interesting and exciting place.

"And you've lost her? You fool, how did you manage that?" Charles-Michel teased. "Franchement mon cher

Robert, that must take some doing on the Camino. All you have to do is put one foot in front of the other."

"Hey, it takes two to get lost," Bob defended himself. "And I seem to remember you losing me a few times in Montreal."

"Well, it was late and it's possible we were somewhat drunk and maybe had a bit to smoke. But now I am a responsible adult and have managed, for quite a few years, to keep up with my travelling companions. Or I choose to travel alone, like now." Bob took in Charles-Michel's appearance. He was not quite as tall as Bob, thick silver hair—it had been dark before—even in his hiking gear he looked groomed. Bob could see that Charles-Michel was still aware that he could be charming in his easy-going sophisticated way.

They started down the path. It was not only steep but rocky with loose stones. Both men were agile, but it would be easy to twist an ankle or send a shower of pebbles down the hill. Bob felt a small thrust of rivalry as he managed the descent. He knew Charles-Michel would not miss the opportunity to rib him if he stumbled or slipped. But the challenge of the path gave Bob a bit of time to get his thoughts together. Charles-Michel was such a large part of his student days, a time of discovery, self-discovery. Taking paths that were interesting but twisted, unlike the Camino that led to Santiago, his relationship with Charles-Michel had not been a clear path and in the end had led nowhere beyond a neglected friendship. Bob really did not want to visit this time of his past, especially not now when he was dealing with a crisis with Brigit. And Brigit will meet Charles-Michel. Even though they were only on day four, Bob saw that pilgrims along the Camino did not disappear but kept resurfacing. Some stopped for their feet and others to sight-see; they would connect again at a fountain or a hostel.

"So what brought you to the Camino, Bob?" There were now scrubby oak and gorse bushes on each side of the path but it was getting wider and smoother. "What kind of pilgrim are you? I don't remember you as a religious soul."

"Brigit is. She's a practicing Anglican, so it was her idea. And, we needed to celebrate. That was the plan but I don't know how well that's working." Charles-Michel looked up to meet Bob's eyes. Bob remembered the interest and empathy Charles-Michel showed his friends and it just seemed natural to slip back into the habit of being questioned by him and giving answers.

"We are just coming out of a financial crisis. Six years ago I invested in Gold-Rush. It's a mining company, or was. I don't know if it made much of a splash in Montreal, but it was enormous in Calgary and of course I heard all about it from Dad and my brother and began to follow it."

"Yes I remember all the hype about that," said Charles-Michel.

"Well I invested in them," explained Bob. "It looked so good. They were prospecting for gold in Myanmar. It had just opened up again, and every day there was news coming in about the assays from this exploration site they had staked. It was all so exciting. It was the Wild West and the Klondike all rolled in one. I got caught up in it. I don't know if you remember the details, but the shares were zooming up in value. I bought some early on and then when the new assay results came in rich in gold I felt I had to buy more so I bought short and took out a loan. You have no idea how easy it is to get money. When you go down that road, they are clamouring to lend it do you—'no problem. You have a steady job, your wife too, you own your house. Here, have a quarter of a million dollars. Have more. Have fun. Don't worry; you'll pay us back when your fortune comes in! You're so lucky to have this opportunity blah blah,' as they shove the money at you." Bob stopped and shook his head as he saw himself signing the papers with such excitement.

"I don't mean to say I wasn't responsible for what I was doing. It's just that there are sharks out there cruising around waiting for the weak and for the regular people who have weak and vain moments, they so are! Anyway, then there was a great silence all of sudden. We were hearing nothing from the exploration and testing site. If I had been smart. I would have sold then and made a killing; the shares had soared, but no. I was waiting for the real gold to come in and push those shares up goodness knows where. Charles-Michel—I was doing this for the family. All the things we could do, buy houses for the kids, a real lake house not a cottage. Travel for us all. I could see so many ways we could use that money in a constructive way. It wasn't greed. I really wanted us to experience a wide world."

"And what happened?"

"News came out that the tests had been fixed. Salting — gold dust added to the samples before they went to the lab. Complete fraud: the stocks crashed overnight."

"Mon Dieu. That is awful. I'm so sorry to hear that. But it doesn't really sound like you, Bob. Was it Brigit's idea?" A pain hit Bob in the chest. It flashed through his mind that he was having a heart attack but the pain was that of a heartbreak. Was Charles-Michel being critical of Brigit to try to make Bob feel better? Well, it didn't really matter. Bob could not stop now. And now this friend had appeared on the path and it was as though he had been sent to hear this whole sad story that had hurt them all so much. He plunged on: "It was me. I didn't tell Brigit. I had to tell her when it all went wrong and I lost all that money. The shares just crashed and were worth nothing. Not only had we lost the savings I had invested, but I had borrowed money. Then came the interest rates and the threats to foreclose. Maybe we should have declared bankruptcy, but Brigit insisted that we hang in and pay back the debt, do extra work, lease out the cottage, and manage with one car."

"Bob, you didn't tell her until it was too late? And she stuck by you?"

"Yes. She was great. And now we have finally paid off the debt. We don't have any savings, but we decided that we could manage this trip and that it would be a chance to turn the page."

"And now you have lost her!"

"I don't know if she's really lost or she just lost me deliberately because we quarrelled."

"Give me a break. You quarrelled and now you've lost her," said Charles-Michel.

"Since we started this walk, she keeps throwing the whole thing back in my face. She was really heroic through all those years and now that it's over, she won't let it go. She sort of made a career over the whole paying back the money thing." Bob cut himself short. He would have liked to have said how Brigit was dawdling and not keeping up and that they had agreed on a schedule and she was not respecting it and that she seemed to enjoy delaying even more to take photos and to chat to everyone they met. But he saw, that in telling the story of the last few years, that keeping to the plan on the trail was about the least of his problems.

****

"Brigit, we didn't see Bob. Have you found him?" It was Mireille. She and Luigi had spent a very nice afternoon sightseeing. Brigit smiled bravely. "Have dinner with us" invited Mireille. They agreed to meet and Brigit went off for her shower. 'Cold water only, really! I don't feel like a bracing shower; life is already ghastly enough today.'

The bunk was comfortable, and she had an extra blanket but

Pardon My Camino

Brigit lay awake imagining the worst: Was Bob hurt? Could he have been attacked, robbed, or even kidnapped? How would they contact me if he was in hospital? Or is he just so fed up that he has gone on, taking the opportunity to get rid of me for a while? She went back and forth in her mind, assuring herself that all was well to various scenarios of disaster. And how did she feel about their marriage? Was she really unable to get over the financial crisis as Bob had suggested? Now on the Camino, full time with Bob and time to think, where was her forgiveness and the fresh start? The money had hurt. She liked the good things of life as much as the next person, but they had pulled through. But what still got to her was Bob's attitude. She felt that for him it was all about the system: the stock market, the media hype, the loan sharks, even his brother and father telling him all about Gold-Rush.

For Brigit, the last years had been all about teaching, correcting papers, running the Drama Club at school, helping with the debating group, extra summer school work. Then there had been the house and the kids. And her church community: Altar Guild, the weekly supper for those in need, the schedule of duties—all things that gave her structure and nurtured her soul and heart. And what of friendships, relationships, and her integrity? She veered away from that—'not now.' She checked her watch: three am. A small stirring of peace began to settle in her chest. It reached her head and down to her gut. A quite voice came to her:

"Brigit. He will be alright. Have faith, just hold him in prayer." She did, and sleep came at last.

She set out in the dark. She had had two hours of sleep at the most, but she felt strong this morning; her mind was dim and she just left it that way—'As long as I can,' she thought, 'I will just walk.' The moonlight showed her the markers and the track through the fields. It was a struggle up El Perdón and she stumbled over stones on the path to the summit with the windmills. She rested and gazed back to Pamplona and the Pyrenees, silver against the rising sun and then turned west to the great landscape to come. She was alone with a row of cut-out sculptures of pilgrims, one with a donkey, marching along the ridge. She made her way down the steep rough slope. Once down the hill she followed a gravel track between orchards and small cultivated fields. A blue Renault van passed her with men with black plastic crates all piled up in the back. She came upon them further up the path and stood and watched. They were working in a small sloping field covered with heavy black plastic. The men peeled back the plastic on a raised row of buds, pushed curved knives into the soil and drew out stems of white asparagus that looked like fat white straight worms. As they worked, they packed them in the black crates, neatly, pointy ends up.

She came into the village of Uterga and now she was hungry. It was well into the morning and according to her guide she had walked twelve kilometres. She saw there was a bar-restaurant and went in, gladly took off her pack and ordered a coffee and selected what she had come to call the breakfast tapas — various finger foods made of egg and ham. The local Pamplona newspaper was lying on the bar. She took it to the table and as far as her Spanish went, she could see no news of dead pilgrims or other disaster that might have befallen Bob.

She was surprised at how good it felt walking alone. There was still the whole Bob problem but it was so much easier to walk than stay still and worry. She would walk to Puente de la Reina today and if he wasn't there, she would deal with things then. She found a new rhythm with the Camino: the footsteps of the pilgrims through the thousand years gave her energy and fuelled her imagination. She thought of Chaucer's pilgrims to Canterbury. A time when, for ordinary folk, the idea of travelling for pleasure did not exist and going on a pilgrimage was about the closest people came to tourism. And then poor Don Quixote, eager and valiant at every turn.

"Don Quixote when he saw the strange garb of the penitents, without reflecting how often he had seen it before, took it into his head that this was a case of adventure."

(Miguel de Cervantes. Part four of The Ingenious Gentleman Don Quixote of la Mancha, Chapter 52.)

7. Off the Beaten Track

It was nearly seven o'clock when Bob and Charles-Michel made it to the albergue in Puente la Reina. The town had three hostels; Bob felt that Brigit would have come to this one by the church that they had chosen during their planning as it was the most historic. There was no sign of her. The albergue had a kitchen and dining area so they bought supper fixings to take a break from the pilgrim meals at the restaurants which were becoming a bit monotonous. They bought some white asparagus, lettuce, tomatoes, goat cheese, olives, bread as well as a bar of dark chocolate and a bottle of red wine. Back at the albergue they met Colin who had just arrived. He too had not seen Brigit. Once again Bob had to put up with ribbing.

"It's just as well you met Charles-Michel. Otherwise you probably would have been wandering goodness knows where!"

Charles-Michel agreed: "To Bilbao, where he really wants to go and his free spirit might have just led him there."

"Well you can be sure, if and when I get to Bilbao, I am not going to walk it and not with you two either," retorted

Bob. 'Free spirit indeed. That was how Brigit was walking the Camino.'

After supper they checked out the other two hostels. No Brigit. Bob did think about calling his children in Canada to see if they had heard from their mother, but he did not want to worry them or answer their questions. He was tired of being asked how on earth he could have lost Brigit. And she was the one who left the cell phone behind!

Colin had already left when Bob got up in the morning. Coffee had been made and Charles-Michel joined Bob in the kitchen "Alors, jeune homme, qu'est-ce qui se passe?" which was Charles-Michel's way of asking Bob what he was going to do about his missing wife.

"I'm going to stay here today and wait for her. She must have slept in Pamplona or Cizur Menor so she'll be here today and be on the lookout for me. I'll explore the town and the other Camino path."

"How about I spend the day with you? I could do with a slow day after walking six hundred and fifty kilometres so far, and there's lots of history to check out around here." They explained their situation to the hospitalario who said they could leave their backpacks at the hostel and, under the circumstances, they could stay another night. Leaving a note stuck on the front door for Brigit, they went exploring. First to the church, "Iglesia del Crucifijo. It belonged to the Templars along with the hostel. "It's famous for the crucifix." Charles-Michel was translating from the plaque in the church, "as it is such an unusual form." In a plain rough stone alcove hung the small crucifix. It was in the shape of a Y. The figure of Jesus was thin and suffering with his long arms stretched up, almost in triumph.

"Jesus, a broken body leaving his earthly form to come back as the Christ to all people through the Holy Spirit" said Charles-Michel. Bob looked at him surprised. "You forget, Bob, that while you were doing your high school I was doing my cours classique with the brothers."

"But you're not religious," said Bob.

"I'm not an organized church person but the Christian faith is such a part of my culture. Unlike some fellow Quebecers of my age, I never felt I had to bad-mouth the church. However, I certainly don't feel I can go around calling myself a true Christian."

"Why not? Bob asked.

"Well, being part of a community and supporting each other is a basic part of the Christian life. It's a big commitment to be part of a church. It's amazing when you think of it, how people from all different walks of life come together with their own time and money to worship, do good works, look out for each other—learn together."

"I've never really thought about it like that" said Bob. "Brigit goes to church and helps and is involved and the services and activities all seems to come together."

"And we turn up for Christmas and Easter and expect them to be there for our funerals. Anyway, there are not many parishes where I would feel comfortable."

"Would it make a difference if you were straight?" asked Bob.

"I don't think so. If it was just the fact that I'm gay that's keeping me from church, then the churches would be full of all you straight people, but they aren't. And if I really wanted to, I could find a parish that would welcome me. But I'm happy to do the fun stuff like the Camino."

After looking around the town they walked back to the previous village where another branch of the Camino, the Camino Aragonés, joined their path. Bob remembered that pilgrims coming from southern France and Italy could cross the Pyrenees further to the east at the pass at Somport: a popular route for Roman armies and merchant travellers. As they set out an old man sunning himself in the main square called out to them. "Aquí, aquí, el Camino esta aquí" and he waved his cane at them and pointed along the path they had taken when they arrived the day before. Bob and Charles-Michel just waved back, smiled and kept going.

"Has that happened to you before?" asked Bob. "It's like the last thing they want is stray pilgrims wandering around the countryside."

"Yup, and at night, they have us all tucked up in our bunks with the lights out by ten pm. Then they can settle down and have their dinner. Like putting the children to bed."

"Then it's lights on at the crack of dawn and we are turfed out and back on the path and they are still fast asleep."

By this time they could see a valley before them: fields either side of a straight tree-lined road, but what struck them was a small church nestled down in the valley.

"It's a perfect octagon, amazing," said Bob, They took in the golden stone building encircled by a ring of arches with the roof sloping down from a simple central bell cupola. Charles-Michel was reading from his book: "Eunate, it's a Basque name. Built in the thirteenth Century. Associated with our friends the Knight Templars. Graves have been found with scallop shells so it is thought to be a burial place for pilgrims."

"For those who perished on the way—they didn't have high-tech clothes and boots and engineered backpacks," Bob mused.

"Are you suggesting we cast them all off and hike in sandals with a gourd for water? Now I would be willing, but somehow, mon cher Robert, I don't see you doing that. But if you will, I will," challenged Charles-Michel.

"Oh sure. I have a good mind to do it just to see you suffer!" said Bob as they took the tree-lined path that led them down to the church.

****

Coming into the village of Muruzábal, Brigit saw a picture of a church painted on a wall. She recognized it from a poster she had seen: Eunate—the octagonal church. It would be a detour from the path, but Brigit saw she could do two sides of a triangle and get back to the Camino further along. It would only be three extra kilometres and it would lead her back to Puente la Reina where she was sure Bob would find her. Feeling brave about leaving the Camino, she set out. As she went down the hill along a winding country road, past a little stone chapel, she was struck at how empty the countryside was; no other pilgrims to be seen. Over to her far right she could see the church; the path made a curve, but the direction was clear. She relaxed and enjoyed the walk and the solitude. Crossing a tree-lined avenue she came to the outer ring of arches. From the backpacks outside the porch of the church entrance she saw that other pilgrims were here. She went in. It was dark inside; the only light was from the candles before the statues of saints. She found a seat and as her eyes got used to the dim light she could see the plain unadorned walls. Voices behind her were reciting the rosary. She sat and listened.

Outside, she saw that it was a group of young Italian men who had been praying. She smiled at them in gratitude. She was feeling in a mellow mood and at that moment all seemed well in the universe; these were the encounters of peace and joy she had expected along the Camino.

Beyond the church was a group of low buildings. Brigit knew there was a hostel here and that she could get a stamp for her pilgrims' passport; she definitely wanted to prove she had been here, done the detour and seen this beautiful church. As she came to the end of a wall, she heard a laugh and a voice, "Touché!" followed by more laughter. She stopped dead in her tracks. Her breath caught in her throat. 'Bob?' She came around the wall and saw him sitting at a wooden table with his back to her, talking to another man she did not recognize. They had a picnic laid out in front of them and they were having a fine time. She supposed she must have felt relief at finding Bob but the emotion that won the day was indignation. Here he was laughing, chatting and eating a delicious lunch.

"Bob," she said, and heard her voice too high, too thin.

"Brigit." Bob jumped up and turned around and at the same moment she saw the other man looking at her attentively. She made a supreme effort to smile and took a deep breath to calm herself. Bob gave her a hug which she managed to return.

"Thank goodness I've found you," said Bob.

"Well, it seems I found you, actually," said Brigit. "Oh lunch!" she added trying not to sound too bitchy.

"Brigit, you've got to meet an old friend of mine. Charles-Michel Legeault. Brigit, my wife." The man got up and came around the end of the picnic table and shook her hand. "Enchanté" he said in a rather formal tone.

"Bonjour," replied Brigit impressed with his style. She took in his well cut hair and his clothes and asked if he was Canadian. Bob and Charles-Michel explained how they had been university friends and Charles-Michel made sure she sat down and had some wine with bread and cheese. She started speaking in French to Charles-Michel and Bob joined in; it gave them both a refuge, hiding behind the formality of subjunctive verbs and adjective agreements. When he could do so politely, Charles-Michel excused himself and said he was going to explore a bit further.

"I'm glad you're okay." Bob broke the ice.

"I'm fine. But you didn't seem very concerned."

"I waited for you, looked for you and inquired at the hostels. Apart from reporting you missing to the police, I don't know what else I could have done. Is that what I should have done? Set up a search party?" he said. "Anyway what happened to you after you went into that café? I was waiting for you and you never came out, the last I saw of you was disappearing into a bar full of men. Of course I was worried. Didn't you get my note at the top of the El Perdón with John?"

"What you are talking about?" shot back Brigit. "I stayed in Cizur Menor, worried sick and then set out this morning for Puente la Reina. I set out early and had plenty of time to do this detour and then when I get here, I find you having a fine time with your friend. You were worried? It didn't sound like it to me."

"I was having the best day yet on the Camino. Taking time to look around and being with someone who is good company. It has been a very nice break. And that does not mean I wasn't worried about you. I was sure you would come to Puente la Reina by this evening. And if not, then I would have dealt with it."

"Anyway, who is Charles-Michel?" Brigit was still really angry. Finding Bob, which should have been a good thing, was just all wrong.

"We told you. We were friends at McGill".

"And he's gay."

"Why do you say that?"

"Because he's charming, polite, groomed, cultivated, and there are very few straight guys who seem to take that amount of trouble, and he is probably totally self-centred."

"Well. Why don't you try for a few stereotypes while you are at it? No he is not self-centred; he's a very generous spirit. Yes he is gay—so what of it?"

"Well, you haven't told me what kind of friendship you had?"

"Where on earth is this coming from? Don't be ridiculous. D'you know, I think you're jealous!"

Once again they stood glaring at each other not sure where to go next. And all of a sudden Brigit found herself laughing. Bob was just as surprised but greatly relieved and he joined in.

"What a mess we are in," said Brigit ruefully.

'Maybe I am getting some benefit from the Camino. I have been able to clear the air, at least for a while,' she thought, but she did not say it out loud.

****

Brigit checked into the hostel and went through the shower and laundry routine. A German pilgrim from supper the previous evening arrived and when Charles-Michel turned up, they told him they had all made supper plans, together. Charles-Michel gave Bob a careful look. When he could, he asked if that was wise as the couple had so much to sort out. Bob stiffened and said they were doing fine but that it was "not as simple as that." But Bob knew that he had to talk with Brigit. "Let's go down to the river and see the bridge," he said. As they sat on the shore, they could see how the arches of the bridge made perfect circles with their reflections in the water.

"What do you want to do?" asked Bob. Brigit was silent. "Are you still angry?"

"I don't know where I'm at. It was really horrible when I lost you, but when I saw you again today I was angry all over again. I don't like being like this, you know, and you don't help me."

Bob just kept quiet. He didn't know what he could do to help and he didn't know if he should anyway. This was Brigit's problem and she had to sort it out herself.

"I really liked walking by myself today," she continued. "I was surprised at how good it felt. I think I would like to do that. Yes, walk by myself for some of the stages."

8. You Take the High Road, I'll Take the Low

Bob and Charles-Michel set off early from Puente la Reina. It was time to get going again and that morning, as the sun came up, they made their way along a rough track by the Rio Arga. The Camino then took a sharp right turn and up a steep climb. The path straggled into various uphill options. There had been rain overnight and it was a struggle up slippery slopes and along narrow muddy ledges. At the top they could see back over the valley.

"View and rest stop," Bob declared.

"And breakfast," said Charles-Michel who took off his pack and got out bread, cheese, and an apple.

"Here comes the sun. Good timing!"

"For you my friend," claimed Charles-Michel.

"Always so modest about your accomplishments and influence!"

Bob and Brigit had spent much time the evening before seeing how they could walk apart yet keep in touch. Bob was worried. He felt Brigit had a rather vague attitude and did not realize that she could not just wander around expecting to find a bed and a meal. They asked about buying a replacement phone but were told they could do that in Logroño. As they planned to meet up there anyway, that was no use. For better or for worse they had cobbled together a plan: they phoned their daughter Elizabeth in Canada and arranged that she would be the contact point. It did seem a bit crazy phoning Canada when they would probably never be more than twenty kilometres apart, but in the end it seemed the most practical. Elizabeth said at least she would hear from them this way. They would both call her at least every other day and would next meet in Logroño. If Brigit was a day behind, Bob would wait for her. Brigit said she would try not to fall too far behind but that she was not going to rush her Camino.

Once out of Puente la Reina and the river valley, Brigit could see ahead a little town keeping neatly to the confines of a hill. Cirauqui. White houses with beige roofs rose up the hill to the square church tower. She went up the narrow shaded streets where many of the houses were decorated with coats of arms or scallop shells. Leaving Cirauqui, Brigit saw she was on the Roman road she had seen in pictures during their winter research. It was narrow, lined with yew trees, the paving stones deeply rutted and it led over a bridge across a very small stream. But further on she could hear the groan of backhoes and bulldozers and the trail skirted along a wire fence to separate it from a highway construction zone. Now the path was blocked and a detour pointed up a steep hill, around a vineyard, and down the other side. When Brigit got back down again she could see that the blocked-off point of the path was about fifty meters away and that it had taken her half an hour and much climbing up and down to get back here.

She was frustrated and angry and felt that it was a mean and unnecessary decision by someone who had never had to walk that detour with a pack on a hot day, or maybe, she thought, they are sick and tired of having all these people walking through their work site. She wondered how Bob and Charles-Michel were getting on— they probably just cut through and ignored the signs. And then Bob would be pissed off when she fell behind.

The detours didn't end there; Brigit came across construction for a new housing development and had to make her way through ugly orange plastic fencing and little makeshift arrows. Finally, at the town of Villatuerta, she decided to find the albergue for the night. She was about four kilometres from Estella, where she had been aiming for, but the good thing was she did not risk bumping into Bob and that was just fine.

****

The next morning she made it to Estella and in the large town square found a café for breakfast. From her table she could watch the smartly dressed men and women standing around the bar having their coffee and croissants before work. She would have liked to phone Elizabeth but knew it was still the middle of the night for her. Elizabeth had studied agriculture which was rather a surprise for her parents. Then straight out of college she had married David, a fellow student. They now had their own farm north-west of Ottawa. Brigit and Bob were very proud of them, not only as farmers but as entrepreneurs, and this, along with their young granddaughter Stephanie, had been a great consolation for them through all their recent hard times.

Not for a moment had Elizabeth let Brigit and Bob think that they would not get beyond their problems and move on with their lives. Sometimes Brigit felt their roles reversed; even though Elizabeth was only twenty-eight years old, she seemed to have wisdom and determination beyond her years. 'But maybe it's her generation,' and she wondered if she herself would have launched into such a business venture. 'When I was her age, getting a teaching job was considered a very successful and responsible thing to do,' she thought. Thinking of home, she wondered about her church and the challenges there: the finances, the building to maintain; and then there were things, or more to the point, a person around her church life she didn't want to think about at all. Though the Camino was far from home and home issues should be out of sight, it wasn't working out like that. There was her whole blow-up with Bob, unresolved. He had said to forgive him and move on. 'Oh, if only he knew!' she thought.

A modern stone wall, and below an alcove with a pilgrim statue, a coat of arms and two taps offering wine and water for the pilgrims. This was the famous Bodegas Irache. Brigit got out her tin cup and turned on the brass tap. It tasted like Beaujolais nouveau. Other pilgrims came by the winery and marvelled at this wonderful tradition started by the monks. Brigit took her mug and found a bench in the garden. "The gift of wine." She thought of how Jesus at The Last Supper, had told His disciples to drink the wine as a symbol of His blood and the pact of the new covenant of love with His people. At her church she was always full of wonder when she served the wine at the Eucharist and went from person to person offering the chalice — The blood of Christ, the cup of salvation — and they would look at each other with awe and amazement in their eyes. It never became a routine or lost its reverence.

Brigit kept walking, past gardens and oak woods until she could see in the distance a fortress on a hill, then a church spire and then a village emerged up from the landscape: Villamayor de Monjardín. What a wonderful name. Coming into the village she saw pilgrims sitting at a white plastic table in front of a building opposite the church. Mireille was there.

"This is a little parish-run albergue. It's really charming. Come and see."

Brigit decided to stay for the night. Once organized, they hung their washing on the lines set up in the church yard, then they went into the church, putting a Euro in a slot to turn on the lights. "That's a good idea" said Brigit always aware of church finances. They explored the rest of the village, found a café and sat outside drinking a beer. There was another albergue in the village and in the end quite a few pilgrims joined them in the square, enjoying their beer after the day's walk.

Brigit had spotted a public phone booth and, after supper, balancing her note book on top of a tiny shelf, she punched in the number for the Canada Direct service. It was very strange to hear, in this Spanish village, a voice down the line: "Welcome to Canada. Bienvenue au Canada."

"Hi Mum." Brigit caught up on the news: Stephanie their granddaughter, the farm, some late snow. Elizabeth had already heard from her father that evening. He was in Los Arcos and left a message for Brigit to be sure to phone the next evening as there may be a change of plans for their meeting in Logroňo.

"Mum, what's going on?"

"We are just walking separately for a while."

"Yes but what happened? You and Dad set off for this adventure and you prepared and planned the whole thing for months together. And now you have quarrelled and you're wandering around by yourself and he has met up with some old school chum."

"We didn't quarrel."

"I don't know what else you want to call it. You are both rather distant and polite when you talk about each other and you have decided to spend part of your holiday apart.

Sounds like a quarrel to me. Is it still about the money business?"

"Yes, I suppose it is." Liz could be so direct and she's oversimplifying things as usual, thought Brigit.

"Mum what are you going to do about this? I don't think it's the money anymore. I saw you get through that. It wasn't easy but you did and you seemed closer then than now. Mum, have you told Dad?"

There was a silence. Brigit felt she had to fill the transatlantic void.

"Told him what, dear?" It was her thin voice again. What was Liz asking? What did she know?

"About your relationship with that man. I don't know his name. But Mum, you know who and what I'm talking about".

Brigit froze and for a moment thought about denying everything and laughing it off. But if Liz was talking about it, she must know. She would never just throw out theories.

"I think maybe you're exaggerating," Brigit tried, "and what do you think you know and how?"

"Oh Mum I don't want to sound like some wronged spouse, but I suspected something for quite a long time. When we all came to the church at Christmas that year when there was the great snow storm and everything was running late and people missing. You all had to reorganize who was doing what. I had taken our coats out to the hall and when I was on my way back I saw you talking to this man. He looked like he was the warden on duty. And I heard you,

Mum, and honestly it was just too intimate and cozy for a regular church conversation. After that I just observed you and the odd excuses to make phone calls when you were out with us. And you seemed all of a sudden to be excited about life when it was still a really tough haul for you, or would have been. Does Dad know? I thought it wasn't that hard to see really, when we are so close to you."

Brigit felt herself gag. Was she going to throw up? Maybe Bob did know. "It's all over. It was nothing really," she managed to get out.

"Well, I'm glad if it's over. But I don't think it was nothing. Does Dad know?"

"Damn it, Elizabeth! He doesn't know. At least I don't think so. And really, it's over and it wasn't such a big deal anyway." Her voice was croaking by this time. "I'm going to end now. I promise I will call you tomorrow evening. I can't manage any more this evening."

"Okay, Mum. I'm sorry I upset you. But you know you can't just ignore this."

"Elizabeth, this really isn't your business," managed Brigit.

"You bet it is. You're my parents. I love you, both of you, and you've put me in the mix now as your contact point, so, I'm sorry, but I've decided that I have to speak out."

"I'm going to say goodbye. I can't talk anymore. I'll call tomorrow. I promise."

"Be sure you call. I love you, Mum. Take care. Take care. I'm worried about you."

9. Tread Warily

The church clock rang out the hours and the half hours. Brigit lay in her bunk in misery, groping her way in and out of tears. How could she possibly sleep now that Liz had thrown this in her face, and was Liz right? Did she have to tell Bob? This whole confession and laying everything bare. It's almost self-indulgence; is it really love to confront him with my mess? It was over and done with and she had decided to put this episode behind her. That was how she felt she could move on. 'Wasn't that what all this was supposed to be about— their Camino? Damn it! All this shit just keeps coming back.' She raged to herself and the universe in general that life was sending her more than her share of misery. "Oh God, help me get through this." Her instinct was to hide this whole thing away, bury it, laugh it off, have amnesia, run away, whatever it took to not have to face it, especially not to have to tell Bob about it. 'Can he forgive? Do I want to give him the opportunity?' They had never faced cheating in their marriage. As well as she knew Bob, she did not know how he would react. She was scared, very scared. 'Would he leave her? Would he be able to forgive her?' If he did, what would their life be like? Brigit put her head in her pillow and cried tears of fear and regret.

****

Brigit thought back to the moment when it all started. "I really like your hair like that," Earl whispered to Brigit as he slid passed her to get to the other chair. What was this? Here they were, by the high altar, the choir was singing, the priest was preparing the wine and the bread for communion, and sunlight came through the stained-glass windows making coloured patterns on the floor. Brigit's mood suited the solemnity of the moment. She was preparing to be one of the chalice servers, and so was Earl. That's why they were up at the altar. Brigit loved these moments. She felt her soul soar. What on earth was Earl saying to her? She just stood there, rigid, certainly not looking at him but she could feel his body next to her. Now the priest was ready to start the prayers for the communion and she did her best to join in. How could he be up here and say something like that? Brigit had always felt it was a gift that she could become so involved in the beauty of the prayers, the music, the ritual. "Like your hair…" It kept intruding.

"Brigit. I think I upset you. I didn't mean to be flippant. It's just I found you looking so beautiful, I had to tell you." Earl had come into the Altar Guild room. She was alone tidying everything away after the service.

'Oh my God,' thought Brigit, 'This is turning into a Gothic novel.' Her plan had been to keep clear of Earl and let the whole thing blow over. And here he was telling her how beautiful she was. Earl was a church warden, and this was one of his Sundays on duty so he made sure everything was ship-shape before locking up. It was hardly surprising that he had caught up with her. Some of the women at the church were quite intrigued by Earl. There he was, a rough diamond, stocky, strongly built with short dark hair and an elaborate tattoo on his right arm of an angel holding up a cross. Now in his late fifties, retired, he explained his former professional life as a sports impresario. He had been a kingpin, bringing race-car and motorbike events to towns all over eastern and central Canada; he even seemed to have been involved in beauty pageants. But his real love was boxing.

"I don't fit into that world anymore," he had told Brigit and Bob when they had had a group from the church over to dinner at the house. But Earl did not give up on boxing—he coached at the boys' club in a gym in lower town.

"You missed out on coffee. So did I. Why don't we go out and have a cappuccino? My treat. Let me make up for being so insensitive."

It would look petty to turn Earl down. Brigit had essays to mark but she did have time. Bob was on a work trip out west and spending the weekend with his parents and would be back on a plane that evening. It was February. There had been snow overnight and the sidewalk was slushy and slippery. As they came out of the church to walk to the coffee shop just around the corner, Earl took her arm.

"Watch your feet here. I don't want something happening to you," he said.

'Enough yet!' But she let him guide her through the icy slush. What was she supposed to do—jerk her arm away?

****

"Elizabeth? Hi there. Yes, it's Dad. How's everything going? Did you hear from the people in Montreal?"

"Good to hear you, Dad. Yes, big news. We got a contract with them. They have three restaurants and they want our bison meat. We've still got to work out the delivery details. But it's great."

"Well done, you guys. Breaking into that market. Bringing the wild west to Montreal. You can be a proud Albertan."

"I'll leave that to you, Dad. I'm just Ottawa Valley. Listen, I talked with Mum last night after you called so I've got an update on her progress."

"Good, because we are planning a bit of a detour."

"But you are to meet up in Logroňo? I'm following you on Google Earth. It makes sense. That was your plan."

"Well, as Mum is behind, we are going to visit the San Millán monasteries. UNESCO World Heritage site, lots of history. We'll take a bus there from Nájera. This means we will overnight in Logroňo and then keep going. We can catch up with Mum in Santo Domingo de Calzada."

"Hang on. Let me write that down. Spell it for me, Dad. You haven't even asked me where she is now."

Bob had suggested the detour. He had seen a poster of the two San Millán monasteries at a tourist office.

"And you're willing to deviate from your famous schedule?" Charles-Michel enquired.

"Yeah, yeah, very funny. I guess I must be learning from the Camino— are you happy?

They made it to Nájera, took a local bus out to San Millán and found a pension in the village for the night. Next day they visited the cave up on the side of a hill where San Millán had lived as a priest-hermit in the fifth century. The lower monastery was a far grander affair, and a guide told them it was here, in the tenth century, what was now considered standard Spanish, had been written for the first time. When siesta time came and the whole village closed down, they set out to find their way to Santo Domingo de la Calzada. It was going to be a cross-country trek, but the hospitalario in Logroño had photocopied a page out of a guide with a map. They walked through the forest, meeting no one as they climbed a steep hill and came through to the next valley to the west. They were silent as they walked. They had at least twenty kilometres still to go to Santo Domingo.

Elizabeth had been right. Bob had not asked where Brigit was. It was so easy to get involved in the trail and enjoy Charles-Michel's company. As he walked in silence, the thought that he may be meeting up with her this evening forced him to think about their situation. He had told her he would not put up with her continuing attitude of blame, but he had not thought beyond that. They had been married nearly thirty years He knew it had been a good marriage over most of that time.

They had met on Canada Day at the Canadian Embassy in Washington. She was there with her family. When they got chatting, they found out they were both students at George Washington University. Her father's parish was in a smart suburb in Maryland. That day was also the unveiling of a portrait of Lester B. Pearson, the Canadian prime minister who had been awarded the Nobel Peace Prize for creating the UN Peace Keeping Forces. The portrait had been painted by Brigit's mother. She had commissions from Canada and the States for portraits of leaders in public life, business people, couples, and children.

"But I don't do pets," she told Bob. "Pity really. There is quite a demand for horse and dog portraits and their egos don't extend to how they think they should look."

It was not love at first sight for Bob. In fact it was her parents who caught his interest. They could have been a couple out of literature— the striking clergy man: commanding presence but with a deeper side beyond most common mortals. As for the mother, Isabelle, she was his idea of a classical artist, a Pre-Raphaelite. She combined her bohemian style with chic: long, well cut hair, and that afternoon, a draped dress in an oriental print, amber necklace and earrings.

"Bob, what are you studying at George Washington?" Isabelle Greenfield asked him.

"I'm doing my doctorate in international trade and public administration. This seemed the place to do it, but I plan to make my career in Canada, I hope with the Federal Government."

She asked Bob about growing up in Calgary. "You must miss the Rockies. I was an artist-in-residence at the Banff Centre. It was the only time I got into landscapes, but the scenery just takes over. It's so majestic—what does that leave for the artist? So I stuck with we flawed human beings." She smiled at her husband and Bob half-expected the Reverend Greenfield to add something about flawed humans. They were, after all, his business too.

"I'm doing my Masters in English literature." Brigit told him. "It is a bit of a paradox being in the States when my interest is the female British writers of the 19th century—Jane Austen, the Brontës, and my favorite: Mrs. Gaskell.

"I have to say I don't know much about her. I rather thought she wrote charming society novels,"

"Not at all. Elizabeth Gaskell wrote rather gritty stuff about the conditions for women in England at the time—all the economic and social upsets.

"What should I read by her then?" asked Bob.

"With your interest in political science, I think you should try *North and South*. It's all about the upheavals around the industrial revolution in the north of England and the misery for the agricultural workers in the south."

"So what attracted you to these authors?"

"I think it's the situation of these middle class woman: well educated, talented, and with a social conscience. They could not go out and get a job, so they turned to writing. Many of them were associated with clergymen: either daughters or wives. Maybe I identify with them. Though I wouldn't dream of comparing my life to that of the Brontës'."

"I keep saying I will be the dreadful brother, Branwell," said her brother Peter who had arrived to hear the end of the conversation. "Though to compare Bethesda, Maryland, with the Haworth parsonage on the Yorkshire moors won't go very far! At least the name has that great Biblical ring."

Bob became friends with the family and was often invited to their home for meals and parties. And he began to be fascinated by Brigit—a mixture of Victorian parsonage and hippie U.S. campus in the seventies. She had long dark blonde hair that she would wear loose or caught up in a chignon. She wore miniskirts and Bob enjoyed looking at her strong shapely legs. As they often met at the pool for a student-date of swimming he got to admire the rest of her figure. She was a good swimmer and wore a one piece swimsuit but it still let him see the outline of her breasts and he was sure she had a beautiful cleavage somewhere under all that Lycra. Sitting outside on campus, sunning themselves on a small patch of grass, he noticed a scar below her right knee.

"How did you get this?" he asked as he stroked the mark.

"Fell off a horse when I was fourteen. It would have been okay but then the horse stepped back onto me."

"Ouch, that's no good. Do you still ride?"

"Not much. It was easy then because my grandparents lived up the Ottawa Valley. They had two lovely horses with a meadow so we could ride all the time when we stayed with them. I think the horses were glad to see us leave."

Bob bent down and kissed the scar. He smelt jasmine flowers and fresh air and sunlight and felt tension from his gut move down his body and settle between his thighs. He cupped her calf in his hand, covering the scar with his mouth, his tongue lingering over the now-faint mark.

Bob could not be sure how much sexual experience she actually had. She lived at home, and as she had not accepted his offer to come back to the house he shared with four other students, he was left in the dark. They talked about morality, sexuality, and the general social upheaval that was going on around them in the city, the ghettos and on campus. It was the 1970s and premarital sex had just kept going from the free love of the 1960s. However, over the weeks Bob did have the opportunity to discover more of her body. He was enchanted and excited and started urgently looking for a way to let them have some rather more serious time to themselves.

10. And the Walls Come Tumblin' Down

Leaving Villamayor de Monjardín, the track led between vineyards and hills. The first community was ten kilometres along so no café con leche yet. Brigit made do with an apple and water. That suited her mood anyway—it should be bread and water. She could have walked with others, but she needed to be alone. She had become totally self-absorbed, her feet, her pack, finding a bed, and this total friggin mess. It was her torment, her Slough of Despondency.

****

After that February coffee with Earl they had started to look out for each other. At church meetings, she would catch his eye when someone said something they both found ironic or amusing. And then they both volunteered to organize a sculpture exhibition that the church was hosting.

"We can make a good team for this," Earl said. "You have the art side and the writing and I'm used to organizing events and we can both work on the publicity. We should get some sponsorship too —some corporate cash. Then we can do a bit of a splash for the opening."

They worked together, setting up the show with the curator and making posters, finding a caterer. They did the media interviews together, early evenings for the supper-hour TV and early mornings for the radio shows.

"Time for breakfast," Earl said as they stood outside the CBC studios on Queen's Street.

It was a Saturday morning, and they went down to the market area. They had fruit salad, eggs Benedict, and coffee. Brigit thanked the waiter as he refilled her coffee. "I haven't had real breakfast out in ages."

"Well you should. It's a great way to start the day."

The exhibition was set up in the church hall. Earl had used his connections well and people from the business world, some politicians, artists, academic and community leaders were there. The sculptures were by artists from developing countries. Two of the artists were present and so was a local TV station.

"Congratulations, you two," beamed the Rector. "We had no idea when we offered to host this that it would turn out to be such a big event." and she headed off to talk with the local member of the Ontario legislature.

"And the Bishop is working the crowd too," Brigit grinned. Earl looked to where the Bishop was talking with a Senator and the wife of the president of a high-tech company.

Pardon My Camino

****

Brigit made it to Torres del Rio that night. It was twenty kilometres to Logroňo and next morning she made an early start. Though the highway was not far away, the path went along earth tracks through vineyards with almond and olive trees placed among the vines. As she came to the town of Viana she got a whiff of something sweet. 'What is that?' Looking around at the ancient church and the tall houses with their decorated gateways she felt welcomed; she found a café and ordered her café con leche and chose a couple of the daytime tapas. Leaving Viana, her path threaded through backyards and garden plots with fruit trees, rosy tomato vines, pepper plants, and raised rows of asparagus, lettuce, and spinach. There was a little stream where people filled their watering cans. "Buenas tardes," she called out to an old man lovingly tending his rows.

"Buen Camino. Pray for me in Santiago!" the call came back.

And now she could smell baking and soon she was walking along the wall of what indeed turned out to be a cookie factory. If the smell was not enough, there was a big sign with a picture of golden galletas. The sky was clear and the path gentle but she needed to stop. There was a pain shooting through her right heel. She found an open area with some shade under a little flowering tree and took off her pack and sat in the grass to rest.

****

After the sculpture show she and Earl became more creative at finding reasons to meet and that is when things really did start to get more serious. At least when they were doing the art show that kept them busy, but now, when they were together, they just centred on each other. Earl had a small house in the Glebe area of Ottawa. It had been his mother's and it was warm and worn in a cozy way. He had taken over the house after he and his wife divorced and his mother died, which all occurred about the same time. Brigit began stopping by when school ended for the day. Earl would wave her in and insist she relax while he made tea. He said after dealing with the teenagers at school, she needed quality-relax time. Earl wanted to hear about the kids, what she was teaching, and the things they said.

"You're going to be one of those teachers they will remember years from now. You know, future prime ministers will say, 'it's all thanks to Mrs. Matthews'." He teased her, and she was flattered. After these meetings she would go home and slip into her role as wife and mother, refreshed and able to cope so much better.

But one day things changed. She had been dropping by for tea for about a month. It was one of those days when you can feel quite confident that spring really has arrived. Ottawa was showing off her tulips in the parks and along the canal not far from Earl's house. Brigit entered and Earl closed the front door. They stood together, in greeting, but continued to hold each other. Brigit broke away, almost shivering despite the warmth. "It is so gorgeous today, and the tulips, such a shock of colour, almost gaudy after the winter." It was her high thin voice. She went through to the living room. The French windows were open.

"It's spring when I get to leave the patio doors open for the first time," said Earl and he came up behind her and wrapped his arms around her and put his head on her shoulder. Brigit put her hands on his, not quite sure what to do. But Earl started to nuzzle her neck with his lips and she leaned her head into his. She turned—he turned her—who knows—but she was facing him, in his arms and he took her face in his hands, they kissed. It was so gentle, she was amazed. Earl, the boxer with his tough, taut body: she had never expected such tenderness. And he kept kissing her, on her mouth, her neck, over her face, still as tender but relentless, never pausing. Brigit felt as though she was drinking port wine. She could feel warmth radiating from her lips and down her chest, along her spine. She hardly kissed back, just stayed there in his touch, in his warmth, drinking in the tenderness, almost immobile. And his hands began to gently move over her body, over her back, her shoulders, her buttocks, around to her breasts. She felt herself melt. She had read love scenes like this. She was mesmerized and Earl did not stop. It became even more like the great romance when he picked her up and carried her into the bedroom. Did she resist? Not at all! She might be passive on the outside, but fire coursed right through her and desire burnt between her thighs snaking into her gut, taking over her whole being, demanding attention. He did not seem to expect anything from her but when he moved his body onto hers, he looked down into her eyes and she eased her legs apart for him.

****

The walk into the city of Logroño was another Camino mixture. The hard-packed path did keep Brigit off the highway but there were plenty of industrial buildings and road works. Another uphill and there was a sign to say it was now the province of La Rioja, the famous wine district. 'Oh shoot!' Now she could feel her heel chaffing in her boot. Vineyards butted right up to the highway and the factories walls. She followed the markers, a new design for the new province: a short grey pillar with a stylized swirling scallop shell. The path went down to the rio Ebro, where a stone bridge led into the city.

"Completo— no room," explained the hospitalaria at the Logroño albergue. Brigit sighed. Other pilgrims were sitting around looking showered and relaxed and here she was hot and sweaty, her shoulders aching from her pack and her foot burning. Now she would have to sort out a pension. The guide book only mentioned this one hostel. She sat down on a bench discouraged, but the albergue lady started giving her instructions.

"She says there's another hostel at one of the churches," a young man with an English accent translated. "They don't open until this one is full but they will have room for you." Three other pilgrims arrived through the archway including Mireille. She flopped down next to Brigit. Between the English man and the kindly lady, they understood that the parish of one of the churches had recently started to look after the overflow pilgrims. The hospitalaria plucked at Brigit's arm.

"Vamos!" she smiled and gathering up her pilgrim-chicks, led them out of the courtyard, back to the Camino and two hundred meters further along she pointed at a church and told them to ring the bell at the house next door. It was one large room on the second floor, a high ceiling, tall windows looking out onto the street with tiny balconies, just enough room to air their hiking boots. She and Mireille took their thin mattresses from the pile in the corner and put them next to each other on the marble floor. Brigit went through her routine: out with the sleeping bag and other clothes: undies, light pants, a T-shirt, sandals. Her fleece jacket went into the sleeping bag stuff-bag to make a pillow. Barefoot, she gave her feet a careful inspection. Sure enough there was a red swelling on the outside of her right heel. There was already a blister. "Oh hell!"

Mireille called her for the shower. There were just two cubicles so no snoozing yet. "There's a great Spanish product for feet called Compeed." Mireille said. "It's a sort of pretreated plaster bandage that treats blisters. We'll look for a pharmacy when we go out. Why don't you have a snooze after your shower and rest your foot."

She must have slept because she could remember her dream: There she is in a wheelchair and Charles-Michel is pushing her up a steep hill. Bob is already at the top and keeps telling them to hurry up and that it's an easy climb!

As they left the house they looked up at the façade of the church.

"Iglesia de Santiago El Real — church of St. James. Real is royal I think," Brigit worked out. "And look there's the man himself — Santiago, slaying more infidels." At the top of the façade was a statue of a man with a sword on a mighty horse riding over severed heads lying on the ground.

"That looks like St. James too, and he looks so much calmer and more benevolent," Mireille said as she pointed to where another statue of St. James stood seeming to point along the Camino. Walking in the city was not painful for Brigit as her sandals had open backs. It was early evening and a Friday. The city was heaving with people. They came to an open plaza with cafés and managed to get a table. When the waitress came, they each ordered a glass of La Rioja wine. It came with a dish of olives. It was fun being with Mireille and Brigit told her of the wheelchair dream.

"You make Bob sound like a monster," said Mireille.

"No, he's a lovely man. Well, most of the time. It was just a dream. By the way, what happened to Luigi? The Italian who was walking with you," Brigit asked.

"Good question. What did happen to Luigi? We were walking together and I was quite touched that he seemed happy to walk at my pace. Well, apparently, he had hurt his leg and was walking slowly to let it heal. And I thought it was for my company!" She laughed. "And he was very charming. How about you? Weren't you going to meet Bob here?"

"It's the Camino thing, learning as we go. Yes we were, but he met an old university friend and they decided on a detour to a monastery. I'm enjoying having time to myself."

"Yes, I can understand that. Still…"

"It is strange because this trip was to be a celebration and reconciliation, with life and each other." Brigit gave her an edited version of their life for the last five years with Bob's investments and the financial struggle.

"Sounds like it was a long haul. What went wrong now?"

"I've been trying to work it out," said Brigit. "Things just seemed to fall apart when we got here. We had made planning this trip such a project."

They ordered another glass of wine each.

"We should have ordered a bottle first time around," said Mireille. "Go on."

"We started out, and everything was getting on my nerves."

"That doesn't sound good."

The waitress turned up with the wine and some more olives.

"Then in Pamplona we got separated. I think it was my fault. It was a shock and I was so worried. And just to add to it all, I had left our cell phone behind on the first night. So he kept going, and then he met this old chum of his, just by chance."

"So where did you meet up?"

"That wasn't a great moment either, but I did keep my cool, more or less. I just stumbled on Bob and his friend Charles-Michel at the Eunate church. There they were having lunch al fresco. I was worried about him and he said he was worried about me, except it didn't look like it with the wine, the Parma ham, cheese, and olives."

Brigit and Mireille started to laugh.

"There I was all covered in Camino dust. They had spent the night in Puente and had just wandered up with the lunch bag, all cool and clean. I had every right to look a bit incredulous and be a bit sarcastic."

"So what is the friend like?" asked Mireille.
"Charles-Michel, charming and sophisticated, doing his best, the poor man. He got stuck in the middle of our situation. He managed to slip away as soon as he decently could. Bob's moving on and that's making it even worse for me. I feel he should be suffering some more. Hell, I am!"

****

"Liz, I'm sure you understand, that though your Dad and I are only about thirty kilometres apart, it's a long way when you are walking, with a pack." It was Brigit's evening call to Liz.

"Mum it turns out Dad's friend had a cell phone at the bottom of his pack all along. I'll give you the number."

"Gracious. Guess he didn't realize it was an issue. I'm just being sensible about how far I walk every day. I have to watch out for my foot. If I fall too far behind, I'll take a bus and catch up. But not yet. I'm still managing." This seemed to satisfy Liz and at least she had not brought up the Earl situation.

11. Midnight in Camino Insomnia

As night is falling, it's getting late.
My God I am afraid to lose the trace of the path.
Don't leave me all alone. Stay here with me.
Because I've been a rebel, I have looked for danger,
I have searched with curiosity on the highest hills, in the
deepest abyss,
Forgive me Lord and stay here with me.

*Hymn from the evening order of service of the Iglesia de Santiago
El Real de Logroño*

Inside the church was deep velvet darkness. A pool of light
lit the pilgrims seated in a semicircle, each in their own high-
backed dark wood seat in the retro-choir. They took turns to
read passages from the evening service, each in their own
language. Brigit read the hymn:

"...because I've been a rebel, I have looked for
danger..." Her voice choked. A rebel, a wilful thoughtless
rebel: she struggled through the third verse.

"How fast the evening falls! Stay here with me! Amen."

97

She glanced at the priest who smiled at her and nodded gently. 'Oh dear God he must know, it must show. Why did he choose me to read this?' The evening service continued, the words weaving through her as she gazed at the hymn on the green leaflet … "in the deepest abyss forgive me, Lord." Would God really forgive her? But how could she forgive herself? How could she find any excuse for risking her marriage and damaging the lives of all those she loved and cherished the most in the world? What would make her betray herself and all she believed in?

Compline was over. The priest gave the blessing, and asked them to pray for the members of this congregation.

In the sleeping area the lights were dim; Mireille was already in her sleeping bag. The night, which had started off so peacefully, got noisier: the lovely windows that overlooked the street also let in all the noise from the Friday night crowds walking past as they left the bars. If they just walked on by, it would not be so bad, but the area in front of the church seemed to be a favourite spot to hang out, chat, laugh, and sing. Then too, there was the church clock; and so it was another sleepless night.

The next morning Brigit carefully peeled the cover off the Compeed and stuck it over the blister, put on her hiking sock, and eased into the boot and laced it tight. She set out alone. It had started to rain overnight and this morning there were no signs of it stopping. Mireille had gone ahead. Her friend Barbara from New York was a volunteer hospitalaria in the albergue in Grañón and she was going to spend a few days with her.

"I feel bad about leaving you but we'll meet up along the trail."

It was a relief to walk slowly and to stop as often as she needed but Brigit missed Mireille. They would have had a laugh over a collection of gnomes in a garden on the way out of town. The rain kept coming. Brigit walked through suburbs and then along the shoulder of the highway, but, she thought, at least it is paved and I can keep out of the puddles. However, after taking a tunnel under an even larger highway, she was back into fields and vineyards and a muddy trail. She could see the town of Navarette in the distance and decided to find a restaurant there for lunch.

She took her time over lunch so the trail was deserted by the time she left the town. The ground was now red clay turned into sticky mud and it caked her boots like a kid's floatie. She did her best to avoid the water puddling along the dirt road but in many places it flooded the whole width of the path. Through the rain she could see rows of vines, monotonous and rigid, like multiple narrow-gauge railway lines. At the edge of the fields there were lean-to huts for the field workers, lunch shelter for shade or from the rain. Brigit decided to rest in one and check her feet. She scrambled up the bank through the slime. The hut was furnished with an old wooden kitchen set—a table and three chairs. She dumped her pack on the table and took off her boot.

"Oh hell!" The dressing hung pathetically from one corner. Her first aid kit was at the bottom of her pack, so it meant getting everything out to get at the plasters. It was no use changing her socks. Her second pair had not dried from when she had washed them the night before. She sat on the straight-back wooden chair looking out at the rain. At least her feet could get some air even if it was damp. There was no sign of any other pilgrims and there were no workers around: all at home in the warm. She sat feeling desolate. 'Where is all this going? I'm getting nowhere. I'm walking less and less each day. Bob is getting on fine without me, and anyway I don't know how to deal with him—or me for that matter. I miss the kids. I'm homesick. I really am,' she realized.

"Oh heavenly Father. What am I going to do? This is all too much for me." She dug out her New Testament. 'Poor old James. Where was I with his letter?' She searched through the Epistles looking for it. 'I don't even know where it comes. Oh here, right after Hebrews.'

"Blessed is the man who endures temptation for when he has been approved, he will receive the crown of life which the Lord has promised to those who love Him…" Brigit read it again. She must have heard this reading many times in her life but she had no memory of it. "Oh I love you Lord but I didn't endure temptation. I just went full steam ahead, into sin." She sat there wondering sadly about her weakness for temptation. "But God loves me regardless." That's what her father would have told her. She missed her father. And sitting there, damp and cold, she cried for the loss of her father, even though it was four years now since his death. She tried to pray. She wanted to, but her mind wandered and she was remembering a summer evening as a kid at the lake with her parents, brothers, and sister and her prayer was left hanging, unfinished.

She put everything back in the pack and stuck fresh Compeed on her foot—trying to make them extra firm—before putting on the damp socks and then the damp boots. She put the rain cover on the pack and swung it on her back. The pack dragged on her shoulders. She adjusted the straps but it was either too tight, or when released, too loose. So she just tightened them up and gave up, scrambled down the bank, over the ditch and back onto the path.

Brigit no longer knew where the wet from outside met the wet inside. Despite the chill, she could feel herself sweating as she climbed a path that just seemed to keep going. At last she reached the village of Ventosa. She followed the main street to the square with the church. As she looked around, she saw people standing in a group. Then a bus came along; Nájera was the posted destination. Almost by instinct, Brigit joined the group and waited her turn to climb on the bus. She sorted out the fare, took off her pack, and sat down next to a teenaged boy plugged into his earphones. 'That was simple, and here I am!' Her foot throbbed, but it was such a relief to be out of the rain and moving forward. She managed to get out her guide and saw that the albergue in Nájera was a new large municipal one. 'Good. Room for me.'

The bus made stops along the way for passengers from hamlets and farms that Brigit could see through the rain. After about twenty minutes, the bus crossed a bridge and came into the town. The next stop was in a square and the bus driver turned around and called out to Brigit that the albergue was here. 'Well, bless him. More looking after pilgrims. No passing under the radar here.' she thought as she thanked him on her way out.

The albergue was a long one-storey building set on one side of the square. It was four o'clock and she could see there were bicycles already standing in the open court yard in front of the albergue doors. 'Almost worst to cycle in the rain than walk,' she thought.

There was an older Spanish man in the office. He took one look at Brigit and told her to leave her boots and coat out in the hallway. He led her through to a large dormitory.

She managed to get herself to the shower. Standing in the warm water was consoling. Drying herself on her small microfiber towel was laborious. Her usual juggling to keep her clean clothes dry, with, as usual not enough hooks, was frustrating.

'Do designers ever use their showers to try them out?' she thought bitterly. Still damp and clammy she made it back to her bed. Her rain-gear had actually managed to keep most of her clothes dry. There were wet rings around the collar and cuffs, her walking pants were wet below the knees, otherwise her clothes were just damp. Her boots were two muddy, soggy blobs. From under there somewhere, would eventually emerge her valiant high-tech warrior boots. At the moment they looked grumpy and useless. 'Just like me,' she thought as she carefully wiggled into her sleeping bag.

"Oh, excuse me!" Brigit woke up with a start from a sharp jolt to find a large man with a big pack looming over her. "Forgive me. I hit your bed." he said.

"No problem," mumbled Brigit, then managed a "Hi." She looked at her watch and saw that she had slept for two hours. Most of her body did feel better but she could feel the throbbing pain in her right heel— 'that place again.' There was the blister, well the former blister, as the top skin had now completely come away and the underneath a glutinous hole was red and raw, and more alarming still, the whole area looked angry with the skin taut and shiny around the wound. 'Oh hell. Not good.' Various scenarios flashed through her mind: go back to sleep, find an enormous plaster and just cover it up and hope it will go away, then horror scenes of gangrene and the foot being amputated, maybe her leg… like the pilgrims who used to die along the Camino. She sighed and brought herself back to reality. 'This is the twenty first century not the Middle Ages. Proper dressings and antibiotics would look after it.' However, that did mean getting medical help. She struggled up and managed to put her sandals on and made her way to the office. A group of

Spanish cyclists were chatting with the hospitalario but there was a woman volunteer there now as well. She looked at Brigit, half smiled and nodded her head back "¿Si?"

"Do you speak English?" Brigit asked. No way could she manage this in Spanish.

The women shrugged her shoulders. "A little, yes."

Brigit sat down at the desk and explained about her foot and that she needed medical help.

"Show me!" ordered the woman.

They both inspected her foot. "That is not good. You should not walk. How can you walk like that? You must be careful."

"That is why I need to see a doctor."

The woman now called across to the hospitalario and rapid conversation went back and forth until he came to look at her foot. He shook his head and looked at Brigit as though she was a wilful child.

"Is there a clinic I can go to and see a doctor?" she asked. Why did they keep carrying on as though they had discovered the wound and she didn't know anything about it?

"Your foot is bad. You have to see a doctor!" the woman told her.

Brigit took one sharp breath and then another. "Yes, can you help me?"

In the end the woman drove Brigit to a clinic attached to the town hospital. She took over the whole situation. Brigit sat there with what she hoped was an intelligent and amiable expression on her face. 'Whatever it takes to get this seen to.' The woman came in with her to the examination room and once again, vivid and assertive explanations seemed to be going on. It turned out the doctor spoke English, and even smiled at her and acknowledged her existence.

"Yes, you have the start of an infection. You should not have let your feet get wet. It is dangerous when you have open wounds." He then inspected both feet. "No Camino walking for three or four days. We will dress your foot and give you a prescription for the infection. "Are you walking with others?"

"Yes, my husband. But he is ahead."

More disapproval, more confusion. Brigit said she would try and contact her husband. The woman said she should rest extra days at the albergue. "You must not walk. Do you understand? Your foot is infected; you must rest it. And you must take your medication. Do you understand?" Brigit was worn out and worn down. "Yes, yes, thank you, thank you." More nodding and smiling.

Back in the dormitory, everyone seemed to have heard of her situation. People came and sympathized with her, telling of others or themselves, with various ailments: pulled tendons, bum knees, blisters—stories galore. And offers of supper: she went to the kitchen area and let others feed her. It was like the loaves and the fishes, except she was only one, but they kept showering her with food. There was even a couple who had been with François from Roncevalles.

"François is ahead but we had to take two days off because I pulled a muscle in the back." explained the wife, and the husband ran his hand on his back to show just where it had all gone wrong.

12. Thy Presence, My Light

Bob and Charles-Michel reached Santo Domingo de Calzada around seven pm. There was room for them at the second hostel. A large no-nonsense Spaniard was in charge; he gathered up their packs under his arm and took them upstairs and showed them into a pleasant dormitory with real beds, well-spaced out. They got the tour: the bathrooms, then the backyard where there was a separate kitchen and dining area, also, a fancy mini-pagoda-like structure with chickens and a white fluffy cock. "¡Los gallinas! The cathedral chickens," the hospitalario told them. On the way back they went through a large, crowded dormitory area. "The first to come sleep in this lower room, and the last ones, who are tired, get the good rooms upstairs." This was different. When the hospitalario heard they had walked from San Millán, and that was why they were so late, he gave them a front door key so they would not have to rush back for the ten o'clock curfew. "Make sure you see the cathedral. The pilgrims' mass starts at eight."

They arrived at the cathedral just as the mass was ending. They looked around the large sanctuary with its columns, paintings, and golden wooden carvings. A railed-off enclosure housed the tomb of Santo Domingo. There was an information sheet in English. "Santo Domingo, hero of the Camino," Bob read. "He lived in the eleventh century. They wouldn't let him become a monk at San Millán because he was illiterate.

"That sucks," said Charles-Michel.

"He devoted his life to helping pilgrims, he built bridges, and he improved roads and founded hostels."

"Their loss, our gain. It's amazing that was nearly a thousand years ago and we are still walking the Camino and remembering him," said Charles-Michel

As they headed back to the main door, a tiny person, as though out of a folk tale, put out her hand and pulled on Charles-Michel's sleeve and pointed to the ceiling. "¡Las gallinas y el gallo!" High up on the wall was a window where chickens were pecking around.

"What did she say? Chicken and the egg?" Bob asked.

"Not the egg—the chickens and the cock, you dumb-wit," laughed Charles-Michel.

"What's with the chickens? I keep seeing pictures of them around too." Bob asked.

It was Colin who unravelled the mystery. "How can you be here and not know the story?" he asked, exaggerating his Australian accent. When he heard they had a key to the hostel, he announced they should all go to a restaurant he had scouted out.

"Well, tell us the story, then," said Bob.

"Not till I have a glass of wine and ordered my food," said Colin.

"Legend has it, or the truth be told, depending where you come down on these matters, that a German couple and their adult son on the pilgrimage stayed the night here. The buxom inn-keeper's daughter took a shine to the son. He was a pious lad on a pilgrimage and spurned her advances. She was pissed off and hid some of the church silver in his pack and then denounced him. He was found guilty and hanged. The parents went to Santiago, no idea what had happened to their son. Then on their way home they saw him on the gallows, and he was still alive! Double surprise. And this is where Domingo comes in. He had kept him alive. So Santo Domingo goes with the parents to the local sheriff and tells him to let the lad go. The sheriff, who was cooking a nice fat chicken over the grill for his supper, laughs at them.

"That man is no more alive than this chicken. Yes you might guess: whereupon the chicken jumps off the spit, reintegrates its feathers, very much alive. And our hero is saved and goes back to Germany with Mum and Dad. And those chickens are the descendants of the original one and that is the truth."

As Bob and the others walked back from the restaurant, Charles-Michel's phone rang.

"Hallo Brigit, yes it's Charles-Michel. How are you? No, we are still up. Here's Bob."

"Hello darling, how's it going? Where are you?"

"It's good to hear your voice. I'm in Nájera. I took a bus here for the last bit. I was so wet and my foot has become a problem. I'm at the albergue and they helped me get my foot seen to at the clinic. I'm going to be okay but the thing is, the doctor says I have to rest it for three or four days."

"Darling, how awful for you. How is it feeling now, are you in pain?"

"It's sore but I feel so much better now that I have had it seen to. I'm pissed off about having to rest. I've been thinking, if I could get transport to Burgos and find a pension, I could wait for you there."

"Can you be seen by a doctor in Burgos?"

"Yes, there is a clinic I could go to."

"Good. I think the Burgos idea is good. But here is what I am going to do. I'll come and find you and we will go together to Burgos and you can rest up there. I don't want you to do that trip alone. How does that sound?"

"Bob, I don't want to upset your walk. I am sure I could manage."

"Don't be daft darling. Of course I'll be there. Just sit tight at the albergue there. Tomorrow morning I'll sort out the bus. We're in Santo Domingo, so tell the albergue I am coming and that you need to stay there at least until noon. Just stay put so I can find you."

"Oh thank you sweetie. I am sorry to be a trouble but it would be lovely. I'll be here. With my foot I'm not going anywhere. I'm at the municipal hostel. It's by the river."

****

Bob could hear rustling noises coming from the chickens. He was in the backyard. Above, the Milky Way dazzled and seemed to beckon him into a great universe. It was two in the morning and with no sign of sleep, Bob got up and slipped outside. Brigit kept coming back into his thoughts. As he sat in the darkness, he thought back to their student days in Washington. It had taken some planning, but at the end of the summer term, Bob had finally managed to organize a trip to New York City for the two of them. They had a friend who played in a string quartet and the group was performing in a festival of Early Music. They would go for the weekend and stay at the friend's apartment in Manhattan, but as the friend was also one of the festival organizers, they did not expect to see much of her. They took the train from Washington on the Friday afternoon, stopped by the apartment, then set out to explore. It was summer and the evening was light and warm.

"Where do you want to go?" Bob asked, his hand stroking her hair.

"Greenwich Village. That would be fun wouldn't it?" She took his arm leaning her body into his. They found a restaurant and had something to eat. Back on the street they floated along with the evening crowd, looking at the art on display, and watching the musicians. Bob buried his face in her hair and whispered, "let's go back to the apartment." He wanted Brigit and this was the time: enough of the delicious anticipation!

"This is a first for me," she whispered to Bob as their hands started to explore beyond each other's clothing.

"Oh you sweet thing," murmured Bob. "We're going to be fine. I don't want you to worry and I will use a condom." Bob had not had many sexual partners but he was experienced enough to be able to take things slowly. Thirty-three years later, as he sat out there under the stars, he could feel the excitement of the intense joy and pleasure of that weekend. She had been so responsive and so attentive, generous and loving. They hardly slept that night. They both wanted more. Brigit would run her hands over Bob's body, over his chest, down over his stomach and between his legs, gently brushing him, still shy to do more than that. It sent Bob wild. He wrapped his legs around her and pulled her up onto his body. She wanted to learn and she let Bob guide her.

"Would your parents be very shocked?" Bob asked as they finally lay together resting.

"They know, or have a pretty good idea anyway," said Brigit.

"No! Are you sure?"

"Yes. Otherwise there would have been arrangements for me to stay with friends. I usually stay with family friends when I go out of town."

"There are always friends available?"

"Oh, you have no idea. We have so many friends from Dad's old parishes, or people who moved away and keep in touch. It's fun and they are always so kind to me. But this is more fun." She tickled Bob and laughed. She was so sweet and so beautiful. Bob was in love. They both were. Bob remembered it all— it really was wonderful to be young. Despite the lack of sleep they had gone the next day to the Museum of Modern Art and then to the music festival and joined up with their friends for a fun evening. Then back to the apartment for more glorious sweet love. On the train back to Washington they talked about getting married. Bob told her that he could not see their relationship going any other way. They knew it was early days yet and they were both students and would not be able to get married for a while. But they would tell their parents. They did not want to hide something so important from them and they thought it might make getting together a bit easier in the meantime.

13. The Land of El Cid

Next morning, Brigit had more offers of food for breakfast from fellow pilgrims. The news that Bob, the missing husband, was actually going to come and join her met with general approval. 'It's like church,' she thought. 'We all care and follow each other's business.' But it was comforting that these people worried that she was going to manage. She spent the morning doing her washing. The albergue had a washer and dryer for pilgrims. 'Such a luxury,' she thought. 'Well, at least I will be washed and fresh when Bob gets here.' As she shook out her washing from the dryer, she did wonder how their reunion would work out. 'I was grumpy when we set out separately from Puente. How long ago was that now? Five days. But he was so sweet on the phone last evening and he sounded like his old self. Well, my putrid foot can bring us together.' And she realized that it had also crowded out her turmoil over Earl. In fact the more distance she had from her Earl adventure, the stranger the whole episode appeared to her. As though it was not her at all who had had this affair, just some gossip she had heard. 'I haven't thought about him since Compline in Logroño. Maybe that was my last agony and now it's over for me and done with. Wow, little foot, you're doing double duty.'

****

Bob arrived at noon. "Yes. Your wife is here," the hospitalario told him. "Go through to the dormitory; she is the only one there."

"Hi, darling. No don't walk, I'm coming to you," said Bob as he saw her at the far end of the dormitory. And they hugged and then kissed and it felt good. Bob insisted they sit on the bed and not stress the foot.

"It's fine when I wear my sandals. I'm allowed to walk a bit."

"Well let's save that for when we really need it. How's it feeling today?"

"Not bad, considering." And she told him about being chastised by the hostel volunteers and the general horror about her foot. "As though I had done it on purpose."

"It did go from bad to worse in a hurry. I guess you should not have walked yesterday. Colin was on at me about the dangers of getting your feet wet."

"Poor you. I don't know quite what you were supposed to do about that. I was not very open to advice from you."

"I hope you— we—have got beyond that now."

"Me too. Silver lining from my poor old foot."

"The hospitalario told me they could help us sort out transport and a pension in Burgos. Do you want to wait here while I talk with them?" asked Bob.

"No, I don't want to be left out."

There was a bus that they could take at two o'clock. It was close on one hundred kilometers to Burgos, so with the stops, about a two-hour trip. As for accommodation, the hospitalario knew of a pension he could recommend. He phoned up. Yes, there was a room they could have for four nights or five if necessary.

"Bob, that's a big stop for you, well for us, but I'm stuck with my foot anyway."

"Darling, it's fine. We'll be in a big city, not like being stuck out in a village somewhere. And I was working it out with the guys, and they will arrive while we are there. What about Mireille?"

The Burgos bus did a loop through Nájera before heading back onto the highway. "It looks like it will be the N-120 all the way." said Bob.

"These seats are so comfy," said Brigit as she settled in. "And I can feel the heater. I don't think I've been this comfy since home."

Bob could see from his guide that the highway and the Camino zig zagged across each other much of the way. At one point, the road went through a deep narrow valley, dark with tree. "Up on that ridge is the path to San Juan de Ortega." He did regret that he would miss that part of the Camino. It was a wild track that left the highway and the

116

valley and went up steeply through the forest to the remote monastery of St. John of the Nettle: "a refuge in a dangerous and wild place for those ancient pilgrims."

They took a taxi from the bus station to their pension in Calle de la Pueblo, a narrow street off one of the central squares in Burgos. On the way they passed a statue of a warrior on horseback with a flowing beard, lance and shield. "El Cid," said the taxi driver waving proudly. The driver managed to drive the car right up to the tall double wooden doors that gave right onto the street. There was a list of doorbells with the pension well marked; a voice came over an intercom. Bob gave their name, and then came instructions about segundo piso. He did not get the rest but second floor was a good start. They made their way up the stairs, Bob with the packs and Brigit managing her wounded foot. An energetic middle-aged woman came out and greeted them and showed them into a hallway. They sorted out keys: one for the outer street door, one for the landing hallway door and one for the room. They paid for four nights and Brigit said the sentences she had prepared that they may wish to stay further.

"Si, si." She pointed to Brigit's foot and shook her head and smiled sympathetically. She had obviously heard all about it when the booking was made. She picked up one of the backpacks, took them down the hall, showed them two full bathrooms and then to the room at the back of the house. There were more demonstrations with the keys, then a little test for both of them as to which key was for which door. Brigit gave a giggle. "Si, si. Keys are fine," Brigit was just able to get out as now she doing her best to stifle her laughter.

"Si si, todos está bien. Gracias, gracias," said Bob trying to politely swish her out of the room. Whatever it was that had set Brigit off, it was not getting any better. The pension lady left with a coquettish smile at Bob.

"Darling, what it is?" said Bob. "You're practically in hysterics."

"I'm so sorry. I didn't think I could contain myself."

"Well you didn't. She must think we are a very strange couple."

"It's when she started in on the keys. You have to realize that there is a whole ceremony around the keys that comes with a practical exam. I ran into that in Torres. Oh my God, it is so good to be with you!"

They clung to each other, relieved at how their reunion was turning out.

"Well are you going to stop laughing enough to let me kiss you?"

"Si, mi El Cid."

"More Ed Cid." And he pushed Brigit onto the bed and found her lips. "When was the last time we made love in the middle of the day in a cheap hotel room?" murmured Bob.

"Too long, but those boots are coming off."

"You are getting so fancy in your ways."

Between them they got the boots off and Brigit flung one across the room with another giggle. Bob was worried for a moment that she was off again but she was too busy undoing his hiking shorts.

Their love making was passionate if a bit scrambled, but they made up in tenderness as they lay on the bed catching their breath and trying to untangle from the pink bedspread.

"Oh my God, your foot! I forgot about it. Did I hurt you?

"Oh thank you, sweetie. No. We had far yummier things to think about than my rotting foot. It's feeling not at all bad."

"I think I should avail myself of señora's bathtubs," said Bob.

****

Bob and Brigit slept in the next morning. They washed some of Bob's clothes and managed to set up a clothes line along the little window balcony.

"I saw a café just round the corner. Can you manage that? We need breakfast." Getting food with Brigit's foot was a challenge. Bob had gone out the evening before and had come back with a pizza.

"Oh yes, I would really like to leave the room, charming as it is," said Brigit. "Let's try that hot chocolate. I've seen people drinking it in the mornings."

The hot chocolate was so thick they ate it with a spoon. It was served in small cups with fritters dusted in icing sugar. "How do you feel about not walking today?"

Bob smiled and hunched his shoulders. "I'm fine and there's lots more Camino ahead of us. And it's good to be back with you, Bridgy. Are we going to survive?"

"Yes Robby, we're good, as the kids say! I know it's a lot for you to give up being with the others, but I just love having you back with me." Her voice broke. Bob took her hands.

"Do you think we ought to go wild and order a coffee to wash down the chocolate goo?"

"No, not yet. That should be our reward after the clinic. But I do need a glass of water to help it along," said Brigit.

The tourist office had given Bob a map and circled the clinic. Luckily it was downtown.

"We need a wheelchair. Then we could go through all these pedestrian streets and I could push you," said Bob.

Brigit remembered the dream she had where Charles-Michel was pushing her uphill in a wheelchair. She wondered about telling it to Bob, but thought better of it. 'He really was not very nice,' she thought, 'it was only a dream, and he would probably find it funny. Leave well enough alone.'

Her foot was much better. The doctor said "more rest, come and see us in three days. You will probably be able to start again with gentle stages then." A nurse applied a new dressing. She watched Brigit walk in her sandals and said that as long as she did not overdo it, they could walk gently in the city. They asked her about a restaurant for lunch.

There was a street that had several good choices and they should go at one pm, before the office workers arrive.

"'Lenguado Imperial': here it is lenguado— sole— don't know what the Imperial is, but I'm going for that," decided Brigit. They sorted through the menu del dia: a set lunch menu with three choices for each course. They had no difficulty eating their way through salad, pasta, the sole— baked with a sauce, asparagus, crusty bread, and flan: crème caramel topped with whipped cream. Bob, with the waiter, decided on a local wine. The restaurant and bar were full of business people with orders being shouted out and banter between tables. Once again it was good to be among the mainstream, even though they were only wayfarers in this ancient Camino city.

Everywhere was still during the siesta heat. They made their way to a park by the river and found a bench and Brigit snoozed with her head in Bob's lap while he read. "I don't know how you can keep your eyes open after our wine at lunch," murmured Brigit.

"Guess I'm in better training than you."

"Yeah, you boys didn't cover all those kilometres by having a siesta after every bottle of wine. I wonder how they are getting along."

"Shush," said Bob.

Brigit got the message but wondered about Bob spending more days of staying put because of her foot. He was being so perfect; and then how much would she be able to walk anyway?

That evening, reading her Camino guide, Brigit saw that there were two monasteries not far from the city. "And look, at the Monasterio San Pedro, El Cid's horse is buried there. You have to go and see that."

"Sending me to a monastery! What's wrong with staying in the city?"

"No, you go and I'll stay here and rest my foot and catch up on email."

14. On the Bright Side of the Moon

Bob set out at nine the next morning, along the river and then headed east; it felt so light walking with no pack. In less than two hours he reached the San Pedro de Cardeña monastery. He had no problem finding El Cid's horse – Babieca's tomb was in the yard to one side of the main entrance. Bob read the plaque: "supposed tomb of...." 'To have your tomb marked after a thousand years is good going for a horse,' he thought. Bob went into the church. He caught a glimpse of a hooded monk in a black habit up by the high altar. From the church Bob was able to walk around the cloisters surrounding a grassy courtyard.

"Buenos dias." Bob turned to find the monk next to him. "English? German?"

"Canadian," said Bob. The monk smiled and asked how he was finding the Camino.

"You know we are famous for our wine here. Would you like to see the bodega—the cellar?" He led Bob through a door at the back of the cloisters, down a stairway, unlocking doors from a bunch of keys till they arrived in the wine cellars. They were immaculate. Raked sandy floors, arched low ceilings, and racks of oak caskets and then rows of bottles. There was a slight yeasty smell. "Always the same temperature," explained the monk. "The wine is called Valdevegón, a very good red wine." He took a bottle that was already opened and gave Bob a taste.

"Good for your health," said the monk. Bob smiled his thanks. By the time he said goodbye to the monk— Father Antoine— Bob was ready for lunch. Finding a sunny corner against a wall, he sat down and got out the sandwich he had bought in Burgos and an apple.

"¡Bob, momento!" It was Father Antoine waving at him. He disappeared into the building and after a few minutes came out carrying a ceramic mug and gave it to Bob. It was wine for his lunch.

"Muchas gracias," said Bob. "¿Y usted?" and he showed his sandwich, willing to share.

"No, no thank you. We have different meal times but I will sit with you," and he hoisted up his habit so he could sit on the grass with Bob.

"It is good you come here and see beyond the Camino," he said. Then Father Antoine told Bob of how Santiago: St. James, had been transformed during the Reconquista times, in the Spanish imagination, into a warrior who came to help Queen Isabelle and King Ferdinand finally defeat the Arabs who had lived in Spain for hundreds of years. "It was a crusade in Spain. It is sad, as there had been tolerance up till then between the Jews, Muslims and Christians—well more tolerance anyway, then it became a time when great violence was done in Jesus' name."

"May I ask you something?"

"You can try. I do not know if I will have the answer."

"Is it difficult for Christians to forgive?"

"You are asking about the time of the Inquisition or now—today? I think you are asking about today," and the monk gave Bob a pleasant smile. "But we do forgive—all the time. But Christians are no better than other people. Do you practise the faith?"

"I guess you could call me an observer. My wife is very involved in her church, and I support her and attend church sometimes, and I know how important it is for her, so I want to understand more."

"Yes. You are right. Forgiveness is fundamental in the faith. You could say we should be better people as we know about God's great love for us and the miracle and mystery of grace. Jesus came and lived among us, and showed us God's forgiveness. But we, like other human beings, have been conditioned and wounded. That is the way we are. That is how we are fallen. And when we ask another for forgiveness, we must be truthful, in our hearts. But you know we do not forgive just for the other person. We forgive others for ourselves, to free and heal ourselves."

"What would prevent someone from forgiving?" Bob asked.

"A big thing in our way, is that we do not forgive ourselves. As Christians we are to seek wholeness in all ways: the spirit, mind, and body. We must be of service to others and be healed through prayer, to let God talk to us in silence. It sounds easy: just sit still with God but in our world there is so much going on in our heads. But this way, there is healing from many of the burdens we carry around from childhood and other life events that prevents us from reaching real Christian and human maturity. But like many truths, it is simple but not easy and it takes time." And he smiled sweetly at Bob.

****

In the city, Brigit too was caring for her soul. Attending midday mass in a chapel in the cathedral she concentrated on the words, recognizing the readings and the prayers. On the high wall of the chapel there was a spectacular modern tapestry of the crucifixion. She prayed, giving thanks that she and Bob were back together and that all was well again. She asked for blessings on her children and her church back home. Earl came to mind and she prayed for him. Had she used him and dumped him? Was he over her? There had been that embarrassing flower delivery just before they left Ottawa. That had been mean. She had done the breaking up. It had all been very polite and muted. He could not have expected her to leave Bob. Love and sex had tricked her: she had been their victim, taken on a twisted path and now left with the guilt of the sex but, thank goodness, no lingering love.

After the cathedral Brigit headed to the library. She downloaded her emails. She did quick individual hellos and then a collective email update, making it all sound such fun and not too many details about the fact that they had walked apart for five days.

On her way out she saw a poster. It was a long and thin with the word GUERNICA along the top. *Guernica,* the Pablo Picasso picture. Guernica, of course, how stupid to be so surprised, Guernica was in Spain. It was still a shock because for Brigit this picture was almost a private domain, actually for Bob and her, it was intimate territory. She sat down on a bare wooden bench in the hallway and continued to gaze at the picture. Guernica meant New York for her, New York with Bob.

****

It's summer in New York City, magic — Greenwich Village, the music festival, wandering the streets and now here at the Museum of Modern Art with Bob. Above all with Bob, they are lovers, his arm is around her shoulders, hers around his waist. They have to keep touching each other. They need to be touching. They have made their way up to the gallery and here they are before this shocking picture. A picture which occupied the length of a whole wall, with parts of people and animals jostled around the canvas. Never have Picasso's disjointed people made such sense to her as in this picture of the bombing massacre of the people of the town of Guernica during the Spanish Civil War. A bombing trial-run by the German high command, a blitzkrieg dress-rehearsal. Her emotions were wide open after their night of love, the cruelty of the picture, and the tragedy of the event poured into her body seeking her spirit. "Dear God forgive them, Dear God bless them." She did not know if she was praying for the victims or the perpetrators.

Bob sees her flushed face and eyes rimmed with tears and pulls her to him to comfort her for her pain and the indignation for humanity, and for himself, for his love for her and now the sharing of her grief.

The time span had no importance. She was there —out of the museum now, in Central Park, laughing, kissing, much kissing, back to the apartment in the afternoon making love assured of privacy as their friend was playing in a concert, a concert they were to have attended. Brigit smiled. She remembered how bold she became with Bob, with their love-making, from a virgin to sex-bomb in one weekend. Oh so sweet!

****

Bob caught a bus back to Burgos. It left him on the other side of the river from the city centre. People were milling around doing their shopping. Bob ambled along taking it in: a grocer with a green plastic crate full of snails set out in front of the store, butchers, bakers, a hardware store with strings of twisted plastic. He had seen them hung in open doorways for privacy, all in different colours. Like liquorice gone wild.

In a supermarket he bought a packet of olives stuffed with almonds, wine in a carton and some cheese for aperitif.

"Al, hello!" Bob called out. It was the American, the one with the ear plugs they met on their first night. "How are you getting on?"

"Hi there. Great to see you. Actually, not so good. This is the end for me. I'm catching a train tomorrow for Madrid and flying home. I'm really in a bad way. My feet, my legs are chaffing, my shoulders are so painful. And the business at home is all going sideways without me."

Bob commiserated with him and invited him to join them for supper but Al had other plans. Bob reflected that if he had talked with Al ten days ago, he might have been tempted to leave the Camino himself. It would have been easy. Brigit had been such a pain. But now he felt different. Brigit was her old sweet self: their relationship better than it had been for several years. Now he was committed to the Camino: the community of pilgrims, the locals they met, the path, the history.

They made love as the evening sun slanted into the room. Bob buried his head into Brigit's hair. Is that Spanish shampoo?" he murmured.

Over supper, Bob told her about the monastery. "I was adopted by this monk, Father Antoine. He told me how St. James came down on his horse with his sword to reclaim Spain for the monarchs and the Catholic Church."

"What else did you talk about?"

"I asked him about Christians and forgiveness."

"Oh my goodness, you did get into the heavy stuff!" she laughed, but did not ask for more details.

After supper they reached Charles-Michel. "We are overnight here in the St Juan de Ortega monastery. Did you get rain? We had it all day."

"No rain for us, thanks. Must be local in those hills. How far will you go tomorrow?" asked Bob.

"Roll out the red carpet, we will be arriving in Burgos. Looking forward to seeing you."

"Hang on, Brigit's trying to tell me something."

"Give her the phone. Hi, Brigit. How's the foot?" Charles-Michel asked.

"Getting so much better; however I am still grounded. Bob's being an angel, but I don't want him to get too antsy. How would it be if he came to meet you somewhere along the trail, and could walk into Burgos with you?"

"That would be great. But are you all right by yourself?"

"No problem. Today I sent him off to a monastery to see El Cid's horse. I'll hand him back to you."

"You see I am getting dispatched all over the place. Where could we meet up?" They worked out distances and timing.

"Looking forward to seeing you," said Charles-Michel. "Good talking with you. It's a bit austere here. À demain."

The next call was to Liz. Bob talked to her first. "Mum's foot is getting better. But we are still grounded for a few days. But we made it to Burgos."

"But what are you doing about medical help there?"

"It's western Europe. Probably easier to get seen to than it would be in Canada. We checked in at the local clinic and Mum's getting good care."

It was Brigit's turn. "How are you really doing, Mum, beyond the foot?"

"Dad and I are fine, happy to be back together and we are having a rest here in Burgos."

"What are you going to do next?"

"When I get the green light, we will get going again. We still have over five hundred kilometres to go: not even half way yet. Soon we will be up on the Meseta, the great plateau."

'Oh Elizabeth,' thought Brigit. 'Why can't she let bygones be bygones and get off my case about Earl? Anyway, what could I say? She knew Bob was standing right here. If she were here, she would see that everything has sorted itself out and is just fine.'

15. Into the Bright Lights

Bob had arranged to meet Colin and Charles-Michel where the Camino reached the river. From the river path, Bob arrived in a community that probably once had a character and heart of its own before it became a traffic corridor. Crossing the main road, Bob decided to wait at a bench next to a bus stop.

"Hola, there mate. Good to see you," said Colin giving Bob a man hug.

"You are looking fine, mon cher," said Charles-Michel. "You missed nothing on this last part of the trail. It was a rough slog over ploughed land along a wire fence."

"How was San Juan?" asked Bob.

"Let's say we are ready for some city comforts," said Colin. "The albergue is in the monastery—very monastic and dour. It didn't help that we had rain most of the day and arrived wet. I don't think the sun ever penetrates those thick walls and there was only cold water in the showers. We skipped those, as we were wet enough already. We arrived just in time for mass and then we were all invited to have garlic soup. It's a great tradition there. It was tasty and warm and came with bread, but that was it for supper. How's Brigit doing?"

"Are you pilgrims? Do you speak English? Oh hallo! You were at the monastery last night." A woman approached them, firmly holding her Camino guide with both hands. "Are you taking the river path into Burgos? I'm finding this very confusing. Which way are you going? By the way I'm Wanda. We didn't get to talk yesterday evening, but I saw you come in later. I'm looking for the Camino markers. Have you seen them?"

The men made room for her on the bench. Bob had to suppress an instinct to stand up. 'Hell no,' he thought, 'we are pilgrims together. But I bet she's a nurse or a school principal or something where she organizes everyone.'

"Where are you from?" he asked instead.

"I'm from Vancouver Island, in Canada. Are you on your way to Burgos? May I walk with you? I am really not comfortable when I can't see the arrows. It says the path follows the river which is somewhere not far from here."

There were no arrows or markers to be seen, but they assured Wanda that as the river flowed through Burgos, she just needed to follow it along. Grass and reeds grew on the river banks but a path cut across the bends between high poplars. They crossed over a footbridge to the city side, right to the locked double doors of an arena. The outside was plastered with layers of dog-eared posters for bullfights.

It was two o'clock when they reached the taller buildings of the city centre. They stood by the white stone bridge with the traffic flowing on each side of the statue of El Cid. They looked at Charles-Michel and Colin explained to Wanda that he was their history nerd. "Yeah, and he's chockers about it and gives us little clues and then just sits there with a smug look on his face—that's about it, isn't it Charlie-Micky?"

"Yes, and be thankful that I am here, you Philistines. El Cid was born in Burgos and this is where he got his coup d'envoi— his career break. He was a mercenary, and his first boss was Prince Sancho. The prince shared the kingdom with all his siblings who had inherited it from their dad who was the king, but this turned out to be a very messy arrangement."

"He is certainly very impressive" said Wanda.

"Indeed he is. Check out the flowing beard and his sword is out and up—magnificent!" said Charles-Michel.

"Let's go to the cathedral square and find a café." said Bob. He explained to Wanda about Brigit and her foot. Wanda was full of sympathy. She was traveling with a friend who had hurt her knee and had been banned from walking for two weeks, so was doing the stages by bus. Wanda and her friend Shirley had decided that Wanda should not sacrifice her walking. "How sensible," thought Bob.

"I guess you've seen all the sights by now." Colin said to Bob.

"We haven't done the cathedral, but I can tell you where the local clinic is."

They arranged to meet back at the Cathedral at seven o'clock and then they would visit the Cathedral and then find supper. Colin and Charles-Michel were going to get beds at a small hostel that was near the cathedral. Wanda needed to head over to the large hostel which was in a park back over the river. She said if her friend Shirley was up to it, she would like to meet up with them for the cathedral and supper and to meet Brigit.

****

Bob and Brigit took a taxi to the cathedral. Wanda and her friend Shirley had also taken a taxi and Mireille was with them.

"Bob this is Mireille." said Brigit

"Hi, yes, we met in Trinidad de Arre," said Bob.

Colin and Charles-Michel turned up. The cathedral stood out like a movie set. The white marble was damp from a rain shower and made deep shadows on the filigree spires which sparkled against the dark blue evening sky. Inside was vast with chapels the size of churches, and smaller chapels with elaborate altars along screened corridors. Their group had split up and it was not difficult for Mireille and Brigit to find a bench in a quiet chapel.

"How come you've caught up? What about Grañón?" Brigit asked Mireille.

"When I saw the weather," said Mireille, "and I did want to catch up a bit of time, I took a bus this afternoon. I'd had enough of the rain and as all my clothes were washed and dried, I was not going to risk getting them wet all over again."

"Good move."

"So that's the famous Charles-Michel. Bob seems to be having a good time. In fact you both look rather relaxed. Are you back on track?"

"Bob came to fetch me in Nájera. I was grounded with my foot. It got quite bad. And then we took a bus here. I was still worried but then everything was fine. It's like we turned back the clock and found the fun again. We haven't talked about anything serious so maybe we won't need to and we can just get on with the Camino and life."

"And speaking of....here they are," said Mireille as Bob and Charles-Michel entered the chapel.

"What are you two doing lurking back here? This place lends itself to a farce or a drama with everyone hiding out in different chapels for intrigues and encounters," said Charles-Michel. "Have you seen El Cid's tomb?" He led them around a circular screen into the large sanctuary.

"I completed missed this when I came in," said Mireille. "It's so vast."

Three great naves went the length of the church and in the centre was the tomb of El Cid and his wife Jimena. Colin was already there.

"I thought he was buried with his horse," said Mireille.

"He was, but then they moved him here, left the horse behind, and brought his wife along instead." Colin grinned and said he had read it in the guide book.

They found a restaurant near the cathedral for supper.

"Bob," said Colin. "So you did manage on your quest to track Brigit down."

"He arrived in Nájera like El Cid, but on the bus," said Brigit. "You should have seen, when we went to the albergue office to ask for help with our bookings, they treated him as the returning hero. It was like his arrival was putting things back in order for all those people who have been saying to me: '¿Dondé está su esposo?—where is your husband?' I saw all those nosy, well-meaning folk lined up along the Camino looking at him with approval."

"Bob with a hero complex," said Charles-Michel. "Just what we need!"

Colin asked Shirley about her knee.

"It is a luxury to have a doctor among us." Shirley said. "Colin, what brings you on the Camino?"

"Such a great way to be a tourist," he replied. "And I love being with you all, makes a community."

"But why the Camino?" Wanda asked.

"I was told to go and do something therapeutic and this seemed to fit the bill."

The three women looked at him expectantly. Finally Wanda said, "You can't open that door and just leave us there. Tell us more."

"Just another Camino story," said Colin. He turned to Wanda. "I work in hospital emergency and it can get a bit hairy. I got caught up in a nasty situation: a mentally unstable man came in for care. He was so stressed and anxious about the wait, he took a female nurse hostage. He had a hunting knife. Eventually he let me take the nurse's place, and it all went on for another thirty-six hours. When it was all over, they decided I may have traumatic after-effects, so they have me on three months leave."

"Gracious Colin, you are such a hero. And you never told us this," said Brigit.

"Well there's not much to tell. I feel fine, in body and mind. But if they want to give me paid leave to come and walk the Camino, fine by me!"

"We should have been looking out for you. And you have been caring for all of us."

"If I had needed help, I would have told you."

"Well, you are a hero," Wanda said.

Other pilgrims saw them in the restaurant and came to join in. Charles-Michel, Colin, and two German men planned to set out in the morning together. There was talk of meeting up in León as Brigit and Bob were thinking of taking the train over part of the Meseta to catch up the time spent in Burgos.

"We have to check in at the clinic," said Brigit. "They think I will be okay for walking again. Let's hope so, but it means we will be starting out later than you guys and we will be going slowly, I expect."

16. Amazing Kindness

"How about we just walk in silence for a couple of hours each morning?" said Brigit.

"Prayers-on-the-go Heavenly Father is not easy for me. Lots of people pray as they walk or jog, I just get distracted, but this is the Camino and that means new ways of doing things."

The doctor at the clinic had said Brigit could start walking again, but not to overdo it and to keep her feet dry. The nurse gave them dressings and made sure Brigit understood about taking all the antibiotics. So after checking out of the pension they were back on the Camino. Bob was ahead, walking between two straight lines of trees, in and out of sunlight and shadows. And, to the right, barbed wire and a guard post—a prison—a prison on the Camino! There's been pain and suffering along this path: illness, death, starvation, theft, drowning, murder. That's enough! You're just being Gothic.' Brigit sighed, reconciling the romance of the Camino with the reality of civic life.

On a footbridge over a freeway, they stood like kids, watching the trucks and cars zooming along under their feet. "Look—that bus, says León," said Brigit.

"Next big city. Let's find a place to have a break and you can check your foot. What do you think about Rabé de las Calzados for the night?" asked Bob.

"That's not very far— only eleven kilometers from Burgos."

"It's day one for your foot and walking. We should not go too far. There's a hostel and it's just on the edge of the Meseta and so tomorrow morning, we'll start right in."

****

There were in fact two albergues in Rabé de las Calzados but it did them no good. The first one had a notice that, for family reasons, they were away. They found the second. It too was closed. Fed up and mystified, they sat on a bench in front of the hostel. The streets were empty. Doors and shutters closed. Bob could hear the murmur of voices and the clinking of knives and forks on plates— lunch sounds slipping through the open window of the house opposite. Half shaded with a blind, he could see people seated at table. Here he was on the outside, in the harsh light, spying on their family intimacy. A wayfaring stranger relying on the hospitality of others. And it wasn't going to be here tonight.

A door opened in the albergue. Brigit jumped up— it was open after all. A man with a grey, striped butcher's apron came out with a floor mat and started beating it against the wall.

"¡Hola! ¿Albergue?" asked Brigit, smiling with great expectations.

"Non!" came the reply. "Vous parlez français?" The man dashed into the house and came out with a printed internet page and waved it in their faces. It was in English but he gave them no time to read it. Bob and Brigit gazed at him bemused as, out of his lips, which were pursed forward into a tight circle, it all came out: a tirade about the Camino and pilgrims in particular. "Why did you come?" he shot at them. "Didn't you know that the hostels are closed? Don't you have the internet in Canada? You should have checked before you came." Brigit was trying to sort out the printed page: something about thumbtacks in hostels. "Qu'est-ce que c'est, monsieur?" she asked. All monsieur could tell them was to look at the sheet of paper. Brigit asked about the other hostel.

"That is a joke. They say a family problem, but it is because they are ashamed. I am not going to go on with this. I opened a hostel to help people but now I will just use my house for myself. I have to close down and I won't be able to open until July and I don't know if I will! Pilgrims, they arrive with their big dirty boots. They hang their wet washing everywhere. Leave a mess in the showers. They don't want to pay for supper but want to use my kitchen for their own cooking. And now this!"

Brigit was looking at the internet page. The headline said, "Thumbtacks close down hostels." "This is one of those search-engine translations," she murmured to Bob, who had no chance of hearing as the man was still fixing him with his eyes full of indignation and giving him more of his hard luck story. Thumbtacks was not the only strange word. What's this about "pilgrims' waitings? What do they mean waitings?"— she started to work backwards: this was translated from French to *wait*— attendre, waiting? Oh it must be attentes, as in expectations, so pilgrims' expectations! Really these translation engines are worse than useless, Brigit clucked. So then what about thumbtacks? In French punaise, une punaise. Then she got it. Then she started to laugh. The man stopped. He and Bob both looked at her.

"Mais qu'est-ce que vous avez, Madame?" The man glared at her.

Brigit managed to say "Punaise!"

Now the awful truth began to dawn on Bob. Une punaise —a thumbtack, a drawing pin, and a BED BUG. The same word in French. Bob looked at the page again. It did made sense in a crazy way. But now it was urgent to get them out of here before monsieur blew a gasket. Brigit was now into a full-blown laughing fit.

"Come on. Let's go." He pushed Brigit's pack into her arms. "Merci, Monsieur. Bonne chance et au revoir." He caught Brigit's elbow and dragged her along.

"But Bob; it's so funny. Do you get it? Punaises? Bedbugs? We must tell him."

"Just keep going, Brigit."

"But Bob, he doesn't know about the confusion."

"I get it Brigit, and no he will not find it funny. I'm not going to tell him and neither are you!"

"Bedbugs— no wonder he has his knickers in a twist," said Brigit.

"I wonder how many other pilgrims have been completely mystified. No wonder he thinks we are all such a dreadful lot," said Bob. "He wants us to return to Canada immediately. He says that's it for the Camino, and the hostels are all closed."

"Oh, he's crazy. They can't all be closed, could they?" Brigit looked at Bob with horror on her face.

"No, we would have heard about that."

"We stayed in the pension in Burgos. We might not have heard."

"The others were staying in the albergue. They would have told us at the tourist office. We knew that bedbugs are a Camino problem, but people keep walking."

"Well I hope you're right. It could be awful!"

They stopped in the main square and sat on the edge of the stone fountain. Bob took out the guide. Hornillos was the next place where they could find an albergue.

"It's another ten kilometres and there's a big uphill. And everyone will be going there as they can't stay here. Where are we all going to sleep?" asked Bob. "And what about food, and your foot?"

"Bob we're fine for food. We did that shopping in Burgos. It will cool down soon. Let's enjoy the walk and there's no use worrying. Santiago, it's up to you. I know you will look after us."

It was three o'clock when they set off up the hill. The gravel track wound up to the great plateau of the Meseta. In the far distance they could see four pilgrims. There were no earthly sounds, only the song of the skylarks high above them. The fields had smooth carpets of fresh green wheat and on the terraces to the right: what looked like barley.

"It reminds me of the prairies— same crops," said Bob.

"It's so wide and still, such a contrast," said Brigit. "To think we were in busy Burgos this morning and we did it all on foot." Another hour on and they could see in the distance a valley with a ribbon of green and beyond that some white buildings: Hornillos del Camino. The climb down was steep and stony. They crossed a small road, over a stream, and met some locals.

"Buenas tardes," all round.

The albergue signs guided them to the church in the small square, and off to one side was the hostel: a low building in field stone. Inside the albergue they made their way down steps to what felt like a cave. Several people were sitting at a wooden table where a small old man had a large ledger and an ink stamp.

"Hola, si si," he said when they asked about staying, but he needed their pilgrims' passports. He carefully lined up his stamp in the next empty square and out came a green picture; proudly he held it up to them. The old man pointed, and twinkled at Brigit's puzzled expression. "Gallo."

"'A cockerel'; we're back with the Camino poultry," said Bob. Their names were entered into the ledger, in ink and with care. Then the old man jumped up, smiled, and signalled to everyone. "Vamos!"

"He's like a leprechaun," Brigit whispered. The hostel was a labyrinth; he showed them the kitchen and the showers. In the dormitories the bunk beds were all festooned with pilgrims and their gear. Brigit looked at the little man and waved into the dormitory. He shook his head, pointing and gesticulating:

"Aqui, duchas y cocina" — showers and cooking. He headed up the stairs and out into daylight with his pilgrim train, along a street then into a narrow stone house. This was the local clinic, but on the upper floor there were piles of thin plastic-covered mattresses and a marble floor: the overflow sleeping place.

"Well, bless them." said Brigit.

"And this floor and the mattresses all look quite thumbtack-proof." Bob said getting a couple of mattresses lined up for them.

They had to wait their turn but managed their showers and even to cook some supper. The whole of the village was overrun with pilgrims, sunning themselves on the church steps, draping their washing over stone walls, drinking beer at tables in the square in front of the little restaurant. In the centre of the square was a stone plinth with a statue of a perky cockerel. They joined the beer drinkers and found Astrid and Sven, the people from Sweden they had met on their first night. When Sven heard about Brigit's foot, he insisted that he give her a foot massage. "Come on, do not worry. I am a healer," and he gently and firmly massaged her feet.

****

Brigit can hear the sound of popping corn. Around her in a circle, people are peacefully eating popcorn out of brown paper bags and looking on. Bob is here, Liz and her husband, the rector from church, other church friends, her brother Peter. Earl is massaging her foot. Everyone is watching, and she's fine letting Earl do this with so many of her loved ones looking on. Earl is attentive and loving. His hands go from her foot, over her ankle and up her calf, to the knee, travelling up her leg. And people keep arriving and taking their place in the circle, watching her and watching Earl and munching. And somewhere in the background more corn is popping.

"Cramp, cramp in her leg, how could it when Earl is taking all that trouble? Oh, pain, bend the foot. Caught in the sleeping bag. Lift up the legs. It's agony. Keep calm. Just breathe. Where have they all gone?" But the sound was still there. She tried to remember what was happening. What were she and Earl doing? How could she have just sat there? Oh, but they didn't know what it meant. Had Earl just given her an innocent and caring foot rub? No it wasn't, she knew, he knew, but the others didn't realize. Even Liz had looked on complacently. Brigit lay there suffering shame and the burning in her leg. What would have happened if she hadn't woken up? She felt her insides curling at the thought of it: his hand moving up the inside of her thigh and everyone just sitting watching. Was this a sentencing circle? Were her peers and elders sitting in judgement of her sins? The clock on the church tower rang. It's four in the morning. The dark cave in her belly flooded with grief.

The popping corn was rain. There must be a tin roof out back of this place, maybe a garden shed. Brigit listened. The sound was now too heavy and constant to be popcorn.

"Bob, it's raining." Brigit was surprised she had managed another three hours of sleep.

"Yes, I know. Don't rush. We'll take our time and go to the café for breakfast. Maybe it will have stopped by then."

"Hallo there! Come and sit with us." It was Astrid and Sven. "We don't hurry, you know. Astrid does not like to walk too far and I do not like to rush. It's perfect. Some pilgrims are so intent. Brigit—how is the foot?"

"It feels good this morning."

"But we are worried about the boots and her feet getting wet," said Bob.

"I have something for you." Sven took his backpack and steadying it on the floor between his knees, opened it and reached to the bottom. "Here it is," he brought out a spray can. "Water-proof for your boots."

"We did some of that in Burgos. You will need it yourself." said Bob.

"You must do it again. More layers is good. And please use it. Then we can get rid of the can. If you do it now it can dry while you have breakfast. Come I will help. Brigit, take off your boots." He and Bob headed out under the awning in front of the café.

"He is so kind," said Brigit to Astrid.

"Yes, he is. That is normal. He is a good man. So is your Bob: a good man."

Brigit thought of her dream and how she did not deserve all this kindness and love this morning. "Yes he is."

"You will see, Brigit. All is going to be well with you. Sometimes it takes time. You have to let it happen."

Brigit looked at Astrid, grateful but embarrassed. 'This is creepy,' she thought. 'Because obviously she can see straight into me—Astrid the clairvoyant.'

17. Into the Underworld

They climbed out of the village, the trail cutting across the side of a hill. Water spread across the fields with green spring wheat sticking up like a rice paddy.

"The ground is saturated," said Bob. The rain was still falling.

They reached the edge of a valley with the path leading down to a stream. On the other side was a grove of trees next to a small domed blue building painted with a large white scallop shell.

"The San Bol hostel. Sven and Astrid were heading there."

But their path was blocked. The stream was flooded and water was bubbling and bouncing over the path and submerging the flat plank bridge.

"Oh hell!" said Bob

"Could we take off our boots and wade through?"

"It's too fast and quite deep right at the bridge," said Bob. No one was around. On their side of the river there were just soggy fields. They could see a road on the other side. No use to them here.

"Let's wait. Maybe it will go down as fast as it came up." Bob realized that this was a bit ridiculous, but what else to do—go back to Hornillos? There were some large smooth stones by the edge of the trail so they sat, gazing out at the rain.

"Brigit, you know when you met Charles-Michel and me at that church at Eunate?"

"Yes, why?"

"You asked me about my relationship with Charles-Michel."

"I'm sorry about that. I was really being snarky."

"I was really annoyed."

"I'm sorry."

"I was annoyed with myself. I was furious to find myself in such a mess of my own making." Bob's voice was thick and low.

"Are you talking about Charles-Michel?"

"Charles-Michel yes. I don't want you to get this wrong. It wasn't anything. It was then and over."

"What was it?

"Nothing really, but…"

"What happened? What are you saying?" Brigit's voice came out off-tone.

"Let me tell you. It's not easy. Just be quiet. Charles-Michel was one of the first people I met when I went to university. We met in a poli-sci course. Then he was a teaching assistant in my French course. You know what fun he is and charming. We became good friends. I knew he was gay. He was way out of the closet and rather flashy about it too. He took me under his wing. He was sophisticated and had lots of friends, gay and straight. He teased me about sex and my sexuality and about how many men were actually gay or bisexual. It was a game. He knew I was straight. He flirted with me. And I let him."

"You let him what?"

"He would touch me— just my hair, or shoulders. Run his hand down my back, nothing more. But one night, after a night out, we did kiss. It was a real shock for me. I guess it was a good thing as it was a wake-up call. I realized that I was not being honest with Charles-Michel, letting him flirt when I knew he would like more. I knew I was not gay. It could never be a physical relationship. So I told him. He laughed it off and said I was scared of just a kiss. He knew I was straight but that it might be interesting for us both. He just ruffled my hair and gave me a push away. After that we just kept being good friends."

"How could you? That would be too strange."

"Not really. I was only eighteen, still a virgin. I had fooled around with the girls at high school. That had been exciting. But you know back then, some were into sex but most of us were just into heavy petting."

"What happened next?"

"We did stay friends. I met lots of girls: many through his circle of friends. There were parties. I began to have sex with females, which was reassuring and it was great."

"What about Charles-Michel? What did he do?"

"He had a good time teasing me. He had lovers. Things were easier and simpler then and wilder with no AIDS. But I was not that wild. It was all going on around me, but I wasn't an angel, either."

The rain was still falling. Bob kissing a guy. She had no problem with same-sex relationships, but her Bob!

"Do you miss that?"

"No. Don't be crazy. That was just fun at university. By the time he left McGill, we were still good friends, but all that flirting and teasing stuff had ended ages before. Then, we lost touch with each other. Over the years and because of work, we would meet at the odd conference but nothing more. I think I had not quite reconciled myself to our past. But it really was good to spend time with him on the Camino here. I enjoy his company. Well, so did you. You saw what he is like. Such a great guy."

There was silence. Bob looked at Brigit but her face was mostly hidden by the hood of her jacket. Bob sighed. The rain was still falling.

There was a splash of bright orange by the hostel. Bob jumped up. A person was walking their way on the other side of the river. Bob waved and took off down to the water.

"Bob, is that you?" It was Sven.

"Yes. The bridge is flooded."

"I saw your jackets. You just stayed there so I came to see what was happening."

"Thank you. I'm very glad to see you. "

"Let me go back to the hostel and see if they have any ideas. This must have happened before." Soon he was back. They had a pontoon arrangement. If they could make their way to the field opposite the hostel, they would be able to get them across. Bob and Brigit went back up the path to higher ground to avoid some of the standing water in the field. By the time they were on the river bank, Sven and another man had the pontoon across the stream. They strung a rope between two trees on either side of the river to pull the pontoon across. The river was wider here. The water spread out, calmer.

"Hallo Brigit. You see we meet again."

"Sven, you are turning into our guardian angel."

They made it over in two trips.

"So Brigit, this is like that famous song: 'The Rain in Spain.' But I think this is quite unusual, all this rain. Now we will go into the house. It is warm there."

There were five young people inside, two girls, three guys as well as Astrid. A fire burnt in a central fireplace.

Bob dug away at the mud packed into the soles of their boots. The roof over the patio kept him dry. He could smell the sweet wood smoke and the fresh rain. An old white dog seemed happy to have his company. He was feeling light-headed; he had surprised himself telling this old story to Brigit. Why had he chosen this time to tell her? The whole thing just seemed to present itself to be told. Brigit had thrown that question at him, not even a question really, just a jibe. However, it must have made a tear somewhere in the fabric of his memories.

"Bob, come in for lunch." It was Astrid. There was a vegetable casserole, cheese, and bread. This albergue was not like any other they had come across. The people here did not seem to be walking the Camino. They were just hanging out. Living here. There were musical instruments in the round room with the fireplace. It was a community. There were bunks for overnight people too. After lunch, Sven and another man took off to help some more pilgrims who were stranded. Bob helped Brigit do the dishes.

"Bob, how far to the next place? Can we keep going?"

"Yes, let's, and the rain has stopped. There are quite a few places coming up with hostels."

When Sven returned, they said goodbye. They put a donation in the box. One of the guys put a stamp in their pilgrim passports. It was beautiful: half owl, half scallop shell with a sword and surrounded with ancient symbols and writing. They made their way along the track back to the Camino, passing the stone ruins of what used to be San Bol's monastery, now covered in wild flowers—white, purple, and blue.

"That was interesting," said Bob. "Sven to the rescue again. I thought you might want to stay. Did you get a bit of a rest?"

"I wasn't comfortable there. It was a bit too hippie. I thought they were probably going to be partying till late and I am not really into that frame of mind at the moment."

"Since when have you had any problems with parties, or hippies for that matter?"

"I've had enough of the blast from the sixties and seventies today!"

Resting at San Bol, Brigit was haunted by visions of Charles-Michel running his hand down Bob's back. Down to his buttocks, a hand on each, pulling him face to face and then the kiss. That song—the kiss—the cinnamon kiss that goes on and on. Better it were a bitter-aloes kiss. Witchcraft seemed to suit the atmosphere at San Bol with enough ancient Camino mystery in that valley to make Bob tell this story.

"So, why did you tell me and now?"

"I don't know. It just seemed the right thing to do. It wasn't a confession but when I was talking to Father Antoine at the monastery, he talked about being truthful rather than just telling the truth."

"'Those who deal truthfully are His delight.' Do you feel it's important that you tell me this, or is it important that I should know?"

"Interesting question. I think I felt it was important for me to say it. It is a part of my past, so part of me. I thought you should know about it."

"We've got on all these years without me knowing," said Brigit.

"I know. But now we are on a pilgrimage and other things have changed and upset our lives in the last few years.

Maybe we should change how we communicate and about what."

"Why did you say it wasn't a confession?"

"Well, a confession is when you have done something wrong."

"So?"

"I haven't done anything wrong to you. I apologized at the time to Charles-Michel as I had not been honest with him."

"I am shocked. It's my vision, my understanding of you, who you are. Did I get it wrong after all these years of being together?"

"I'm not anybody different. I'm absolutely the same person. It is just one of the threads that long ago was an experience that makes me who I am. I am sure it made me more tolerant and understanding of diversity, of my human weakness—all that. It's not an apology that I made telling you this. I am not going to say sorry for anything."

"Why are you so sure that I should not be hurt by this?"

"If you are, that's your own choice. We did not even know each other at that time. I see it as part of our shared morality. We share the same values on acceptance, social justice, and inclusiveness. If it does not go against our values, that is another reason that it would not hurt you."

"You have to give me some time to get my mind around this. I hear what you are saying, but I don't feel that way at the moment."

"Brigit, I think you are being naïve about this."

'But he told me – why now? If we are going in for tell-all, where will this take us?' She felt her insides knotting up and clawing up her throat with a bitter acrid taste. Brigit did not care how far they walked. It had stopped raining but she kept her jacket hood up. It was easier this way, with her face hidden, at least from Bob.

"How about Hontanas for the night?" Bob suggested.

"I can keep going. I feel fine. What is the next one after that?"

"Castrojeriz or then San Antón: very interesting but it is only open in the summer. Let's stop in Hontanas. There are several albergues there."

It was a steep, slippery climb down. As they reached the edge of the village of Hontanas, the path became a sunken earth road. The houses and farm buildings made rough stone walls. They could see into farm yards where hens, ducks, and goats were pecking and nosing around to see if there was anything worth eating. Brigit felt like she was in a movie set for a Bible story. They kept going and found the municipal hostel.

"I like this," said Brigit making her nest in a lower bunk. "When we are organized let's go and have a beer and see if there are people we know."

18. Truth and Truthfully

'No surprise,' thought Brigit as she lay in her rather spacious bunk. 'This is an award winning hostel. The least I could do is honour it with a good night's sleep.' She knew that was not going to happen. Now that Bob had told her about this chapter of his past, it added another great big heaping of manure on the already rather high pile of dung that seemed to have moved back into her life. She admitted this old story made no difference to her now. Bob had left it in his past and moved on. That was her plan too, but now Bob had added this true confessions thing into the mix. Did he suspect something after all?

***

Bob was sleeping well, but earlier that night he had wondered again why he had told Brigit. Was he pushing her buttons with this old story? Had she really got over the money episode? Where had that all gone? 'Let's see what happens next,' he thought. 'These are strange waters.'

Earlier they had met up with Wanda and Shirley and had supper together on the patio outside the hostel. Bob talked with Shirley about her plans. She was still stuck with her bad knee and she was suggesting to Wanda that they take a train to León. Bob was thinking it would not be such a loss to skip the rest of the Meseta.

"What do you think, Bridgy? We could take the train from Frómista. We don't want to be rushed for the last third of the trail."

"My foot is a lot better now. I don't want us to miss parts of the Camino because I have been slow."

But this wasn't a problem for Bob: "Let's catch up a bit of time. It's our Camino. It's forty-five kilometres to Frómista. There's a train leaves at noon. We could do about thirty today, if you can manage that, and stay at Itero de la Vega. Then do an early start tomorrow for the rest of the way into Frómista. And we have Castrojeriz and San Antón today. Lots to see!"

The path out of Hontanas was a dirt track along a ridge in the valley. Despite others on the trail, there was a lonely, brooding feel to the place. They could see, hidden in the hillside, cement slabs with long slit openings.

"Gun emplacements," said Bob. "From the civil war. This valley would be a good line to hold."

"We never hear about the Civil War. It's all Charlemagne and Isabelle and Ferdinand."

Across the stream in the valley, an ancient stone arch came into view.

"San Antón!" they said together.

"I've got goosebumps," said Brigit as they walked under the arch. "The monks would leave food here when the gates were locked so the latecomers had something to eat and could sleep here too." Beyond the arch, a stone gateway led into an open space surrounded by the ruins of a church and other buildings: the remains of a monastery. Bob was reading a notice on the wall: "The Antonine Order helped lepers and others with all those diseases from the Middle Ages. The Order honoured St. Anthony of Egypt. Do you know about him, Brigit?"

"St. Anthony of the Desert, or Egypt. I certainly do; we did a whole study on the Desert Fathers at church. They were the start of the monastic tradition. And Anthony was the founder. Not sure if he was the actually the founder, but at least a pioneer."

"When, and was it in Egypt?"

"Oh, yes. Egypt was very Christian at the time—the third century. These people went into the desert to live as a community. And there were women too— the Desert Mothers. The monasteries attracted followers in the thousands, then a group would split off and go further into the desert to have more solitude. The monks wrote about their faith and their prayer life which was all around the silence of the heart."

"Gracious Bridgy, that is impressive. I thought Charles-Michel had the corner on Camino history."

"Oh, I would not compete with him," she laughed. "But there are churchy bits I'm pretty good at."

"Hallo there, well met. This is all quite Chaucerian!" It was Wanda. "You really get a feel for the ancient pilgrims here."

"You just missed Brigit's exposition on St. Anthony of the Desert. He predates Chaucer by at least a millennium."

"Oh Brigit, tell all!"

There were enough ruins still standing to see where a rose window must have been. The caretaker told them that the monastery had had a mill, an orchard, a dovecote, as well as the church.

"What is this symbol?" asked Bob pointing to a form of a capital T carved in a stone.

"That was the monks. It is the Tau. The symbol of love which guided them in their healing work," explained the caretaker. He stamped their credencial books— a stamp with a crown above a coat of arms and three of the Tau symbols.

Walking towards the town of Castrojeriz they could see a castle on a hill top. The straight avenue of trees gave them shade.

"Oh, a haystack!" Wanda pointed off to the left. I don't miss a good opportunity like that." And she took off for a moment of privacy. "I'm amazed," she said after Brigit had had her turn, "how I can now pee without taking off my backpack. Such a skill."

"They should do something about the whole washroom issue on the Camino now there are so many pilgrims. Bob and I each have a little plastic hiking trowel. It can be a horrible mess behind hedges and walls. The farmers and landowners are fed up. I don't blame them. They post notices asking people to be more respectful and to clean up after themselves. Like when you take your dog for a walk!"

"A not-so-charming side of the Camino," Wanda agreed.

Brigit began to feel her old worry-fiends starting to nag at her. Bob's story: maybe his truth-telling is just that with no ulterior motive, or is he just waiting to see what she'd do next? Was it not enough to do a pilgrimage for her sins? Who was it good enough for? Herself and God, but that was not her only relationship in life.

That evening, after supper, Bob and Brigit headed out to explore. They took a path along the river bank and found a bench. The sun was slowly setting but there was still plenty of light.

"It's interesting to see how everyone connects to the history in different ways. Like San Antón—for Wanda it was Chaucer. I am intrigued with the Tau symbol. They must have had connections with Asia. What about you, Bridgy? What clicked with you?"

"St.Anthony of the Desert—from the third century." They gazed out at the river.

"Bob, there is something I need to tell you." Brigit nearly gagged as she heard the words coming out of her mouth. "Bob?"

"Yeah, I'm listening."

"I had an affair." There it was. But if she expected relief, there was none. Just a great roar in her head.

"But you were a virgin when we met. What do you mean?"

'Give me a break,' she thought. 'He must think I'm doing an ancient history Charles-Michel thing.'

"No, recently."

"You mean on the Camino?"

'Oh dear God,' she thought. 'This is getting far worse.'

"About two years ago. It's all been over ages ago now."

"Brigit, what on earth are you telling me? That you had this affair two years ago? And now you are telling me about it? Apparently, I did not need to know before. Now all of a sudden in the middle of nowhere you decide to catch me up with your life! Who was it? Where did all this happen? Was it at your school? And what was *I* doing?"

****

Bob felt like he was being strangled, but instead of around his neck, around his chest. It was getting difficult for him to breathe. "Well?" he barked out.

"I'm so sorry, Bob. Things just got out of hand. There is no excuse. I just kept going and when I should have stepped back, I didn't. At the time I did not seem to realize what an awful thing I was doing. It just all happened. It was from church when we were putting on that art show."

"At church. Give me a break. There I am thinking you're at church and all the time you were fooling around. Adultery. I can't even take this in." Bob jumped to his feet.

"Bob, I don't know why I told you this now. I guess it is the Camino. Then you telling me about Charles-Michel yesterday. I just thought it would all go away. But I see it won't. I didn't want to tell you. Then I realized that I could not go on like this. It has just been getting worse. I don't want to destroy our lives, but this is too much for me to hide."

"Well, maybe you should have thought of that before you had this fling or whatever it was. What do you think is going to happen to us?"

"I just hope we can work through this somehow. Would it help if we walked apart again?"

Bob sat down, put his head between his hands, and was silent. He jumped up. His face was deeply flushed, his lovely hair a mess.

"No, Brigit. I don't know what we are going to do now that you have dumped this fucking mess on us. You are not going off on your own. I'm not going to have you wandering around in goodness-knows-what state. Do you understand? We are going back to the hostel now. And I don't want to talk any more this evening. Do you understand?"

> *"Come unto me and rest;*
> *lay down, thou weary one, lay down*
> *thy head upon my breast."*
> *I came to Jesus as I was,*
> *so weary, worn, and sad;*
> *I found in him a resting place,*
> *and he has made me glad.*

Horatius Boner (1808-1889)

19. Earth Has Many a Noble City

"Come on, get up!" Bob's harsh whisper broke in on Brigit. She had spent the night in sick turmoil. "Fill your water bottle. There's no shade on this stretch!" Bob hissed.

Downstairs they met Wanda who was taking the same train. Brigit gave her a rather stiff good morning. It was a silent trio who set off, picking up the yellow Camino arrows back to a track of beaten earth between fields of green wheat shoots, vegetables, and vineyards with irrigation systems fed by the river. The path was flat. Up on the ridge to their left was a wind-farm: skeletal white windmills languid in the early morning calm. Above them the still air started to gently vibrate with the sounds of wings, and they could see a great flock of birds circling above pillar-like structures. "Doves and those are dovecotes," said Bob.

"What do they do with them?" asked Brigit.

"They keep the insects down and fertilize the fields. They used to have them at the Monastery at San Antón — don't you remember? Brigit, keep up. This is easy walking. We have the train to catch."

'As though I didn't know,' she told herself. 'Just zip the mouth.' She picked up the pace. They found a café in

Frómista for a coffee and a sandwich. A single church bell was ringing.

"It's Sunday. I miss church," Brigit said to Wanda with a faint smile.

"Really!" cut in Bob.

'Oh shit,' thought Brigit. 'How could I mention church?'

It was disorienting to leave the Camino and join the rest of the world. 'Like leaving home,' thought Brigit. 'Now I'm just a middle-aged tourist with a backpack.' Their next train had originated in Madrid and it was even more alien for Brigit. There were people in suits with their laptops reading reports or a newspaper. Brigit felt closer to the families with their picnic baskets and babies in tow.

*****

The train sped over the Meseta. As they whistled through a station, Bob recognized the name Sahagún, a town on the Camino, and now he could see groups of pilgrims on the Camino path. The train reached León. It was all a bit more of a free-for-all than the orderly Canadian exit routine. Wanda and Brigit got out and stood back from the crowd to wait for Bob.

"Where is he?" said Brigit. No one else was coming out of the carriage. "I'll go and see. Maybe he had to go back for something." Brigit climbed up the two steps and looked in. Bob was there, searching under one of the seats. "Bob, what is it?"

"My pack. It's not here. It was in the luggage rack. It's gone."

"It can't be. Let me look." Brigit searched around. But there were not many places to look. "Could it have been taken to a luggage car and unloaded already? Let me look along the platform." They both got down from the train and explained to Wanda.

"I'll wait here and look after our things. You two go and see if you can track it down."

Bob and Brigit found a ticket collector and managed to explain the problem. Maybe he had heard the same scenario in broken Spanish before. And Brigit's hope of a luggage car and her "?otros vagon para equipaje? only got a sad shake of the head. He waved them to come with him. Brigit went back to tell Wanda. Bob followed the man to the station-master's office. This was truly drowning, and now the loss of his pack. The station official unlocked the door and gestured to Bob to sit down and produced a form. The missing luggage form. Luckily, there were pictures. Bob could tick off the backpack one and wrote in azul for his beautiful blue backpack, his faithful companion.

"Policia?" Bob asked. The man nodded. He got a card out of the drawer and gave to it to Bob: "Comisaria." Bob understood it was the details for the police station. Brigit joined them. "Wanda has gone ahead to the hostel." They looked up the hostel address and showed it to the man. "Si si, monasterio de las Benedictinas." He knew all about that too. He produced a tear-off city map and drew a circle around the hostel and then around the station.

"What should we do first?" asked Brigit, "I was wondering if we should go to the hostel. Maybe they can help us."

"Well, it's on the way to the police station. We might as well, if the hostel is even open this early. Turn here." Bob grunted. The hostel door was unlocked and led into a dark hall. They could make out a registration window with an oak counter and iron grill work. The young man behind the counter said they were too early to check in. They explained that a friend might have arrived earlier and told him about the bag.

"Yes, yes, she told us. You are the ones." He left his desk and came through a door to be with them. His name was José, and he was a volunteer. "I can help you. I can translate. You should go to the police. This is so bad but it can happen. It could happen anywhere in the world, especially on a train."

They thanked him. He told Brigit to put her pack in the office which he then locked and put up a notice saying people could check in after three pm. "What about your money and papers?"

"No, thank goodness. I have my wallet with my money and documents and tickets."

"That is good you have all that, and your boots too." He put a hand on Bob's shoulder and gave him a smile of encouragement. "We can walk. It is less than a kilometer."

Another smile of encouragement and they headed off into the maze of streets of the old town.

"Here we are, arrived!" José led them through the front doors. The conversation was at top speed. José waving a hand in their direction. Bob thought he could make out "peregrino" and "monasterio de las Benedictinas", which is what the locals seemed to call the hostel. Out came the forms. The police officer made notes and at one point made a phone call. "She calls the train station," explained José. Another police officer joined the group. He shook his head and shrugged his shoulders when he heard the details. So despite José's goodwill and all the officials and forms, there was no news of the pack.

They walked back to the hostel. José tried to cheer them up by pointing out city sites and a couple of good tapas bars. Back at the hostel, he took them up to a large dormitory and pointed them to a couple of beds. "Others will be here when the office opens later," he said and then he left.

"This must have happened to other pilgrims before," said Brigit.

"Let's go out," said Bob. "I can't stay inside."

****

It was perfection outside: blue sky, mild weather. In the cathedral square the bells were ringing, groups of people were standing around, some sitting, kids chasing pigeons. They found a stone bench.

"Brigit, maybe this wasn't supposed to be for us, this whole venture. Do you want to go home?"

Brigit looked at him in horror. "What do you mean?" Bob was made of sterner stuff than that. He was a leader, undaunted by adversity. "I know this is horrible. But it's only things. They can be replaced. We can buy new stuff. We can share mine. We can do with less."

"I don't know if we can take any pleasure in this anymore. I can manage. But you should go home, Brigit. I will keep going." He got up and walked away from her over to the cathedral.

'Go home! Sent home like a truant child! Strange,' Brigit ruminated, 'they say you know when you reach rock bottom and then things get better. But it just keeps getting worse. How can it get better if there's no rock bottom?' As she sat there, she had a vision of herself: sitting on the bench looking rather ordinary and even making room for a woman with some stupid little pampered dog. And she observed herself in this distant way. 'This must be like a near-death experience. Can you have one with grief? Well why not, like extreme grief. Could I just float away?' Taken up by the angels outside the cathedral. Her body would be found lifeless among the Sunday crowd: no apparent cause of death, no wound, no organ failure, just no life and no spirit. Her poor family: it would be unfair for Bob and the children. They would take her ashes home. The church would have a beautiful memorial service for her. Maybe Liz would want the ashes scattered over one of her meadows. No. She should be buried with her parents.

It was the little dog sniffing around her feet that forced her back to the present. Her neighbour gave her a smile, inviting her to admire the dog. Brigit did her best not to scowl. 'What does he mean, for me to go back? He was the one who said we had to stay together come what may. This is the loss of his pack and it's no one's fault. So, what has changed?' But Brigit knew that this theft felt like a broken trust, another betrayal. 'We should never have left the Camino' she thought. 'We were safe there. We just brought along our own troubles, not new evil. We must stay together because if we are not together, we will just have all our mess, but we won't be able to sort it out, and my life will be over.'

"Oh dear God. Help me, Help Bob. Please let us find his bag. We are really suffering here. Please stay with us." She sat there in the sun. Half in prayer. Half in reverie and misery. What advice did I give the kids? "Chunk it down!" She used to tell her children that when they had a problem and told her, "there's no way, Mum!" Deal with a bit at a time. Start with what you can, and then you will have another part you can tackle. You can't solve it all at once, but you can start. "You had better follow some of your own advice, Brigit!"

20. Dead Stop

Stepping into the cathedral from the sunshine Bob expected to be in deep shadow. He caught his breath. The large open space was flooded with blue jewelled light from rows of stained glass set in soaring windows, two great tiers of them, scenes of trees, flowers, snakes, birds, a hunting scene— lords and ladies in flowing medieval robes. Bob stood there and the beauty kept going, now with scenes from Bible stories on the upper windows. There was a gentle Sunday movement of people: visitors, pilgrims, several priests and nuns, muted conversations and greetings. Other stained glass presented itself: long sets of windows with abstract patterns of leaves and petals in the most intricate designs. And then higher still, the circular rose windows came to light: saints and apostles, feet to the centre and shoulders to the outside, with garments in deep blues, reds, yellows, and the black lead tracing.

All this beauty and his life a friggin' mess. What did Brigit call these times in a vacuum? Liminal space? When God can work on the pathetic clay that we are and transform us— into what—more understanding, more patient people? That wasn't going to happen. She had screwed that up.

****

Outside, Brigit watched the sunlight play across the west front of the cathedral lighting up spires and arches, catching the many statues. The windows were dark against the golden stonework. As the blue sky deepened, the cathedral became more golden still. She had to put her nagging mind aside with this beauty before her.

"You're in the same place." Bob joined her.

"It's so perfectly beautiful."

"We've hardly eaten all day," said Bob. "We might not feel like it, but we should find some supper."

Eating supper. They could both understand that and set off to look for a restaurant, but all seemed closed. "They were open at lunch and full. I guess that's when people have their main meal on a Sunday—makes sense. What about those tapas bars José recommended? Could we find them?"

"We can find them, but I think we need something more substantial—might be our only choice," said Bob. Back through the old city they found one of José's tapas bars. It turned out to be perfect. The owner insisted they start off with a glass of sherry, blond and sharp and it came in a large wine glass, full. It was a lot of alcohol on an empty stomach, but it was delicious. He took over the choice of dishes— shrimps and mushrooms in garlic and said he would have a tortilla made up too. The bar had been empty when they arrived, but now it was slowly filling up. There was music, not live, but Spanish pop: flamenco. It gave an upbeat atmosphere without demanding anything of them. The owner suggested a glass of Rioja Tempranillo red wine. "You have walked there," he pointed out.

"This is a crazy time and city," said Bob. "My pack stolen, your fiasco, and yet this afternoon has been astounding with the cathedral, and José's help and now this meal and hospitality."

"Bob, I am not going back. You said we must walk together. I'm staying on the Camino and with you!"

"I'm suggesting you do go back. I don't know where you think we are going with all this. You should go back."

"Well, I'm not. Discussion closed. I'm staying!"

The host turned up with the glasses of Tempranillo. "We had better call it a night after this," said Bob. "We still have to officially check in."

With the May evening light they found their way to the albergue.

"Any news from the police?" Bob asked José.

"No, but you must not expect it. It is Sunday."

'Which seems the answer to everything today,' thought Brigit.

José added, "I am sorry that there is no pilgrim blessing tonight. For the nuns, Sunday is their day for themselves. But I told Sister Alicia about you and she wants to talk with you in the morning. And we have some things for you." José darted back into the office and came out with a small pile balanced on his hand: a bed sheet, some pyjama pants, and an old Hard Rock Café T-shirt, all well-worn and well laundered. Also a towel and wash cloth, a bit grey and thread bare. "There are blankets on the beds and also pillows."

"Thank you so much, José. That is so kind," Bob and Brigit both chorused in a mixture of Spanish and English.

"It is the nuns; they care greatly. You will meet them tomorrow."

****

It was the morning getting-up: packing packs and general shuffling around. Bob lay there for a while, nothing much to get up for. He had slept well. 'Doesn't make sense with all this shit going on,' he thought. He looked over to Brigit's bunk. It was more a bed as there were no upper bunks here. 'Good not to have someone looming over you as they pack up."

"Brigit, are you getting up?"

"I guess we'd better. How'd you sleep? "

"José said there's breakfast. We'd better put in an appearance."

Downstairs, there was a crowd of people anxious to get going as soon as they managed a tea or coffee and some bread and jam.

"Hi Brigit. How's the foot?" It was Shirley.

"How lovely to see you! Foot's doing fine, thank heaven. Bob's getting us coffee. I haven't seen Wanda since the train. I expect she told you about Bob's pack."

"She sure did. Wanda's over there. Come and sit with us." They managed to squeeze onto the bench. "We have wonderful news. I can start walking again."

"We went to a community clinic first thing this morning and they say she's good to go!" said Wanda.

"I was wondering if I was ever going to be a proper pilgrim again or just become an expert on Spanish public transport," said Shirley. "It has served me very well, but that definitely wasn't my plan. Now tell us about the bag. Did you see the police? Oh, hello there, Bob."

They gave them the pack update, which really did not amount to much and as for their plans, they were even sketchier. "Well, at least you have good news," said Bob. "I'm going down to see about meeting this nun. If I don't see you before you leave, have a good Camino." Bob got up and threaded his way between the tables, benches, pilgrims, and the packs piled up on the floor.

"What's this about the nun?" asked Shirley. Brigit explained.

"I do hope they can help and advise us; this is such a blow. When your life is so few items already and then they are taken from you, you feel bereft. I'm sure one of the lessons for pilgrims is to let go. I'm afraid I would prefer to hang on."

"You poor things. It's just horrible. But I'm sure the sisters will be of help. I've been throwing myself on their mercy at many albergues and they have been wonderful and very practical. They must have helped with so many situations with pilgrims. A lost pack will just be run-of-the-mill."

Brigit went back to the dormitory, brushed her teeth, and tidied her pack. She felt like having a cry but spoke to herself sternly: 'It's just seeing Wanda and Shirley setting off, and here we are stuck and no plan. Would they have to find a pension?' She hated the idea of leaving this community; they seemed their only hope. Bob came back looking gloomy.

"Sister Alicia can't see us till eleven. There's another volunteer on duty. But she did say that they are expecting us to stay tonight. It will take us at least a day to get sorted. She said not to worry and not to buy stuff yet, which means just more bloody delay and hanging around."

"Let's go and see the Antoni Gaudi building," suggested Brigit. Out in the street, the Monday morning city workers were striding past them into the large glass and steel office buildings.

"It's quite Gothic," Brigit took in the facade of the Gaudi building.

"It's Neo-Gothic, but the inside is Art Nouveau," said Bob. "One of Gaudi's first contracts—1892. It was a department store with apartments upstairs. It's the head office for a bank now. We can go in and look."

Back outside, they headed down a wide avenue to Plaza San Marcos. The palace, a long stone building with a square tower at each end and an imposing arched entrance, was now a posh Parador hotel. They walked around the square looking at medallions set in the pavement that had scenes from the Camino.

"Do you love him?" Bob turned to look straight at Brigit with his question.

"No. I never did."

"Well, what the hell is it all about? You haven't told me anything. All I know is you screwed around with some jerk from church."

"You remember that art show we did with artists from emerging countries? I worked with Earl on that project, and we spent a lot of time in the planning and everything. We just got close. I know it's ridiculous, but it just—kept going."

"You mean that boxer fellow? You can't be serious!"

"He's not a boxer. He coaches boxing to young people. He's an impresario." She was just about to defend Earl as a person of worth, but her pride on this issue would just have to be swallowed. 'Better he thinks of him as the hunchback of Notre Dame if that would help.'

"But why? Are you unhappy with our life?"

"Yes, I was at the time. It was all so grey with the finances. I was just tired and lonely."

"Oh, so we are back to the money now, are we? I guess it's my fault. You are blaming me and still feeling resentful. I thought we agreed we are putting that behind us, but no. You have to dredge it all back up again and use it as an excuse for your appalling behaviour."

"You asked me and I'm telling you," she said. "And you've decided it is all in the past, but it wasn't the hell then.

I was depressed and fed-up and Earl was interested in me and he was kind and sweet if you must know. It just felt so good to be cherished. And no, I am not blaming you. But don't pretend it never happened now that we've paid the debt. I don't love him. I never did, but he saved me at that time when I was so miserable."

"Apparently not that miserable. Playing Madame Patron of arts and sleeping around. Anyway, why didn't you tell me instead of fucking around with this guy?"

Brigit felt herself wither.

"Don't you have more self-esteem than to behave like that? What would your father have said? Your parents never gave you an example like that? They would be ashamed of you and so am I."

The pain just got worse. He was right but it was such a low blow: her priest father, her artist mother, her perfect childhood family life, two brothers and a sister to look out for her, friends and community. Surrounded by good examples. She the preacher's daughter: some smart-ass said that preacher kids are either goody-two-shoes or sluts. She had been a good little girl, a diligent student, the lovely wife, loving mother, even heroic in times of crisis. How did it happen that the slut had turned up in her life? She sat there bemused as she saw how this drama had unfolded.

"What is it?" Bob barked.

"I was just thinking—about being the preacher's daughter, and where I am now."

"Are you blaming your father?"

"Oh, stop. I'm not blaming anyone. I've told you I regret it. Like you've told me you regret and are sorry about the money, and I accepted that. I ask for your understanding and your forgiveness."

"Do you think it's tit for tat? That I should just ignore or forget all about this because I screwed up on the investment? But there is a big difference. I was trying to improve things for the family and you were just out to destroy it and our lives. And you want me to cancel out your adultery with my investment mistake. Oh no, Brigit. It doesn't work like that!"

"You are so unfair, and not being honest. I've told you a thousand times it wasn't so much the money but that you didn't ask me. Didn't tell me till it was too late."

"A thousand times, you are right about that! You just harp on with the same old song. Well look at you now — who's the guilty one? Anyway, I have to go back to the albergue. Are you coming? And what should I call her? Is it Sister?"

"Yes, that should be okay. 'Thank goodness for the missing pack,' thought Brigit. 'Maybe it will save us, or at least give me a break here.'

Sister Alicia was in her office. She was in her early fifties, she wore a black habit with a leather belt, and her hair was covered by a simple coif with a white band. She said how sorry she was that they were suffering this inconvenience and that they were not to think badly of León or Spain because of this. They both reassured her of the hospitality and goodness of the people they had met along the Camino.

"I phoned the police station this morning but there is no sign of your pack. This is the help we can give you: we have some equipment that is left behind by pilgrims." She explained all this in her straightforward English. "The volunteer will take you, Bob, and you can see what is of use. The rest you will have to go out and buy. There is the Corte Inglés in the town. They are good and the prices are fair. Brigit, I would like you to stay. Bob, the volunteer is in the breakfast room. Her name is Julia. Goodbye and good luck. But I will see you at the pilgrims' blessing this evening in the chapel." She opened the office door for him. Bob looked back at Brigit, thanked Sister Alicia, and did as he was told.

Sister Alicia closed the door and smiled at Brigit. "I think we need a coffee," she said, and led her through another door to a scullery area where a coffee pot was set up. Once back in the office she told Brigit to sit in an armchair and she sat across from her in another.

"I asked your husband to go alone as I wanted to talk with you. My daughter, I can see you are unhappy. I know the Camino can be difficult, but I think there is more. Am I right?

"Yes, Sister. Thank you. I have been very stupid and foolish and I am hurting so much." The kindness on this woman's face swept over Brigit like an enormous tide of emotion. She felt her whole being crumple. Her nose blocked. Her shoulders slumped and great sobs rose from deep down in her gut. The crying just took over. She had no control over it. It felt like pain and ache, relief and misery, all at the same time.

"Brigit, you must cry. This is good. Take your time." She put a box of Kleenex on the little table next to the coffee mug.

"Good. Are you feeling a bit better? Brigit, tell me: do you go to church?" Sister Alicia was back.

"Yes, I do." She explained she was involved in her church, and then she found herself confiding that her father had been a priest.

"That is good. It means I can talk to you in the language of our loving Saviour Jesus Christ. Now, my daughter, you say you have been very foolish and stupid. Is that really so?"

"I am sorry Sister, but it's worse. Stupid and foolish are really not the right words. I sinned and broke my marriage vows."

"Well there are reasons and circumstances why we sin. We are blessed knowing that we are forgiven by Jesus, whatever we have done. He loves us as His precious children. That is our comfort and strength. Of course here in the world it is not so clear. Let us talk about what went wrong."

Brigit gave her the bare facts: the money, the struggle, her affair and then how it was all going sideways on the Camino. She did her best to be objective and honest. Sister Alicia's face stayed impassive.

"It is good you are on the pilgrimage. God does heal in effective ways, but not always in the way we like. Do you and your husband want to stay together?"

"I know I do, desperately, though I should have thought of that before. Sister, I cannot imagine my life without Bob: that our family would break up. I can't believe I could do this. What was I thinking?"

"Brigit, talking this sorry-regret manner is not helpful. You must reconcile this with God. You must truly pray about your sin, ask His forgiveness, receive the Sacrament and know you have God's forgiveness, grace, and love. Then it is your work to make it right with your husband. He has blame too, but yours is a serious act. That does not mean that you cannot come through. You are his wife. You know him best. You know what is important for him. Now, go and have some time for yourself. I suggest San Isodoro church. It is more peaceful for prayer than the cathedral."

21. No Walking Yet

Julia, the morning volunteer, and Bob went through the collection of abandoned gear.

"We don't keep everything. People bring too much and leave it: air mattresses, tents, extra coats. They arrive with great big packs, so full and heavy, but some things we know will be useful." They found socks, a pair of flip flop sandals, a rain jacket, and a microfiber T shirt. "It is a surprise what gets left behind on the washing line. But all the better for you. What about these trousers?" She held up a pair of light-weight track pants. But the best find was a backpack: not very high tech but it would do.

Bob was glad about the backpack. At the Corte Inglés department store he saw some really great packs, but very pricey. And his lightweight sleeping bag— it had been perfect for the hostels. He could keep the sheet from last night and most hostels had blankets, so he could manage. He also missed his two draw-string packing bags that had kept things tidy in his pack. It would have to be plastic bags. And his notebook, that was lost too. In the end he only needed to buy a few toiletries and underwear. But he still felt bereft. The loss of his gear and the train wreck that was happening to his marriage: what was left? Back through the city centre, familiar now. 'Feels like we've been here an age—it's only twenty four hours.'

Several packs were already lined up in the entrance hall of the albergue with boots and poles.

"Bonjour, mon cher Robert. How come you have got here before me?" Bob quickly abandoned his plan to organize his pack and he and Charles-Michel headed out. "As you have been here a whole day already, you can be my guide. And where is Brigit? Don't tell me you have lost her too—again."

They made their way to the cathedral and admired the outside, but before tackling the inside they decided to find a restaurant and have lunch. Over coffee, Charles-Michel tilted back in his chair and gave Bob a knowing smile.

"You had better tell me what's going on. Apart from the fact that I know you rather well, you wear your emotions on your sleeve, and I can see that you're actually in a bit of state, despite the poor attempt at the brave face."

Bob sighed. "Things seemed to be going so much better. In fact they were going very well. As we had lost some time, we skipped part of the Meseta and took the train from Frómista. That evening, Brigit dropped this bombshell." Bob stopped. How he could talk about this, even to his old friend? It was just so humiliating. Shit, he could not even look after his pack, so why not tell his friend? It was all pain anyway.

"And…so?" Charles-Michel prompted.

"Brigit had an affair!" The words came out sounding as though from a stranger.

Charles-Michel looked at Bob in shock. "Mon Dieu, Bob. I am so sorry. Do you mind me asking when this all happened? Would you prefer not to talk about it? I don't mean to intrude into your private affairs."

"She tells me she ended it about a year and a half ago. I am just sick and it disgusts me and I'm in a rage the whole time. Can you believe it? He was some prick from her church."

"I can understand that you would feel that way. Were you still struggling with the debt situation at this time?"

"We were just coming through it. Why did she have to wreck everything? She brought up the money thing, as though that could be an excuse, which is so pathetic and dishonest."

"But you are both still walking together?"

"Yes, we are. I'm not going to have her wandering around by herself, getting her feet in a state again and goodness knows what else: befriending some stray lonely pilgrim. And what am I supposed to tell the children? And now this pack business. I did suggest she go home but she said no."

"I think you are doing the right thing. And you don't have to tell your kids anything at this time. I know you don't want to hear this, but I am sure she is really suffering too. Just don't rush into anything."

"How could I possibly rush into anything when I am stuck here without my pack?" Bob said bitterly.

****

Brigit had a heavy rough stone stuck in her rib cage. Now that she had told Bob and Sister Alicia, the reality of what she had done was fully dawning on her. She knew before she had been stupid, wrong, and self-centred but it had just been her own foolish business. As for Earl, frankly he could look after himself. She did not indulge herself by blaming him. It was the shock and horror of discovering, this sickening version of herself who had disregarded the well-being of those she loved the most. She sat in San Isidoro church; people came and went. Now she could see a priest moving around the altar area, maybe getting ready for mass or prayers. She looked at her watch: half past five. She had better get back to the albergue. She certainly did not want to cause more trouble by going missing. But what was she supposed to do back there? She would need to eat. This evening, there would be no welcoming Tapas bar in a charmed escape bubble. What was Bob doing? He would have done his shopping and got himself organized.

The Albergue was hopping, a whole new batch of pilgrims. And there was Mireille; Brigit felt a jab of joy come through her darkness.

"Brigit, when did you get here? Is Bob around? So good to see you. Where did you walk from today?" As Mireille waited in line to check in, Brigit filled her in with the update for her foot, the train, and now the lost pack. "I haven't seen you since Burgos. Tell me how was the Meseta?" asked Brigit. "You've made great time!"

"I got a bit of help. Did you go to that albergue at San Bol? It wasn't like any hostel I'd been to before. Sort of Tolkien—Bilbo's Bag End."

"It felt more like the Mad Hatter's tea party down Alice's rabbit hole to me!" laughed Brigit. "But they really helped us as the river was flooded and we were stuck and they came and ferried us across. We spent some time there and then kept going. It was all a bit too hippie for me."

"Oh I didn't take you for such a woose. They were lovely people. I decided to take a day off and stayed an extra night. Most of them were musicians. Yes it was quite bohemian; good to know there are still enclaves of free spirits left in the Western World."

"I am surprised you left at all. You could have settled in. Were Sven and Astrid there?"

"Yes, they were. Interesting people and they fit right in. Everyone was sweet and hospitable, but the age difference did begin to catch up with me. I can't sleep in till noon any more. There is only so much hanging around and wondering if I should cook some food, or if they plan to get up and do it. Then they have a drink or smoke instead, and I am still wondering if there's any chance of food during daylight hours. I know this sounds old-lady-sad. But it was fun for the time I was there."

"But you have made it here in such good time."

"Well not quite: Philippe at San Bol gave me a ride. He was heading out for supplies and he gave me a ride to Carrión de los Condes. I have been walking from there, four days. So it looks like we all got a bit of help over the Meseta."

By this time they were at the head of the line for registering. José was on duty. He told Brigit that Bob has met a friend earlier, and they had headed out. The women went upstairs and Mireille was able to get a bed near Brigit. "Let me have a shower, then I want to look around the city."

"Okay, and maybe Bob will be back by then. I do want to check in with him." She lay on her bed and closed her eyes. She felt so much better since she had met Mireille. She thought about what Sister Alicia had said: "You know what's important for your husband." She thought back to the lovely summer holidays and weekends they had all spent at their cottage on Blue Sea Lake, up in the Gatineau, north of Ottawa. "Thank you, God that we have been able to keep the cottage." An American diplomat had taken it on a four year lease. It was theirs again now. 'We must get in some good times there this summer,' she thought. 'But will I be there with them? Or am I going to be an outcast, back in the city, in a sad little walk-up apartment, on a hot Sunday afternoon, all by myself? Bob is an attractive man, and charming too— he could find another woman with no problem. She imagined her family there but with her replacement. She felt a wave of anger and resentment—how dare they, how dare he! I don't care what I have to do to keep us together, but I will!'

When Colin turned up in the evening, a picnic supper was organized. They ate in the plaza in front of the albergue and then went to the pilgrim's blessing in the chapel.

"I was given a clear expectation by Sister Alicia to be here," said Bob.

Charles-Michel watched Bob sort his new gear. "Well, you are really in the pilgrim spirit, just a few humble second-hand clothes."

"So next I'll be shuffling along on my knees. What is it the Buddhist pilgrims do—the serious ones, three steps forward and then prostrate themselves? Can I keep my pack on for that?"

"You're travelling so light now that you could manage that. But I guess you went to the chapel this evening so maybe that's enough penance for the time being."

'And,' Bob thought, 'all the rest of the misery I'm going though.'

****

She is on the Camino, walking in the road. Coming towards her is Bob. He has his pack, and his feet are dusty. He does not see her. They walk past each other, but she keeps watching, and as she watches, his face crumples, and he starts to cry. She can see his whole face and body being drawn into the pain.

She feels compassion for this man's suffering. It is so real. Is our suffering one great shared pool, out there, in orbit around the earth? Another wave of hurt and love for Bob. She got her bearings: in the dormitory, still in León. She had arranged with Bob that they would get up early and use the public phone to call Liz. She had e-mailed Liz that she had told her father about the affair, that it was very painful, but she was doing her best to sort things out. She warned Liz that her father was not aware that she knew of the affair, and that he had enough to deal with without knowing that. Brigit was into damage control.

"Hi Liz, Mum and Dad here." Bob was on the phone. "Yes, we are still in León." They told her about the pack and how they were managing to get Bob's gear together. She wanted to know about Brigit's foot.

"Dad, get Mum close to the phone so she can hear. We've got news for you. Big news! We're expecting again. We are thrilled!" Brigit and Bob looked at each other with joy, the joy of another grandchild. Bob and Brigit babbled in love— "how wonderful, so happy, so proud, due when, how are you feeling? How about Stephanie, how is she feeling about this?"

"Stephi is so excited. She's so sweet, and keeps making plans for what the baby will do and where it will sleep. It's different from when Stephi was coming. We are more comfortable and confident about it all. I haven't told Paul or Don yet. We wanted to tell you first."

22. Sacrifice and Chivalry

Sister Alicia, Julia, and José were there to see them off. Julia asked Bob if his pack was good, and if he had all he needed.

"Enough already. When can I get out of this city? Shake the dust from my feet. I have been here an age, and it's not as though this place is full of wonderful memories," said Bob as they got going.

"You ungrateful son-of-a-bitch!" Charles-Michel exploded. "And that bit about shaking the dust from your feet is what Jesus said to his disciples when he sent them out on their own. That was the instruction if they weren't shown hospitality. You have been shown nothing but kindness, hospitality, and given tactful help. You have also just had amazing news about a grandchild. I will never get news like that. You are blessed in your life."

"Yeah really lucky. Cheating wife, losing my pack, victim of a mining fraud."

"Bob, just stand up. Face your demons or whatever, and grow up. Your finances are back in order. Your pack is trivial. And has it occurred to you it's your turn to do some forgiving?"

"Oh, fuck you!" said Bob and strode ahead.

He could have taken some shortcuts, but he followed the yellow arrows, past the cathedral square, San Isodoro church, left and to the Parador San Marcos hotel. Places that had memories of conversations and show-downs with Brigit. And now Charles-Michel getting on his self-righteous high horse!

Once over the river, though it was rather neglected, they could tell they were on the ancient Camino, with crosses and a chapel to Santiago.

"Look! Storks!" shouted Mireille. She pointed to a pair of large grey birds, with long beaks, like an illustration from a fairy tale. There they were organizing a tatty, twiggy, great big mess of a nest on top of the chimney of an abandoned workshop. "That's a sign of good luck. And they bring the babies— like your new grandchild."

"Time for coffee. Bob, we're taking a break." Bob stopped and came back, reluctantly, and joined them at the café table. Charles-Michel bossing around again. La Virgen del Camino, on the edge of León, seemed to be its own community with a large modern church.

"Okay Charles-Michel, what's our history lesson?" asked Brigit.

'Just look at her, sucking up to Charles-Michel—his friend,' Bob thought as he sat down.

"Though this church might look rather new— which it is, from the 1960s, La Virgen Del Camino was a pilgrim site in its own right. A shepherd boy had a vision of the Virgin and persuaded the Bishop of León to build a shrine. And then to make it even more special, in the fifteen hundreds, a certain Alonso, on a crusade, was captured by the Moors. He prayed to the Virgin that if he was released, he'd make a pilgrimage here. The Moors thought that was a big joke. They chained him up and put him in a chest. But he had the last laugh. The Virgin had the chest transported here, along with some church bells that rang out when he arrived. The statues on the outside of the church—the Virgin with the Apostles—are renowned."

"Yes, there's Saint James with his shells all in a row. And look, he's pointing along the path," said Mireille. "I love the Camino, but keeping all the names straight is beyond me! If it isn't a Santo, or a San, it's Del Camino or La Reina or las or de las or del Real or some other variation or other."

"Wanda and Shirley took the path to Villadangos del Páramo. Another good Camino name, but I'm reading it off the guide," said Brigit.

"The original Camino trail," said Charles-Michel.

"See what I mean about the names," exclaimed Mireille. "Just along this part of the path we have Fresno del Camino, Oncina de la Valdoncina, then Chozas de Abajo, and then we finally get to Mazarife— all within about seventeen kilometers. So don't bother to give me a test." Finally they were out into agricultural land. The path was flat and uneventful through brown fields with mounds of sugar beet looking like large earthy potatoes. Eventually they came to the river Órbigo and the bridge.

"Wow!" said Colin. "This is amazing." The bridge was built of hewn stone and two wide arches spanned the river, but it did not stop there. The bridge kept going; a dozen smaller arches marched across a large flood plain and right into the town of Hospital de Órbigo.

"They hold jousting tournaments down there," said Colin. The bridge was paved with cobble stones; a man with a donkey came towards them. They checked in at the parish hostel and decided to cook their meal and sorted out tasks and food—canned lentils, cherizo sausage, salad, and wine.

After supper, as they sat around the courtyard table chatting with other pilgrims, a priest came and joined them. This was his parish and he lived on the upper level of the albergue building. The albergue was sponsored by the German pilgrim association and was dedicated to Karl Leisner. His name in modern cut out stainless steel lettering, was across the front of the building. Karl Leisner, the priest explained to them, had been active in the church in Germany during the 1930s, mainly as a youth leader. His ambition was to be ordained a priest. However he was critical of Adolf Hitler and did not hide his opinions and in 1939 he was arrested and eventually ended up in the Dachau concentration camp. He was not the only cleric there. Over two thousand priests, students, and lay brothers were sent there. Among this group, Leisner continued to be instructed in theology. In 1944, while still in Dachau, he was ordained as a priest by a French bishop who was also interned. He only got to celebrate mass once inside the prison, in fact only the once in his life. Dachau was liberated in April 1945. But he was so ill with tuberculosis that he died a few months later."

Everyone was silent for a while after hearing this story. "He would be so pleased to have the hostel named for him," a German pilgrim finally commented.

"Yes, he is declared a Martyr of the Catholic Church," the priest added.

"It is such a reminder of what is recent European history when you hear of a life like that," said Bob.

"But to talk of another kind of history," said the priest, "do you all know the history of this town and the bridge?" Though most of them had a general idea of the story they asked the priest to tell them.

"It is one of those Romance stories from the Middle Ages about a knight who was rejected by the lady he loved. He was from León and his name was Suero. To gain back his honour, he received the king's permission to send out a challenge to any knight to come and fight him. It was the summer of 1434. The Knight Suero choose this place as he knew there would be many people on their way to Santiago. The news of the challenge spread. Knights, their servants, and horses came from all over Europe and a whole camp grew up by the river. Can you imagine—the colourful tents, flags and banners, the armour, such excitement. The field was prepared for the fighting which was jousting with lances on horseback. The jousting lasted for days: in fact several weeks, with great crowds to watch. Suero had set himself the task of breaking three hundred lances from the knights who challenged him. Each day Don Suero won. In the evening there would be feasts and celebrations. He kept winning and made many enemies from among these warriors. Finally in August, he reached his goal of three hundred broken lances and declared the challenge over. He led a procession back to León to show how he was now free from his oath; then he set off on the pilgrimage to Santiago."

"Why did he give himself this challenge if he had been rejected by this woman?" asked Colin.

"He swore a vow to the lady that he would fast and wear a heavy iron ring around his neck until they were married. When she changed her mind, he had to find an honourable way to free himself from the oath."

"It all went together—the bravery, the love of the lady, the oath—it was your word and that made your honour," said Charles-Michel.

"Absolutely," agreed the priest. "To be a knight, you had status and privileges. But this came with a price: your fidelity to your king or local lord, and to the lady whom you chose to love."

"It all comes back to courage" said Colin. "He could have just done a pilgrimage or some other sacrifice to redeem himself, but no, he put his whole life on the line, risking everything. Imagine if he had been beaten in a joust on the first day of his challenge."

Pardon My Camino

"And how he dealt with the betrayal from his lady, she put him a position where he risked all to overcome that disgrace," said Bob.

"The pursuit of my calling does not allow or permit me to go in any other fashion; easy life, enjoyment, and repose were invented for soft courtiers, but toil, unrest, and arms were invented and made for those alone whom the world calls knights-errant, of whom I, though unworthy, am the least of all."

(Michel de Cervantes. The Ingenious Gentleman Don Quixote of La Mancha, First part, Chapter 13)

23. Change Is a Comin'

Brigit lay in her upper bunk bed, awake: her usual pattern lately. She managed about three hours sleep, then woke up and lay there, tired but awake. She thought about the story of the knight. Did Bob see himself as the knight in the story, betrayed by his lady? What would it take to restore his pride? Could she be part of it? She had seen on the walk from León, now with their pilgrim group—her pod, like the whales—that she and Bob could just keep going and never actually talk together, and therefore never start to sort things out. She had to tell Bob that they must have time together, every day, one-on-one. She just hoped that Bob would not shut her out.

They were all slow the next morning. The plan was to walk to Astorga, about fifteen kilometres. As they were clearing up breakfast, two young German men arrived at the hostel.

"We are looking for Bob and Brigit Matthews." Everyone looked up. Bob stepped forward and Brigit said, "Yes, that's us."

"Oh, that is wonderful! We are very glad to meet you. Hallo! We have been trying to catch you since St-Jean-Pied-de-Port. We had to stop because of my feet for two days," one of them explained. He had an open face and was smiling. "My name is Manfred and this is my friend Leopold. We are army cadets that is why we can walk fast. We have come from Villar de Mazarife this morning," Manfred said. They all shook hands and introduced themselves but finally Bob asked, "How do you know about us?"

"Oh, but we have your handy—your cell phone. You didn't know we were bringing it? At the hostel in St-Jean, the owner asked us to bring it. It was a week after you had been there. But the owner knew we were going fast and would catch you. It has been an adventure as we have been asking for you at the albergues. Then we would lose you. Their system works well when the pilgrims' names are written down in their books," said Leopold. "We had a good time, like a detective movie." And he retrieved their phone from the bottom of his pack and handed it over to Bob. "And I have the charge cord. That is how it was left in St-Jean."

"Yes that was me. I left it behind," said Brigit. "Thank you so much. We had no idea. The hostel owner said they were going to send it on to Santiago."

"You guys are great. Why don't you walk with us today," said Colin." The others all made inviting sounds.

"Yes that would be good, but we have to go fast. We will stop in Astorga to eat and then on to Rabanal for the night."

Charles-Michel was looking at the map. "But that will be fifty kilometres for you today."

"Yes, that is a big day for us. Rabanal has a very nice hostel, run by the English group. But most days we do at least forty kilometres," said Leopold. "And now we will be lighter as we won't be carrying your telephone!" said Manfred and they both had a laugh as they put their packs back on and took off. "Tschüss. Buen Camino!"

"Oh shoot," said Charles-Michel, "We should have asked them if they had seen your pack along the way!"

Brigit was heartened to see that Bob had a laugh about this too. And finally they all set out.

The return of the cell phone let Brigit team up with Bob. "Some good news. I really was careless leaving it behind."

"We've managed quite well without it," said Bob.

"Bob, I have been doing some real thinking. I am trying to understand myself over this horrible affair; it's not easy for me. But I have to do it for me and I hope for you. So though we are walking with the others, which is lovely, I am asking that each day we can have some time. The two of us. To phone home. To talk. I know this is a lot to ask."

"Brigit, I can't imagine what you can say to make anything better. But I guess I can't say we can't talk. If you really want to."

'Oh goodness thank you for bringing the cell phone back at that very time. That just let a bit of light in. And I had my plan ready.'

"Do you know about the Cruz de Ferro?" asked Charles-Michel. "It's the highest point on the Camino. People leave a stone there. Some bring one from home, but there is a tradition that you take one from the next hill and carry it there."

"That's fine. As long as I can take a small one," said Mireille. At the top of the hill, they stopped to take in the view. The city of Astorga was below. But beyond that they could now clearly see mountains: to their left, to the right, and beyond.

"This is the end of the great plain we have been walking over," said Charles-Michel. "And what is maybe more important for us, now there will be some serious uphill."

"We had better find our stones for the Cruz de Ferro," Bob reminded them.

****

They were shown to a round central table with white table linens and two glasses each. The old-fashioned dining room was decorated with heavy drapes, padded panels on the walls, and chandeliers.

"You know what's lovely," said Brigit. "They're not hiding us away in a corner." The owner of the hotel Gaudi in Astorga was a big supporter of the Camino and he welcomed pilgrims in for lunch. So for ten Euro, they were served a charcuterie platter, fish, salad, and a desert called a San Marcos tart. "Sort of like a rum baba with cream filling and caramel on top," said Mireille. And they ordered a Rioja wine and finished with dark strong coffee. The chairs were comfortable. It was such a gracious moment.

It was a bit of an effort for Brigit not to doze off as she sat in the cathedral. She had arranged for this solitude and it was no time to indulge in a snooze. After their perfect lunch, Brigit went first to the Bishop's Palace while the others started with the cathedral. The Palace was another Antoni Gaudi building. It was a museum now with artifacts from the Camino, a collection of religious statues and art work. Brigit was so taken with the building that she did not give the displays much attention, just taking in the luminous and harmonious space around her.

Inside the cathedral the sandstone had a soft pink hue from the late afternoon sun. Brigit sat in the main nave. It was not easy to work out how she could order her thinking into some sort of understanding that would be of use talking to Bob. In the end, she decided to start with something he had asked her: "Why are you telling me this?" Phew, why had she? It has been two years since the affair, and so far she had gotten away with it!

"Brigit, listen to yourself! You are so juvenile: 'Getting away with it'. You make it sound like some kid's game. This is your life, not hide and seek. This is really it, Brigit."

'Oh dear God, just preserve me from myself.'

By the time Brigit made it back to the hostel, it was coming up to six pm. Mireille was there. "The guys are still out sight-seeing. I gave up after the Episcopal Palace but they were off to the Roman walls. How are you? Good to have some time on your own?"

"Yes it was, and the cathedral was cool and peaceful."

"You two really are having an adventurous Camino. And Bob's pack, he seems to be taking it quite hard."

"Oh Mireille, if it was just the pack. You know I told you how all this crap was coming to the surface in our relationship. Well it's far worse. The shoe is on my foot now! I have to say this about the Camino: you can't hide emotionally, at least for me. It all bubbles up to the surface and hits me in the face. It's like Sven said: it has an energy and tricks all of its own. Having all this time to think. Being thrown together. And all these stories of heroes and saints. It's turning out to be a big messy soup! I'm really trying my best to sort it out. But I won't burden you with all the details."

Bob and the others arrived back with food to make a light evening meal.

"We bought salad fixings," explained Bob.

"And the piece de résistance—voila!" said Charles-Michel producing bunches of white asparagus.

"And some really nice looking pâté here," said Colin. "I think it's duck but couldn't be sure. They had me taste some, and ducky or not, it's fine."

"Pan integral and Rioja red!" Charles-Michel said.

"More wine! Are we going to be able to walk tomorrow?" Brigit wondered.

"Of course we will. We might not be able to sleep much in this charming but very crowded dormitory, so we might as well be happy," said Colin. "I think the Camino runs on red wine, all those vineyards—and it's good and cheap."

"Bob, how about calling Liz? Do we have time?"

"Yes, of course you do. Supper later," said Charles-Michel. "I could do with a relax."

Liz was feeling fine: just a bit queasy in the mornings but nothing too serious.

"How's Stephanie? I do miss you all," said Brigit.

"We miss you too, Mum. Stephanie keeps asking after you both. Dad, how are you managing about your pack? Any news?"

"No, no news. I'm making do with donated items. But we did get one thing back: the cell phone." And they told her about the two German army cadets striding across Spain to catch up with them.

"How kind of them," Elizabeth remarked.

"Oh I think they were having quite a good time of it. Like a quest, their Camino Holy Grail," said Brigit.

"Well Mum, I think it was exceptionally kind of them to go to all that trouble."

"Yes dear. You're quite right," said Brigit.

"Bob, can we talk? We've got time before supper."

"Well we should help with it."

"We've still got plenty of time anyway. There's a bench behind the Episcopal Palace. We can admire a bit more Gaudi as we chat." They found the bench that Brigit had checked out in the afternoon. It was delightful in the evening light. "Thank you, Bob, for agreeing to let us talk. I do appreciate that. I know you feel bitter."

"Oh, so this is our heart to heart time, is it? I don't think much has changed since León."

"I agree. The facts haven't changed but I am trying to change and grow."

"That's not going to change the past. You think a few cozy chats are going to make it better—dream on, woman!"

"You asked me why I have told you about the affair. And I wondered too. Did I tell you for me or for you?"

"That's a load of crap."

Brigit chose to ignore this comment and went on: "Did I tell you because I thought it would help me with my guilt, or did I tell you because in the end I respect you too much not to tell you? I know it is right that you should know."

"Where was the respect when you were screwing this boxer? Tell me that."

"Though it did seem to be my secret, that does not mean you would not have found out. Someone could tell you. And that would be just too awful. For you and for me. 'Truth will see the light.'"

"What do you mean 'your secret'? The boxer knew and I'm guessing Liz knew. How embarrassing is that? Shameful. And what is this quotation? Do you think this is the time to be clever?"

"Well it's Shakespeare and Cervantes. You know they were contemporaries. In fact they died on the same date."

"Brigit, just listen to yourself. You're in la-la land."

"Bob, give me a damn break here! I'm trying to manage this as best I can! I know I'm the guilty one. But I have been your wife for thirty years and the mother of your children. I love you. I'm trying to manage and if it comes out wrong sometimes, it's because this is so, so hard and I'm hurting too. Yes, Liz knew. But she is such a wise and understanding person she has taken it in her stride. She loves us and keeps telling me to sort this out and that is what I am trying to do here. It would be a double betrayal if I had not told you. It's bad enough I have waited so long. Imagine if you had found out from someone else. Don't you agree?" Brigit did not know if she could keep it together much longer.

"I think my worse guilt is for the mistake, or sin in this case. That I could have prevented it but I didn't. But I could not go on living with a lie. I don't know what our future together holds. I realize I have to face that. It is up to you. But we could not live together with such a lie. It would have ripped us apart. I would have known why, and you would have just been the victim all over again."

There was silence. Brigit managed not to cry. Bob sat, hunched over. She would have liked to have touched him. Rubbed his shoulders. Take his hand. But she did not dare.

Finally Bob said, "Let's go back and help the others with supper."

24. New Heights

"Today we have a choice of doing a detour and visiting a reconstructed village. It's a national historic site," Charles-Michel explained.

"I'll keep on the main path," said Brigit. "I want to go back to having quiet time in the mornings."

Bob and Charles-Michel voted to go to the historic village. Mireille, Colin, and Brigit would keep on the regular track. The cathedral bells were ringing as they went through the Puerta Obispo in the old city walls. An overpass led them above the autopista highway onto a track out of the city, over a river and into a small village.

"This is where your path to the heritage village branches off," said Colin. "By the way, Mireille, I see there are several good place-names for you along here."

Bob and Charles-Michel branched off to the right and in the distance they could see Castrillo de Polvazares: their destination.

"What do we know about this village? I keep seeing this word Maragato."

"That's the name given to the people of this region," said Charles-Michel. "Nobody seems to know for sure where they came from or their heritage. Maybe because the soil is so poor they were left in peace. Nobody wanted their land."

When they reached the village it appeared deserted, sitting peacefully in the morning light. Cars were parked on the street which was paved with round stones with a channel down the middle for rain. The houses formed a continuous wall of hewn stone with arched double doors that led into court yards.

"Hola! buenos dias, ¿peregrinos? A man's voice called out.

"Si, somos peregrinos" said Charles-Michel, "Buenos dias."

"Bienvenido, ¿de dondé estan? English?"

"Canadiense," said Bob.

"Ah! Quebec? English?"

"Hablamos englese y francese." Bob was getting into his stride.

"Muy bien. I think my English is better than my French. Welcome to my village. I have the hotel, come and have a coffee. Be my guests! My name is Emilio." Emilio looked like he could have been an athlete in his youth, not tall but muscular. He led them through a gate into a courtyard with tables and parasols. "Coffee, yes? ¿café solo, con leche? Yes, con leche is good in the morning." And he went inside and they could hear him shouting out the order in a cheerful voice. Soon a waiter appeared with three coffees, little cookies, and glasses of water. Emilio in the meantime wanted to know about their Camino.

"I am very glad you made the detour to this village. You see it has been restored as it is an important part of the heritage of my people, the Maragato. We have been here for many centuries. When the Romans arrived, we worked for them for their gold mines. Along the road from here."

They had a second cup of coffee, and thanked Emilio and explained they had to keep going to reach Rabanal that afternoon.

"When you were in the washroom." said Charles-Michel to Bob, "he invited us back to dinner this evening."

"Really, how did he think we would manage that?"

"Well I think it was actually me. He said he could come and get me in his car and bring me back in time for curfew, or next morning! It's only about seventeen kilometres by road."

"Oh my, Charles-Michel, he was making a pass at you. And not even very subtle."

"I rather think that was the idea."

"What did you say? Are you tempted?"

"No I am not, but thank you. I think a night with Emilio would be too much of a good thing."

"Well he might have made a real effort and worn a traditional Maragato costume for you. I think you are being a bit hasty just to reject his offer like this."

"I am happy to see Bob that you are able to have a good joke again. So much easier when it's at my expense."

"You could have accepted under the condition that you bring along your friends. How did he know? I mean, you're pretty straightforward."

"That is a sweet way of putting it. Especially the straight bit. Well actually he asked me right out. I guess he has pretty good gaydar. 'So Charles-Michel, I think you are gay. It is so?' Just like that."

"Emilio has gone up in the estimation. Good on him I say."

"Yes, I agree. Refreshing to find someone so direct. Anyway he insisted I take his card."

"Hope yet! Is that your first pick-up on the Camino?"

****

They joined the Camino along a country road and found a grassy bank on which to eat their sandwich. Below them was a pasture enclosed by a low stone wall with a large flock of sheep, a shepherd, and a sheep-dog; all moving like a great wave around the field.

"So much activity. Seems like they use all the energy they get from the grass just rushing around," said Bob.

Approaching Rabanal, there was a new path, rough with stones and roots. They had all agreed they wanted to stay at the Gaucelmo hostel. The one run by the British group.

"Hallo there, and welcome." And if the British accent had not been enough, a tall man in a kilt greeted them.

"Yes, your friends arrived about half an hour ago. One of them, Mireille, had a bit of an accident. We are sorting it out."

"Oh no. What happened?" they both asked.

"They are all in the second dormitory. Go through and join them. Mary, the other volunteer, is there."

When they came into the dormitory, Brigit meet them.

"Brigit, whatever happened? How is Mireille?" Bob said taking her hands.

"She's going to be all right. She tripped on a stone and her forehead came slap down on a root that was sticking out."

Mireille was on a lower bunk and Colin and Mary were with her.

"It was dreadful when it happened. She was in shock. Thank goodness we had Colin with us."

"Hi there," said Mireille in a rather weak voice. "I'm going to be fine and I am getting all the best help."

"Yes, you are going to be okay, but it will be sore," said Colin. "Mary, you have quite an impressive first aid kit here."

"It comes with the hostel. We are pretty well organized, I must say. We don't have much in the way of drugs. We can manage Aspirin. That should help with the pain and help you relax. Maybe even a snooze. What do you think Colin? Two pills and maybe a hot tea?"

"Fine. I'll try and have a sleep. But wake me up later on. I don't want to miss out on anything."

"We'll see how you do. You're in shock. A sleep and some tea will help." said Colin.

The hostel had a courtyard garden. Bob and Charles-Michel tracked down some beer and they all sat outside in the sunshine.

"I just had a look in on Mireille and she's having a good sleep. We're putting the new arrivals in the other room while we still have space."

"Mary, thank you so much," said Brigit. "We are so grateful to be at this albergue when this happened, with you wonderful volunteers."

"We have a good kitchen. I suggest you go to the local tienda and buy groceries for supper to cook here. That will work best for Mireille. And it will give you time to attend the Vespers at eight pm which is quite a treat. We have some Benedictine monks here and for Vespers they sing the Gregorian chants.

"Well, do you think we have another school teacher? There was no hesitation about the instructions," said Charles-Michel.

It was Bob and Brigit who went to the store. "Glad I can take a turn with the shopping and cooking. I haven't done my share lately," said Brigit. "How was your day, Bob?"

"Fine. We'll tell you about it at supper."

They decided on eggs for omelets, boiled potatoes and something that looked like kale.

"Look, kiwi fruit. We could have some with cheese for dessert." Brigit inspected them.

"I've just checked on Mireille," said Colin. "She's fast asleep and looking good. We won't wake her for supper. We can cook something for her later in the evening. Mary says we can break all the rules about using the kitchen late as long as we clear up. Aww, look you got kiwis. Did you think that would make me feel at home, not quite, but close enough. Thanks, guys!"

"Oh you think we have such a choice and no smart comments about the greens. They're turnip tops, and bound to be healthy," said Bob. "Colin, you pour the wine," Bob said as he brought the serving dishes to the table. "I want to hear about your day."

"It was great," Colin said. "Bit of climbing but so good to be up on that plateau — the view and the wind."

"Quiet roads most of the way, villages all with stone houses. We stopped for lunch in El Ganso," said Brigit

"We just walked straight through as it looked abandoned," said Bob.

"The main village is off the path. There's an albergue, a church and a bar where we got beer for our lunch. It's called the Cowboy Bar."

"Oh Bob," said Charles-Michel. "We missed that, so sorry. You would have wanted to go there. It would have been like home on the Prairies for you, or at least downtown Calgary."

"Oh really! Well let's talk about our day. We are lucky to have Charles-Michel's company this evening. He had such an interesting offer for a dinner date." And Bob gave his version of their meeting with Emilio.

"So what was his plan? That you have dinner at his hotel. Did he realize you are a pilgrim, walking?" asked Brigit.

"Oh yes. He had it all worked out. He would fetch Charles-Michel here by car. Then bring him back, but probably the next morning. Ready and refreshed to walk again."

"I guess it's only about twenty minutes by car. Maybe he has a routine," said Colin.

"Ouch! That's not very nice, when I thought I was so special and attractive."

"Just to let you know. It's coming up to eight pm if you were planning on Vespers. We'll keep on eye on Mireille. Don't worry."

"Thank you, Mary."

25. Now as We Come to the Setting of the Sun

Sitting in the small church listening to the monks, Bob agreed, was a treat. Only two monks were chanting, and they alternated lines, their voices pure. As well as the chanting monks, there were three others monks in different habits. After a reading, prayers, and a blessing, the simple Vespers service was over. Bob took a few minutes to look around the church. Going out the door into the evening sunshine he found Charles-Michel and Brigit talking with one of the monks.

"So you had Jesuits with you today?" Charles-Michel was commenting.

"Yes, they are visiting. So you know the orders?"

"I am from Quebec, Canada. I was educated by the Jesuits," explained Charles-Michel.

"Ah yes. The Jesuits, the great educators.

"Indeed. And you are Benedictines."

"We are from the Benedictine monastery near Burgos. That order is a contemplative order. Some of us felt we wanted to be of service in the community. So we came here to serve the pilgrims and some villages in the area. It is, how can I say, an experiment. I am not sure if we will be here forever."

"I went to your monastery: San Pedro," said Bob.

"This is my husband, Bob," Brigit introduced him. "We must get back. One of our group hurt herself today," said Brigit.

"I am sorry to hear that. If you need my help, let me know. I am Father Estevan. Bob, have you a minute?"

"It is just a detail but San Pedro de Cardeña is actually a Trappist order. Our monastery is Santo Domingo de Silos. It is south of Burgos."

"I do apologize. Is that the same San Domingo as in San Domingo de Calzada? We stayed there, at the albergue."

"Yes, absolutely. He was very active on the Camino and is an important saint in Spain. And his humility is an inspiration. Bob, that is very good that you went to San Pedro. Did you meet any of the monks? I know some of them."

"Yes, I spent some time with Father Antoine. He showed me the cellar with the wine making."

"Yes that is Father Antoine, I know him well. Tell me, what did you talk about?"

"Oh—okay, em— well actually I asked him about Christian forgiveness."

"That must have pleased Father Antoine. Though they are not directly on the Camino, he does like to be of help to pilgrims. El Cid's horse helps attract visitors there for him." He laughed. "It is amazing how God works. I should say, takes advantage of the strangest opportunities. El Cid's horse and the chickens at San Domingo de Calzada: did you see them?"

"Yes. I was puzzled until I heard the story."

"It is a wonderful story. So how are your reflections on forgiveness, Bob?"

Bob was aware that, here he was, again, having a heart-to-heart with a complete stranger who happened to be a monk. "When I was talking with Father Antoine, it was my wife who was very annoyed with me. I was upset because she did not seem to be able to forgive me for a mistake I made several years ago that I thought we had resolved. Now, she has told me about something, a terrible thing. I'm just so upset and angry with her. I can't forgive her. I don't even know if I want to. It's so painful."

"Bob, pain is very real. You must respect it, in yourself and in others. Have you talked about this forgiveness with your wife?"

"She is anxious to talk about it and I am finding it difficult."

"You have to give yourself time. If this is recent, please be kind to yourself and realize it takes time. I admire you and your wife if you are looking at your problems. The Camino gives you the space and time, even if it can be rather too intense for comfort. And you will meet people along the way who can help."

"I don't even know if I want any help or advice," said Bob.

"You will know if the advice works for you or not and when you are ready. It may not be advice, but a meeting, an event, a place. Just remember that forgiveness is as much for your sake as for those to be forgiven."

"Father Antoine said that too."

"Well, there you are. It must be right, you will see."

****

Brigit lay in her bunk, awake. There were twenty people sleeping in the room and that meant a fair share of snorers and wheezers all snuffling and grunting their way through the night. Still it had actually been a good day—apart from Mireille's accident. She had not had her heart-to-heart with Bob. He seemed better today. Better than he had been for a while. His day with Charles-Michel had been a success.

"Dear Lord, thank you for everything: the Camino, these friends, and the strangers we meet who help us in so many ways. Thank you for the monks this evening and bless their ministry. Help Bob and me with our problems. Guide us. Help Bob to forgive me, please."

****

Next morning Brigit and Bob were up early and were soon joined by Charles-Michel.

"Do we know how Mireille is this morning?" he asked.

"I looked in on her but she's still asleep," said Brigit.

"We will have to see how she's doing and how she feels about walking."

"Brigit, what time do you want to call Don?"

"How about four o'clock our time? It's our son's birthday, the youngest, twenty-two today," she explained to Charles-Michel.

"Well, congratulations to the parents, I say. How blessed you are to have children."

"Thank you, Charles-Michel, you are so right. I never take it for granted that I am blessed with children and now grandchildren," said Brigit.

Breakfast was provided at the albergue but it was not for another half hour.

"I saw that the store opens early. Why don't I go and get some fruit for today?" volunteered Bob.

The tienda was quite busy. Bob was checking out the fruit selection. Maybe just some apples. They travel well.

"Bob, buenos dias, ¿como estas?"

Bob spun round. 'Who the….?

"Emilio! Hello. What a surprise. You are out so early."

"Hallo, my friend. Yes, I come here to buy honey. It is the best in this whole area, from local bees, of course. How nice to see you. How are your friends? How is Charles-Michel?

"We are staying at the Albergue Gaucelmo. One of our group fell yesterday afternoon and hurt herself. We are not sure how she will be today."

"Tsss, that is bad. Where is she hurt?" Emilio asked.

"She fell on her face. She had a shock and is quite shaken."

"Let me come with you to the albergue. I can be of help for this poor lady."

"Oh please don't worry. You have your hotel to run." Said Bob.

"We are not too busy. I have some good staff. Let me put the honey in my car, you buy your things, and we will walk to the albergue."

When Bob turned up with Emilio and introduced him to Brigit, Colin, and Mireille there was much interest and a few coy smiles over in Charles-Michel's direction. Once again, Emilio seemed to have a grand plan.

"Mireille, you must be French with that lovely name. You Canadians, all French and English mixed up. I love it. Mireille, after your accident, it would be better for you not to walk today. It is a difficult part of the Camino. First there is a high climb, with a path with rocks and stones. Then another hill up and then a steep drop down. It would be an honour for me to come and collect you in the afternoon and take you to meet up with the others at the end of their day of walking. This is a good idea. I think so?" and Emilio smiled around the group.

There was a moment of silence. In fact, it did seem to be a good idea.

"Emilio, that is so generous of you," said Mireille "I could not possibly impose on you. You don't even know us.

I am sure you must have important things you need to be doing."

"Of course I know you. Bob and Charles-Michel came to my village yesterday and they told me about the friends they are walking with. I feel we are already good friends. I will be there for the lunch service, and after that my manager can look after things. It would be such a pleasure to spend time with people from outside."

"Mireille, when I took the bus for my foot it was just the right thing to do," said Brigit.

"And Mireille, we will have a good time. The road is near the Camino. We can stop and see bits of it, like La Cruz de Ferro, where you can leave a stone. And there are some beautiful panoramas. And I have another idea: I will bring the mini-van from the hotel. When we meet up with the others, we can all fit in and I can show you some places around."

Bob was trying to catch Charles-Michel's eye to get an idea of how he was reacting to all this, but Charles-Michel was standing to one side. Staying out of it all. They decided that they would walk the twenty-five kilometres to Molinaseca, which got them past the heavy-duty climbing and descending.

"That is a perfect arrangement. You can stay till this afternoon," said Mary. "We make allowances to help the injured. It's usually their feet. Quite a novelty to have a face injury. Yes. You do have a rather bad bruise. What a helpful person Emilio is."

"I heard you chatting away in Spanish," said Colin

"I'm a professor of Romance languages. And it's lovely being here. Think of all the stories I will have to tell when I get back for the university term.

"Mary, is there a history to this building?" asked Brigit.

"Quite a history! It was the Hospital de San Gregorio in the twelfth century. Pilgrim Picaud stayed here and mentions it. He wrote what could be called the first Camino guide. I must get on with the chores."

"Hey guys, is this arrangement with Emilio okay?" said Mireille. "I was getting a bit of a vibe. Am I missing out on something?"

"Mireille, it's just fine," said Charles-Michel. "We just have to let the kids have their fun. We met up with Emilio yesterday and he offered us dinner at his hotel."

"Well, that's only half the story." said Bob. "The offer of dinner was directed at Charles-Michel. He took a real fancy to him."

"Oh Charles-Michel, I have put you in an awkward situation. Maybe we should cancel. Let me do that. I have his number."

"Absolutely not! This is a perfect arrangement. And you know it'll be fun. We can do a bit of tourism together. And you'll all be there to protect me."

"Yeah. Mireille. Don't worry about Charles-Michel. He can look after himself very well."

"It's worse putting up with your sly little smiles and giggles than dealing with Emilio. But you do have to give the guy points for initiative. What was this about honey at the store?"

****

Leaving Rabanal was like walking on a table top with mountains all around. Today they would climb up to a height of over one thousand five hundred meters. It was Brigit's quiet morning time. She was trying to understand how she apparently did not know herself. She was so tempted to say, "that person who had an affair with Earl was not really me." But the sad and puzzling truth is, it is, or had been, her.

"Here you are, little stone," said Brigit as she placed her pebble on top of the pile. Cruz de Ferro was marked with a cross on a tall pole rising out of a hillock of stones and pebbles left by the pilgrims over the centuries. 'I wish I had brought you from home and carried my sins to be left here. But that would still not make it better with Bob.'

26. Things Mostly Ancient

The walkers reached the albergue just after three pm. Brigit and Bob finished their showers. "Shall we phone Don now?" said Brigit.

"How's it going, guys? Is Mum keeping up? How's your foot?"

"So much better. We have covered two-thirds of the way."

"And we have teamed up with a nice group. But tell us your news." said Bob.

They talked about his plans for the evening with his friends. His upcoming final exams for his industrial electrician ticket and the contacts he had made to work in western Canada.

"But I'll not go out until the fall. Now we have the cottage back, I want to spend time together there before I leave. I can get a summer job. Okay, guys. Thanks for remembering my birthday from distant Spain. I love you both. Come home safe!"

"There's a camping field area behind the hostel. Can we go there and talk?"

" Bob, what I have been trying to work out is, that I thought

I knew myself, but that person I thought I knew would not have behaved like I did. But I did. I have to accept that. I am not excusing myself. It was still despicable behaviour."

"Brigit. Where did this all take place and when?"

She realized that for Bob, along with the awful shock and anger of it all, he was still trying to piece it together. "It was at his house," she managed. "And usually after school. He lives in the Glebe."

"Oh, that's very convenient. Just across the canal!"

"Well, he did go to the church so it's the same neighborhood.

"Oh, I know that. You don't have to remind me."

"He goes to another church now. What I was trying to say was that I am working on recognizing this other aspect of me. What seems like another person. And I'm acknowledging this. Taking responsibility. Not just saying, 'well that wasn't really me.'"

"Do you have an explanation for this mystery person whom you claim you don't know?"

"It's horrible and stupid. It feels like I was being a rebellious teenager. Except I never was. And then this snake came out and twisted around inside me. Made me forget who I really am. What is so important in my life."

"Don't you think you're a bit old to have this sort of sick fantasy? You make everything sound like a fairy tale. Another thing I find so hurtful and deceitful is the whole secrecy. That it has taken you so long to tell me about this. You said you told me to prevent me from getting more hurt, but two years to tell me and such a betrayal. It's just so much crap and hypocrisy!"

****

Emilio and Mireille entered the albergue after five pm. They met Brigit.

"Mireille and Emilio! You made it."

Emilio went to the desk and talked with the woman in charge; they seemed to know each other. Mireille asked if there would be a problem for her to get a bed as she was arriving by car.

"Of course not," Emilio had reassured her. "People have injuries. I have to say with your bruise. Everyone can believe you."

"Thanks, Emilio. You're swell!"

"Ha, I understand *swell*, from old American movies! I will wait here. Tell them to come and talk with me. Don't forget we are going on a tour."

"Hi there, Mireille," said Colin. "All well? How do you feel? Nice bruise: got a little bluer since this morning. That war wound should get you some respect."

"Yes. I'm feeling fine now and will be able to walk tomorrow, no problem."

Charles-Michel came to join them. "Yes, it's impressive. What did you do with Emilio?"

"He's waiting for us and said not to forget he is taking us on a tour. I've got a bit to organize. I won't take long."

"I'll go and join him," said Charles-Michel.

Pardon My Camino

****

"I do not want you to get sad and think you are going backwards," said Emilio, "but I plan an interesting tour, along the other side of the river Maruelo from where you walked today." Charles-Michel sat up front and was given a local map so they could see where they were going. They parked the van and followed a path through trees to a group of low stone buildings with the stream beside them.

"This is Herrería. It is a forge for iron that dates from the medieval times, but was restored and it still works," said Emilio.

"This must have been an important installation in the Middle Ages," said Bob.

"Ponferrada in Roman times was the mining centre; in fact this area was the most important mining in the whole Roman Empire," said Emilio.

"As far as I can make out, they smelt the iron and do the forging here. Must be a labour of love," said Bob.

"Maybe they do art work, like one-off wrought iron items. Think of all those balconies that need railings," said Brigit.

Dinner started with white asparagus. "I have become addicted," said Brigit. "But they don't grow it around here, do they, Emilio?"

"No. But they do to the east. You think because you have walked that everything is far away. But one hour on the autopista, and olé! You have your asparagus! And we will be having lamb, and that is very local. You may have passed them on the way today." Emilio had taken them to a restaurant in Acebo. "Here we are on the ancient mountain pass over the Monte Irago. For the pilgrims it was very dangerous. The Knights Templars were here to protect them from thieves and bandits."

"I see this word Bierzo," said Bob.

"Yes, this region. And Ponferrada is the capital. Most people think of the wine when they hear the word Bierzo. The Romans brought the vines and the valleys have a unique soil and climate. It is excellent. We will have some."

"Emilio, have you lived in this area all your life?" asked Colin.

"Yes and no. I was born here and went to school in Astorga. I went to university in Madrid. It was just after General Franco had stepped down as president and dictator and Spain was opening up. It was a great time to be at university. I worked in Madrid for many years and then I decided to come home and was able to open the hotel and restaurant here. It is successful. Our whole area has opened to tourism and the Camino helps. There are people who want to see the Camino and have a Camino experience. So our hotel is a very good place for them. We are a little wild but close to Astorga and all the comforts."

"You are very knowledgeable about the history in the area."

"My family has been here for generations, though sadly my parents have died. I am a member of the rural council for this area".

"So, you are a politician."

"No no. Don't call me that. I am just trying to be of service. To keep the contacts. I am a business person."

"This has been such a lovely evening. Thank you, Emilio," said Brigit. "We must watch the time. We don't want to be locked out."

"Yes, I know it is important that you have your rest. They will not lock you out. I told Matilda at the albergue that you may be a bit late."

27. All Things Bright and Dark

Maybe it was the wine and the good times of the evening before, but it was a rather silent group that set out in the morning from Molinaseca. They made an early start as they planned some sightseeing in Ponferrada. Brigit was doing her silent morning routine. Charles-Michel seemed deep in thought. The others walked together in front, warning of puddles and slippery, muddy bits. It had rained overnight.

'So lovely in this valley,' thought Brigit. 'I feel close to God here.' "Thank you for that comfort, dear Lord, as I carry my heavy heart for Bob and our future." Brigit's God was the God of creation and nature. She thought of how her DNA reached back to the Big Bang and how fire and the energy of love had breathed into the mud to start life: all life—plants, animals, and then humans. 'So we all come out of the same matter, united and yet diverse.'

And Christ has been there since the very beginning— "Christ of the Big Bang." where had she heard that? An amazing thing for Brigit was that, in earthly terms, Jesus had been a failure: tortured, murdered hanging on a cross, deserted by his friends. But that was only the beginning. Then Christ had been resurrected, ascended, the Holy Spirit

231

had come, and Christianity had spread throughout the world. Jesus never behaved like a failure. He didn't pass on his pain. He transformed it. He stopped it there, with him, with no call for revenge but a call for peace: "Blessed are the meek!"

'What is this about?' Brigit caught herself up. 'Okay. I should stop my judgemental mind set towards Bob and myself. Start including us both in the great universal cycle of failure and redemption. Use wrong to do right. Take motion forward into love. So am I just going to give up with Bob? Hell no! But trust in the great movement of humankind towards enlightenment. Trust myself. This is a new starting point.' Brigit felt a shift.

The trail crossed over the road to the village of Campo on the outskirts of Ponferrada. Looking south there were rolling hills with a narrow white road that wound through vineyards following the contours with the now-familiar backdrop of snow-capped mountains.

"Here are the Bierzo vineyards Emilio was boasting about," said Colin.

They crossed the river to reach the city of Ponferrada.

"Wow, that is my idea of a castle!" said Mireille.

"It looks like it belongs in a fairy tale," said Brigit.

"Cracker Jack! I saw one just like that in Las Vegas," said Colin.

"It does look like Disney," said Charles-Michel. "But this is the real thing, or was."

232

"I love it. It has ramparts, turrets and towers and a draw bridge," said Colin.

After exploring around the outside, they found a coffee.

"Charles-Michel. How come the Knights Templar never got to use the castle?" asked Colin.

"They did use it, but only for about twenty years. They were given the site to build a castle, as great protectors of the Camino and Christianity. They finished it in 1282 so it's a true medieval castle. The order of the Knights Templar was amazingly successful with around twenty thousand knights in Western Europe, especially in Spain. They kept pushing back the infidels and were rewarded with land and money. So by the twelve hundreds, they were very powerful and rich. Despite the fact that they were fighting for Christianity, the Pope and various monarchs decided they were too powerful and independent. Imagine, they were like an army and church all of their own only owing allegiance to themselves and God. And they were mystics, but the Vatican never liked that: too much free thinking. A smear campaign started: that they were profane, blasphemous, secretive, demon-worshipping, sodomites, you name it! And then on Friday October 13th, 1307, a force, organized by the pope and the king of France, arrested the leadership of the Knights, and stormed and raided their castles and residences. There was an enormous massacre and the leaders were executed. Their lands and property were seized, and the order of the Knights of the Templar was decimated. It is tragic. Scholars say they held many of the ancient mysteries of the Camino."

"How are you feeling, Mireille?" asked Brigit when the others had left to visit inside the castle.

"Pretty good actually. Wasn't that a fun evening with Emilio? I will be surprised if we don't see him again."

"Yes, I think there is potential there with Charles-Michel."

"I had a lovely afternoon with him. Does Charles-Michel have a partner in his life?"

Brigit hesitated. "Do you know, Mireille? I'm ashamed to say that I don't know. I have never asked him, and I could have. Bob and I have just been wrapped up in our situation, and I know Bob has confided in him. We are so self-centered."

Brigit went to the Basilica. Carved in wood at the altar, in elaborate Baroque gold, was the Virgin Mary surrounded by the golden leaves of a tree: La Virgen de la Encina—the patron saint of the Bierzo. As she turned and walked out to the back of the church, Brigit saw a grouping of statues that caught her breath. There was Christ on the cross, then Mary holding the body of her son on her lap and there was Jesus in a coffin, but no glamourized version, but a true dead corpse, cold and stiff. Brigit went back to her thoughts of the morning walk: "the failed Jesus, the risen Christ." How did the people of this church and city get strength over the centuries from these images? Was it consolation to see Mary in dire suffering and Jesus rotting in the tomb?

Outside in the square, Brigit looked at a contemporary statue of a figure, maybe a pilgrim, holding—was it the Christ child? And next to that, the second part of the statue, a tree trunk with strange small figure—the Virgin again? "So Encina: a tree?"

"Yes, actually a Holm Oak," said Charles-Michel when they joined up. There was a write-up about it in the castle. They used to grow all around here. How was the Basilica?"

"Beautiful, sombre, amazing statues."

"There's another church that I would love to visit: Santa Tomas de Las Ollas. It's a perfect Mozarabic but it is three kilometres off the path. I might come back to this region after Santiago and catch up on it all."

"Does this have something to do with Emilio?" said Brigit and everyone looked at Charles-Michel expectantly.

"Yes, dear friends, it probably does. He did suggest that I come and visit and look around."

"I think that's wonderful. He is such a dear," said Mireille.

"Don't get carried away. This is just tourism with a friendship benefit."

They smiled, wished him well, and refrained this time from teasing.

Out of Ponferrada the land was flat and the path wove through small farm and garden holdings. Mireille and Colin walked ahead and the wide track let Charles-Michel, Bob, and Brigit walk together.

"Charles-Michel, why are you doing the Camino?" asked Brigit. "I'm a bit embarrassed that I have not asked you that before now."

"Don't blame yourself, Brigit. Most probably I didn't give you a convenient opportunity to ask."

"Oh, that sounds rather private. I don't mean to intrude."

"Of course you don't, dear Brigitte. You are all sensibilité, and most tactful. And I seem to know so much about your recent lives, maybe I could talk about mine."

"We, or maybe I, have burdened you with all my problems. I should apologize," said Bob.

"No way. I offered to be there for you. Although it was all a bit more than I had bargained for!"

"But you, Charles-Michel?"

"I could plan some free time, an extended leave of six months, which is a great gift after all those years of work. I had a partner, Matthieu. We had been together about two years when he became ill. He was zero positive, HIV. How dumb is that? I mean more than two decades after the start of the AIDS scare. But he died."

"How dreadful! But are you well, Charles-Michel? I know people can live symptom-free now. The treatments are so effective."

"Yes I'm fine, clear, healthy. Our relationship was not getting along very well for at least a year, which is ironic as it saved me from the disease. Matthieu had started to play and sleep around and got infected. I don't know if I was angrier with him or myself.

"Charles-Michel, you can't blame yourself. You were both adults," said Brigit.

"Yes, but if I had committed to our relationship or ended it when we grew apart, maybe he would not have behaved in such a reckless way. But I didn't and he got sick. He could not tolerate the drugs. They made him horribly sick, and just overwhelmed his whole system. Nothing worked. He just wasted away. We were provided with good home care. I forgave him. Otherwise I would not have been able to nurse him. I was sort of on auto-pilot, which is not the image of the angel of mercy. We muddled along until we got to the point where our case worker said he had to move into a hospice. It should have been a relief, but it wasn't."

"Charles-Michel, I am so sorry to hear you have been through this," said Brigit, her voice catching. She stopped and wrapped her arms around him in a tight hug. She could feel him trembling. She stayed there holding him.

"How long ago is it since Matthieu died?" asked Brigit.

"Nearly two years. Seems I have been living in limbo. That's a bit of an exaggeration. I was getting my life together this past year. Actually planning for the Camino has been a great therapy."

"I know. I loved the planning and anticipation," said Brigit.

"I think the others will have stopped up ahead in Camponaraya. And there's a big wine cooperative there: Emilio's Bierzo vineyards," said Bob.

Mireille and Colin had staked out a picnic table.

"I heard rumours of wine," said Charles-Michel. They bought bread and ham, tomatoes and Belgium endives, and a bottle of the local white wine.

"So what do you think about the albergue in Cacabelos? It's about another eight kilometres. That will be twenty-five for today which I think is good. How are you feeling, Mireille?" asked Bob.

"I'm fine. We can go further if you want."

"Cacabelos looks good," said Bob. "The albergue is beyond the town another kilometre. No kitchen, but I am sure there is a pilgrim meal available nearby. Maybe after our gourmet meal last night, we should have a bit of pilgrim humble pie."

And that is what they had: kale soup, pasta, fried fish, and a pot of yogurt. Basic pilgrim fare.

"Look here, señor doctor, for the future don't trouble yourself about giving me dainty things or choice dishes to eat, for it will be only taking my stomach off its hinges; it is accustomed to goat, cow, bacon, hung beef, turnips and onions."

Miguel de Cervantes, The Ingenious Gentleman Don Quixote, Second Part, Chapter 49.

****

On the walk back from the restaurant, Brigit was able to be alone with Bob. "I was wondering, now we have the cell phone, if it's worthwhile phoning the albergue in León to see if there's any news of your backpack and giving them our number?"

"I guess there's no harm. I could do that tomorrow."

"You know," said Brigit. "I feel guilty about Charles-Michel. We have been with him off and on for nearly a month. He has been so kind to me. Not taking a side or being judgemental, just supportive. And there he was, all along, with his recent past. I have been so self-centred."

"I'm the one who should feel bad. But on the other hand, he had to be ready to tell us when it was right for him. Rather ironic that he said that knowing about our shit let him tell us now."

"Bob, with all my self-examination I really haven't told you—what it's really all about for me now—it's my great and passionate love for you and the family. It is up to you. I know what I want more than anything in this world. It's to live our family life together and you and I as a couple. I am telling you this. You will have to decide what it is to be. I will fight for you as much as I can. In the end it's your decision. I'm going to go in now. Otherwise I will start crying."

Inside, in the dim light, there was the sound of quiet voices and the movement of people getting themselves organized for the night. How extraordinary to sleep like this, all together with strangers and friends. As she lay in her bunk, Brigit thought back. Bob seems so much more energized. He is back to being the organizer, which is more his old self. What could have changed? Talking with Charles-Michel? Does he see that other people have problems and tragedies in their lives too? And has she really forgiven him over the debt when she had felt so bitter? Has the Camino worked on her and she was able to cast off materiel concerns? Hmm: that was expecting a lot!

"Oh God I do hope I got through to him. Please let me move his heart back to me."

28. Camino Allsorts

"Cacabelos, important in Roman times, hence the straight main street," explained Charles-Michel. It was breakfast time. "In the Middle Ages there was a leprosy hospice here. Pity we can't get into the Ermita de las Angustias. There's a picture of Jesus as a child, playing cards with St. Anthony of Padua."

"Have you been tempted to jettison your history guide book to save on weight?" Colin asked.

"It's more the bulk, but I labour on. What I did was just bring a map and a list of the albergues and no regular Camino guide. And look how it works. I teamed up with you guys with all your different guide books, and before that I would just ask people if I could look at their guide. People are happy to share and chat. It's the spirit of the Camino. Set out and trust."

Vineyards to the right, vineyards to the left. Bob was feeling better, lighter, but did not know why. "Give yourself time": that's what the monk had told him at Rabanal. Easy for him to say, standing there in his monk's habit and his celibate life. And what about Charles-Michel? Could his troubles make Bob feel better? That does not sound very noble. But as he walked along, Bob saw that Charles-Michel's story had shown him a bigger picture. Oh hell. Here I am into my fifties, doing crazy things with money—to prove what? That I can be a high-flying entrepreneur, apparently driving my wife into an affair, ignoring my friend's needs and pain. That about sums it up. Despite this litany of misery, he felt better.

"At Pieros, coming up, there's a choice of paths." said Colin, "about the same distance, but one looks more rural."

"If we wanted to take a six-kilometre detour, there is a tenth-century monastery and a castro," said Charles-Michel.

"What is a castro?"

"They were the fortified villages of the original Celts, centuries before the Romans. The Romans just took over any promising villages and defences and then forced the locals to work as slaves."

They took the rural path and stopped for a rest in a hamlet with houses of worn stone and warped wooden balconies. An old lady shuffled out and headed their way. Mireille made room for her on the wooden bench. Long skirt, shawl and black head scarf, she sat in silence. Various other old people drifted out of doorways.

"Wow. That was the valley of the ancients," said Mireille. "I distinctly got the impression she thought I was completely crazy traipsing around the country side with a big pack on my back. She might have a point."

"Look at these vineyards. These folk could be running a flourishing wine business and doing very well, thank you!" said Colin pointing to the hills of carefully tended vines.

It was ten o'clock when they reached Villafranca del Bierzo: time for a coffee in the Plaza Mayor.

"This is the entrance to the narrow valley that leads to the next pass," said Charles-Michel. "It's another special place for the Camino. The pilgrims who were too sick or exhausted to continue could go to the church we passed, through the Puerta del Perdón, go to confession and mass and receive forgiveness as though they had made it all the way to Santiago. There used to be several hostels. Amazing, that in the eleventh and twelfth centuries, at the height of the Camino, there would be as many as five or six different hostels in these towns and villages. It was a prosperous time in Western Europe, that all crashed when the Bubonic Plague arrived in 1347, their pandemic."

"Let's get lunch supplies." said Bob. "Brigit, if you do that, I'll phone the people in León."

"Salut! C'est la belle Brigitte!"

"François! How are you? I haven't seen you since, where? Pamplona maybe."

"Yes, and you were looking for your husband. Did you find him? Where is he?"

"Oh yes, I found him. Thank you. He's phoning the albergue in León. His pack was stolen and we hope they may have found it. François, let me introduce you."

"Ah, d'autres cousins canadiens!" and he launched into big chats with Charles-Michel and Mireille.

"Not me, mate!" said Colin.

"Brigit, you don't have the lunch supplies," Bob joined her. "What's going on?"

"It's François. You remember, from Roncesvalles."

"Oh, him!"

François caught sight of Bob and greeted him with a hearty handshake and a slap around the shoulder. "But Bob, you must take care. You lost your wife in Pamplona and now your pack in León. It is important to watch out. Even though it is a pilgrimage, things can get stolen, hé!"

"Hello François, and how are you getting along? Where is your group? I hope you haven't lost them."

"Non non non, bien sûr que non. René is still walking with me. Some had to go home and another hurt his back. So you see not everyone is chosen to make it to Santiago. Which path are you taking, along the valley or up the mountains?"

Bob wished he knew which way François was going. "We have not quite decided yet but maybe the mountain route."

"Ah, alors, bon courage, mes amis. We are going to take the valley road. But your path will be more beautiful and peaceful. Maybe we should come with you. But my friend is a bit tired. I don't want to lose another one. Not like Bob, hé!"

Bob made a quick retreat to the grocery store. "Okay. You can all stop laughing. That man is just effing awful."

"He's not that bad," Brigit managed through her laughter.

"Oh he is, and worse. Self-righteous and self-satisfied. I know he's your special friend, but really, that crack about me losing everything."

"I think you're right, Bob," said Mireille. "You missed him going on about la belle Brigitte!"

"Fucking cheek of him," said Bob.

"Are you jealous, Bob?"

"Very funny, Charles-Michel."

"Well, he's a style of Frenchman who has to set everyone right, especially the colonials from Canada and Quebec," said Charles-Michel.

"And he kept on about me losing things, obviously to cover up his own inadequacies. I mean what happened to his merry band of pilgrims? They couldn't stand him and left. Just one poor soul left standing and he is failing by the sound of it. The last thing we need is for François to end up by himself and want to join up with us."

"We will hide up in the hills. I thought he was rather funny, but I couldn't understand most of it," said Colin.

"You didn't miss a thing. The pompous ass!"

They picked up the yellow arrows through the town, past elegant houses, a convent, a modern pilgrim statue, and over the fast-flowing Búrbia river. They found the path with no problem and started the sharp steep climb up a lonely track of beaten earth. To each side were flowers: clumps of bright bluebells, other blue flowers that looked like feathers, a bush with pink blossoms. Below they could see the autopista with tiny cars and trucks speeding along. The hills beyond were heavy with dark forest. The trail narrowed and they walked single file until eventually they started down through a plantation of trees.

"Sweet Chestnuts. That's why they are called Spanish Chestnuts," said Bob. Several of the older tree were pruned right back to about a metre above the ground. From these gnarly stumps there were new branches. "You'd think they would not survive that pruning."

The end of the downhill became a set of stairs into the village of Trabadelo. The trail along the valley road was better than expected; there was a pedestrian path by the river for part of the way. Soon they could see a highway bridge soaring above them, spanning the valley. They decided to stay at Vega de Valcarce.

"That's twenty-seven kilometres today. Good going with the hill climb," said Bob.

"And tomorrow into the land of the Celts: Galicia. I am excited about that," said Brigit.

"I fancy a beer," said Bob. They found a café beside the river.

"Look at that castle perched up there to defend the valley," said Brigit.

"And maybe charge a toll as people went through," said Charles-Michel

"That water is really rushing over those weirs. It's all open. Could be a bit dangerous. The locals must be used to it," said Brigit.

"Do you get back to Mont Laurier?" asked Bob.

"Yes, I do," said Charles-Michel. "I grew up there," he explained to Brigit. "My mother's retired now and still lives there. My sister lives just outside Mont Laurier and has two children. I get up there quite often and for a stay in the summer."

"What about your father?"

"He worked in forestry. He was an engineer. That is a tough life. He had a heart attack and died twelve years ago; he was only seventy. He was a good man. When I came out, he was very supportive. I moved to Montreal for university and McGill. It was a good match for me. I needed to improve my English and be in a wider community."

"So, where did you meet Matthieu?" asked Bob.

"At a gay parade."

"I didn't see that coming."

"You are so right, mon cher."

"It's two years; do you have anyone else in your life now?" asked Brigit.

"No, there is no one."

"I saw how Emilio is taken with you."

"Back to Emilio. I thought he was rather flashy to begin with. You remember, Bob. But I got to see him better when we were together. Yes, he is special."

29. Game Changer

Brigit was in bed doing her review of the day and her life. Good chats with Charles-Michel, which let them spend time together having a reasonable conversation. Bob does seem a bit happier.

****

She is in the staff room. School is over for the day and most of the teachers are here. There is fresh snow and the afternoon sun slants in from the west. She is off to one side with her laptop. At the table are her fellow teachers, most with a cup of tea or coffee, laughing and chatting. Earl is telling them about one of the kids who had suggested that the class do a trip to the Rockies to go ice-climbing.

"He had the whole plan. We would fly to Calgary, spend a couple of days there, and then off to Banff for ice-climbing. Have to give him marks for his research. Can you imagine the school board giving us the green light for all those kids to climb up the side of an icy gorge?"

"Oh, Earl!" Brigit pipes up. "It sounds wonderful. I could come along as a chaperone. I know Calgary and the

Rockies. Bob's from there. We often go there." Earl smiles at her warmly. "Brigit, I don't think it would be a good idea seeing as how I'm your lover."

Dark. At home. No. This is not her bed. Where is Bob? She felt the side of her bunk and it came back. The Camino, a hostel, Bob in another bed. It was a dream, of course. How could it be so vivid and so casual at the same time? She climbed out, thank goodness for the lower bunk. She shuffled her way to the door, to the corridor, to the washrooms. There was a harsh light and a grey mirror. Was that her? She sat on the toilet with the acrid smell of a shared facility. Throw up? That would feel better, but that relief did not come. Earl—he didn't have anything to do with the school. He wasn't a teacher. After two years, what business did he have intruding in her dreams and when she was doing the work to reconcile with Bob?

****

The morning was misty but the sunlight filtered through. Cows munching: did they ever take a break? Brigit felt bruised, the dream still vivid and yet here she was among friends as though her life was normal. 'I will just feel pathetic a bit longer, and then pull myself together.' A chat with Mireille would have helped—maybe a gossip about some of the people from the hostel last night. As she was the one who had instituted silent mornings, she was stuck with her own thoughts.

The walk continued, in and out by the river and through bright green meadows. And the animals: chickens, sheep, dogs, cows and even a docile bull. In one field the lambs were chasing the chickens.

"Those chickens look pissed off. Do they have to go through this every spring?" sympathized Mireille. As the path climbed, they could see the river below slithering through the green valley like a sun-sparkled serpent.

"Wild daffodils and primroses," said Colin, "and look at that fern." It was hairpin bends now up the steep slope.

"Keep an eye out," said Bob. "Soon we will finally be leaving Castilla y León!"

There was no missing the crossing into Galacia. A large cement marker with two coats of arms and a cross that looked like a sword and under that the Camino signs: the stylized shell of St. James and the circle of stars of the European Union all in blue and yellow.

****

'A hundred and fifty two kilometres to Santiago. Then what?' thought Bob. Brigit had thrown down this gauntlet that it was up to him. Father Estevan had told him he was to take his time. 'That's not reality.' Bob felt that he had to resolve things, or at least make up his mind, here on the Camino. How could they go home and face the kids if they didn't know their future? Again the thought of the family breaking up made him sick and dizzy. Then thinking of Brigit with that scum made him bitter and filled with bile. Here, they were in a cocoon of friends and walking, but eventually they would reach Santiago. He was now dreading that. How dare Brigit do this to him? Then a nasty little voice said:

"Did you precipitate this, Bob? You and your search for gold, for easy riches, a short cut to the treasure at the end of the rainbow? You don't get anything for nothing; it all has a cost. You stupid fool!"

It could have been suggested to Bob that a Celtic spirit, an evil solitary fairy, one of the not very nice little people, was jerking him around.

****

The village of O'Cebreiro was perched at the top of a ridge of land that made up the mountain pass.

"Seems strange that the pass is at the top of a mountain," said Charles-Michel.

"It must be the easiest way over. I'm sure they didn't want to make life any harder just for the view," said Bob.

"Crikey. It's like a museum up here. Look at those houses," said Colin.

"Those are the traditional ones with the swooping roofs to deflect the wind. They're called palloza," said Charles-

Michel. "Not sure how it's pronounced. In Galacia, do they say the Spanish double LL like Y?"

"Well, if you don't know, there's not much hope for the rest of us," said Colin.

"Iglesia de Santa Maria Real." Brigit was reading the plaque outside the church. "Let's go in." The simple stone building had archways and plain wooden benches that led up to the sanctuary and the high altar. In a side chapel, set back in the wall behind glass, was a chalice. Brigit and Charles-Michel were still reading the history when the others gave up. "Look for us at a café!"

"It turns out," said Charles-Michel, when they had all got their coffee, "that there was a miracle here—very Catholic, very medieval."

"You could call it the story of the devout peasant and the cynical priest," said Brigit.

"Well, let's hear it!"

"A young peasant boy made his way over the mountains and through the snow to come to mass and receive the Eucharist. Just as he arrived, the priest was consecrating the bread and the wine. Seeing the lad, he mocked him for coming all this way in a snow storm. At that moment the bread and wine truly turned into the flesh and blood of Christ," explained Brigit.

"This has been linked to the Holy Grail. There was a tradition that the goblet of the Last Supper was hidden in this village," said Charles-Michel. "They don't say that the chalice here is the Holy Grail, but related to it. The miracle was approved by the pope, and Galacia has the chalice and host—the goblet and the bread—as part of their coat of arms."

"I saw that on the border marker," said Mireille.

"So that's the chalice we saw in the wall, from the miracle," said Colin.

"I have been hearing great things about the private-run albergue in Fonfría. That's about twelve clicks on. I'm voting for that," said Colin.

Coming out of the village they had a wide view of the valleys far below to the west and the north: patchwork fields and the autopista on high bridges linking hillsides. The yellow arrows sent them along a trail with stunted trees, daffodils, an orchid nestled in the grass, then out onto an exposed lookout with a larger-than-life pilgrim statue of a man, striding along, holding onto his hat in the wind.

"These clouds are catching up with us." Brigit waved to the west. They put on their rain gear as the wind drove the rain sideways.

"It must be milking time. The cows are on the move," said Mireille. With the cows there was a donkey and a chicken, nibbling the grass on the high stony bank.

They stayed up on high ground. Through the rain they could see long thin fields bordered by stone walls going straight down into a small valley. A large white and black hen with a scarlet crest was poking around in the undergrowth.

"Galacia is different," said Mireille. "It reminds me of Ireland, all that green and the rain."

"It's that western edge of Europe," said Bob.

"It's more than just the scenery," Mireille continued. "The animals are all over the place and they seem part of village life but not in a sentimental Bambi way."

"Good choice, Colin," said Charles-Michel when they reached the spacious dormitory. "Modern rustic with all the comforts, and central heating. Our gear can dry out." They could relax as they had signed up for the evening meal that was served in a building across the road; it was a modern take on a palloza: round with a thatched roof.

"Brigit, I checked the phone. We missed a call. It's local, as in Spain. I'll go on the veranda and see if I can call back."

"Maybe it's news about your pack." Brigit settled in the cozy bunk.

"Thank you, Lord, for this refuge and this comfort. Bless us along this path and our friends. Bless Liz and…" Brigit went through her list of loving prayers

****

"Bob, it is good you called. José here in León. Sister Alicia told me to telephone you."

"Sorry I missed your call."

"We have news of your pack. It has been found!"

"That is wonderful news."

"The police contacted us. It was handed in. A woman found it in her daughter's room and knew it was not hers. She took her down to the police station to hand it in. Good, you agree?"

"Yes and good on the mother. Do you know if my things are in it?"

"Just some, not everything. Your toilet bag has gone. Your sleeping bag is here and some clothes. No shoes."

"Thank you. Please thank Sister Alicia for me."

"Bob, we have a plan. Where are you?"

"Fonfría, just beyond O'Cebreiro."

"That is perfect. A priest from the parish here is going on Wednesday to Triacastela. That is ahead on your path. You must wait there for him. He will bring your pack on Wednesday, in the morning. His name is Father Juan. He will come to the municipal hostel. Make sure you go to that one. Can you do that?"

"Yes, of course. I will be there for Wednesday morning."

"It is not far from where you are. It will be fine."

Supper was served at a long communal table with a yellow checked tablecloth, baskets of bread, bottles of water and wine, and real wine glasses. They ate with the other pilgrims and shared the story of the found backpack. After supper, the group got together to plan.

"Looking at the map, Triacastela is only about ten kilometres further on," said Bob.

"You know what this means," said Brigit in a small voice. "We are going to lose you guys. We will wait until the next day for the pack to arrive. This is so sad."

"Our little travelling universe is about to be shattered," said Mireille.

"An exercise in Camino letting go," said Charles-Michel. "Before we all burst into tears, we have phones; we can communicate. Who knows, we may be able to join up again, with fresh tales and adventures to share."

'All alone with Bob' thought Brigit, 'The pack was a bit of a distraction but that would not last.'

"Well, the day had to come. I mean we can't continue just to hide from reality behind you guys." Mireille and Brigit were in the women's washroom.

"Why not, if it gives you time."

"Well, it has given us time. But it means we are heading into the moment of truth. Or maybe Bob will not resolve anything."

"Actually it has not been very long. We only left León seven days ago," Mireille pointed out.

"Are you serious?" They counted the night stops they had made along the way.

Brigit wasn't sleeping.

'Only seven days,' she thought. 'Shit! I guess I can't expect a decision from Bob in that time. What do I expect? Did I just want it all: marriage, family, to be the central hub of the home and the illicit thrill of going beyond all those boundaries into an exciting unknown? And now I want him to love and respect me!'

****

Bob was also awake, thinking of what lay ahead. Brigit was going to nag him about this. She would confront him to make a decision. 'How am I supposed to know?' he thought. 'I still haven't had enough time. At the start of this trip it was all about me and my wrongdoings. She doesn't talk about the money any more or what we have lost. Is that it? Now it's all about her love for me and the kids. Where does her sordid affair fit in? It doesn't make sense. It's all just fucking rubbish!'

30. Devices and Desires of Our Own Hearts

Brigit broke the silent morning routine. This was their last time together as a group, until... maybe never again.

"Colin, how are you feeling now about your hostage experience at the hospital?" asked Brigit.

"I'm fine. Still fine I should say. Maybe the Camino effect has given me more compassion for the guy."

"That's healing too. Colin, any chance of you coming to Canada?"

"I'd love to, don't know when. I'll have to do some work when I get back from this trip."

"It would be so lovely if you could come and stay with us in Ottawa and we could go out west and to the mountains."

"You're sweet, Brigit. I will not let you forget that invitation." They gave each other a hug.

The path was muddy from yesterday's rain. Brigit could see violets in the hedgerow and springs forming little waterfalls down the banks. Sheep in the meadows were wreathed in mist. They stood aside to let cows returning to their pastures after milking pass by. In the village of

Biduedo, a tractor was parked in an impossibly narrow gateway. A "Buen Camino" from the farmer.

"Look at that tree," said Mireille. "Out of *The Lord of the Rings*." There it was, beyond gnarled, standing guard by the gate of the ruins of a stone farm house, strange and twisted among new shoots. It was a steep descent into Triacastela between rows of chestnut trees.

"Let's do coffee," said Colin.

Only coffee time, so much of the day ahead. Brigit sighed to herself. Twenty-four hours until the bag comes tomorrow.

"Let me see if there's not at least some homework for you today." Charles-Michel had out his history guide. "The only thing that gets a little mention is a mill one kilometre on the way out of town,"

"Have we decided which route we are taking?" asked Colin. "So tied up with our parting of the ways we've neglected the Camino. The longer one includes Samos, a monastery which seems to get a lot of attention. Do you have something about how pilgrims used to carry limestone from here to a place further on and it was used to build the cathedral in Santiago?" Colin was deep in his guide book.

"They took it to Arzúa for the kilns," said Charles-Michel.

"That's another four days on. Was there anything those poor pilgrims didn't have to suffer? Now lugging rocks around. No wonder there were hospitals and cemeteries for them."

"I know, Colin, but your soul would have been saved. Think of that," Brigit pointed out.

"Thank goodness I'm a doctor. Maybe I can just save lives instead!"

"I don't know if it's that simple."

"Come on. It must be an excellent start, and here I am doing the Camino. I reckon I'm well on my way to paradise."

"Maybe you should pick up a big rock, just in case," said Bob.

But the moment came to say goodbye and for the three of them to continue on out of the town.

****

"What do you want to do?" asked Bob trying to fill a sudden loneliness.

"Cry really, but I guess that's not much of an option. We could go and check out the albergue. Maybe we can at least leave our packs."

The municipal hostel was on the edge of town in a field overlooking the river and made up of several stone buildings. A man doing the cleaning took them to another building, shouted upstairs and a woman came down. They explained as best they could but she got the picture straight away. Yes, Sister Alicia had phoned from León. They could leave their packs, but not have beds until later in the afternoon. There was a beautiful church they should visit.

They stood on the banks of the rio Ouribio, looking at the remains of the large water mill. "We could go a bit further along. This is the Samos Camino," suggested Bob. The path followed the river which curled along flooding the edge of a meadow, along diversion channels over small weirs and sluice gates. A few pilgrims passed them. It felt alien to be walking the trail but with no pack.

"Wonder if they think we are those day walkers who come in a car or get dropped off by a charter bus," said Brigit.

"Are you turning into a Camino snob?"

"Of course. So are you. Think how snooty you were when we met that group of tourists on our way to Acebo. They had all been let loose from their bus."

"I politely said 'Buen Camino' to a woman who was completely blocking the path. She turned around all surprised and talked to me in German. She obviously thought everyone on the path must be from her bus."

"Well, there you are. Just some poor tourist trying to get her Camino experience."

"Is that a bench up there?" said Bob. It was just beyond a bridge and gave them a peaceful view over the river. Though all seemed calm on the surface, Bob had been weighing how best to deal with the next inevitable conversation with Brigit. He saw that he had been a passive—well passive aggressive—partner in these "times to talk properly" as Brigit called them. This was not Bob's style. Heavens above, at work he facilitated difficult situations all the time, aiming to be fair but looking out for the interest of his side of the issue. He had to get beyond his raw emotions despite how he felt betrayed, cheated, and wounded. But if he could call on his training it could be more productive, and he would feel better.

"Brigit, there's something that seems to have been lost. At the start of this journey you were so bitter and accusing about the finances. We thought we were beyond it, but obviously you were not. So where did that go? You said the other night that is wasn't important for you any more. How come?"

"Yes, I know. I was snarky. It was a shock to me too. It was like you couldn't do anything right. Then you got on my nerves and the whole thing seemed to degenerate. Then I wanted to walk by myself. For the debt thing, along the way, something changed. I think the Camino really did help me shed that. I handed those feeling over to God or the trail. I just know that all of a sudden your screw up with the money wasn't an issue any more and that was an enormous relief."

"Or was it that when you told me about your affair, that the pain you gave me felt justified because of the money? Were you waiting for the right moment to tell me about that to get maximum damage?"

There was a black hole. Brigit was short of breath again. No crying. Did she do that? Is it possible that she was storing it up? No!

"No, Bob. That was not how it came about. It was so difficult for me to tell you. I should have told you before but I could not face it. Finally I got to the point where not telling you was so much worse than telling you. It was not to unload my guilt or to get revenge. I knew it was a great risk. I had to tell you for both our sakes."

Their silence was filled by the burping and croaking of the frogs in the meadows.

"I should not have said that to you. I am trying to be constructive and that did not help."

Again Brigit caught her breath, but with surprise and hope.

"I'm sorry too. I should not have used words like 'screw up.' That was not helpful."

Another silence.

"Well I did screw up!"

Brigit waited for the other shoe to fall… "and so did you, far worse", but it didn't happen.

In this comparative harmony and with time on their hands, they decided to phone the family.

"Dad, great news about your pack," said Liz.

"Let's hope it's not damaged."

"People really seem to care and look out for you pilgrims."

When they called Don, he said, "Mum and Dad, you're nearly there. What are you going to do with yourselves? You're just walking machines!"

"I wouldn't have put it quite like that, but it will be strange when we get to Santiago."

"It's just great you two doing this. But we're gonna have an awesome summer all together, time at the lake. Oh and my big news: I've got a job with the city: it's perfect. I do a ten-day shift then I get take ten days off. It's split-shift part-time. I'll be doing the electrical set up for the outdoor summer events.

"Hello Paul. Glad we caught you before work."

"Hi Dad, yes all well. When are you guys coming home? We miss you."

"A couple of weeks now. Just talked to Don and he has all sorts of plans for the summer."

"Yes, Dad. You're going to have to make sure he doesn't turn the cottage into party central with all his chums. Divya and I are really looking forward to spending some quality time with you both and the rest of the family. Such great news about Liz and the new baby!"

They checked in at the albergue. The afternoon still stretched before them.

"I'm going to wander into town and check out the church," said Brigit.

"I'll catch up on my notes."

The church was open and Brigit went in and sat on one of the wooden seats. Another pilgrim was there looking around. The church had simple whitewashed walls; the high altar and retablo was golden Baroque but other than that it had a plain simplicity with open wooden rafters and a couple of saints on a wall with their candles. So peaceful. Brigit sat and prayed. "Dear Lord, show us how to trust again."

****

"Bob, it is you! So good to see you again!"

"Wanda, Shirley. My gracious, look at you!" Bob gave them both a hug. "Not since León. That was ages ago. How are you?"

"Never better."

"Where have you come from?"

"We started today from O'Cebreiro. We love Galicia, very different from other parts of the Camino. And here's Brigit!" They arranged to meet up again in an hour.

"And we can get some beer. I just passed a tienda on the other road," said Brigit.

"I have to ask you about the pack. So dreadful when it was lost in León," said Wanda.

"Well, talk about Camino timing, here you are, for what we hope is the end of that saga." Bob explained about Father Juan arriving with the pack the next day. "We are stuck here, so it's really nice to meet up with you. You've made good time."

"Well we have, but confession, we were offered a ride from Hopital del Órbigo to Astorga and we took it. It was great as we had plenty of time for sight-seeing, and then after a wonderful lunch we managed to get to Santa Catalina de Somoza and the next day to lovely Rabanal," said Shirley.

Over supper they gave Wanda and Shirley more news.

"Emilio sounds lovely," said Wanda.

"He is," agreed Brigit. "To begin with, we did doubt his ulterior motives and we teased Charles-Michel. But from what we've seen, we think he really is a good soul, so we hope that maybe there could be something there."

"You and Mireille have visions of Charles-Michel becoming a co-hotelier in Spain up on the windy plateau."

"We just want him to be happy. He is such a lovely person and he has been through some horrible times. And why not? He could take early retirement." The others burst out laughing. "Does he know this is the plan?" asked Shirley.

"Wouldn't be surprised," said Bob. "If you had met Emilio you would see he is a man of great ingenuity and planning. Almost thought we would have seen him again by now," said Bob.

"They are texting," said Brigit.

"How do you know?" Bob asked.

"Charles-Michel let something slip."

"Poor man. Seems impossible to keep a secret on the Camino. It's a kind of moving village along with the gossip," said Wanda. "Can you imagine conducting a romance on the Camino?"

"Believe me, it happens," said Brigit. "I've heard strange noises from some of the bunks at night. Not us oldies. The young ones, when they think we are all asleep."

"Are you serious?" said Wanda. "But why am I surprised? Me a high school principal. Young people, fresh air, a bed, far from home, exotic locale."

"Brigit, I mean how often?" challenged Bob.

"Okay. Not an every night occurrence, but at least twice that I suspected. Don't forget I teach high school too. You don't know what goes on, Bob."

Bob gave a laugh and remembered how good it could be to just have a fun conversation with Brigit.

****

'Am I looking for redemption?' It was three am, and Brigit was in her "sleepless on the Camino" time of night. People think redemption is forgiveness, but it's more than that. St. Paul says it's turning, as in a new start. Starting afresh, which must mean letting go. It was true that she had let go of her anger around the money. And how would she feel about letting go of Bob? NO! But she had handed it over to him. That was a big risk. Did she have a choice? But as she felt her stomach in free-fall, a clear inner voice spoke to her: "Brigit. You'd be alright. You wouldn't like it, but you would be okay. You can rebuild your life. You would still have the children and friends, church, your profession, and your pension-plan." She almost smiled that the pension had come up. But look at all the money she earned to pay back the debt. If it was all over with Bob, it was good to know the finances would be in order. Though the possibility of losing Bob made her faint, she could feel a small warmth that let her know she would survive. Do more than survive. Life would not end. If she had to, she would let him go.

31. It Takes a Village

Bob was up early. He wanted to see Wanda and Shirley before they set off.

"Good morning. How did you sleep?"

"Mornin', Bob. Slept okay. My sleep expectations are not high in albergues," Shirley replied.

"I see you have the guide book out. Have you decided the route you are going to take?"

"Not sure. Any advice?"

"I just received a text from the others. Charles-Michel says 'Samos amazing, albergue damp. Look but don't stay.'"

"Good to know," said Wanda. "Anyway, Samos is a bit soon to stop. The other way is quite a bit shorter so we could probably make it to Sarria tonight.

At ten o'clock, a young man dressed in casual clothes came bounding up to them and introduced himself as Father Juan. He handed over the pack, and apologized that he could not spend time with them as he had an appointment. He would be pleased to take the borrowed items back. With their thanks and a "Buen Camino" from him, they said goodbye. The backpack seemed none the worse and Bob found his notebook.

****

They followed the path they had walked the previous afternoon along the small river, which was still in flood. They wanted to see Samos so had chosen the longer path.

"Did you see the date? It's May twenty-seventh. That means we have been on the go for four weeks," said Bob.

"Four weeks. That's good going."

"Yes, it is. We are a bit under our six week estimate—even with our delays in Burgos and León, but we did take the train and the bus." Now they could see the bridge and the bench where they had talked yesterday.

"I need to adjust the straps on my pack. I thought I had it, but there's too much weight on my shoulders. Either I have changed shape or our charming thief really had a go at it." They stopped at the bench and Bob took off his pack.

"I'm just going to wander up and see what those kids are up to," said Brigit.

Brigit could see four children playing by one of the diversion channels. Apart from the children and themselves, the village street was empty. "Why aren't they in school?" she thought, "and what are they doing climbing down the bank?"

Screaming. One child is not there. She threw off her pack and ran along the road.

"Bob! Bob, help!"

The children are telling her something. Pointing in the water. Where is the fourth child? In the water? A bit further along a sluice gate is half up. Brigit scrambles down the bank, plunges in and swims in the current along the narrow stream. Nothing to see through this swirling muddy brown water. She reaches the sluice, takes a deep breath, and dives under.

****

Bob hears her call. Urgency and panic in her voice but he can't see her, looks to the other side of the river — no. Now he hears the children. He sees Brigit's pack. He reaches the children, no sign of her. "Where is Brigit?" "¿Dondé es la señora? La señora dondé?" Trying not to shout, mustn't scare them. A boy points at the water, fast running, clouded with mud. Impossible to see beyond the surface. A child in the water, swept along? "God what is she doing?" He runs to the sluice, down the steep bank into the water. It is far deeper than it appears from the bank. He dives under. Now he can feel something, Brigit? He can feel her legs, works up to her waist. He can't feel her arms, are they around the kid? He grasps her around her waist and pulls back against the current away from the sluice. Now he can get one hand forward and hold the child too, a leg. He keeps pulling back, up stream. It is hard against the current. The water is so deep he cannot brace against the stream-bed. Bob struggles, kicks up to the surface. They hit the surface and into the air. He supports them both still kicking fiercely to get to the bank. Brigit is gasping, grabbing reeds at the water's edge, anything to keep from sweeping down again. She is managing but the child is limp and his face is blue.

"Get him out. I'm all right." Brigit chokes. Bob drags the child up the bank. The older boy pulls at Bob's shoulder, trying to help. The two little girls are screaming and crying. Bob quickly looks back and sees that Brigit is making her way up-stream to where it is easier to get out. He lays the child down, searching his mind on giving CPR to a child: "not too much pressure: mustn't crush the ribs." He starts mouth-to-mouth. Chest pressure. Hell, nothing. More mouth-to-mouth. Keep going. Bob looks at the children. "Telephone!" He can't remember the word for help or ambulance or doctor but the older child is not here. He hopes he has gone for help. He must keep pumping blood around this child and breathing air in, as best he can. Back to rescue breaths. Chest rising, listen for breathing, nothing.

"Bob, I'm here. Is he breathing?"

"No. I can't get him to breathe. His lungs must be full of water."

"Turn him over and get his head down."

"Okay, help me. Let me finish this round of compressions. Here we go."

Between them they lift up his little body, turn him over, his head down, and Brigit firmly taps his back. Water is trickling out of his mouth, just a trickle, but it keeps coming. They lay him back on the ground. "I'll keep going. Go and get help."

Brigit makes it as far as the bridge where an older couple is running toward her with the older boy.

"Doctor? Ambulance?" No Spanish words come. But they understand.

"Si si," the man manages. They are both distraught: grandparents?

They reach Bob. "Help me turn him again, I think he is trying to cough."

They are all on their knees, helping to support the boy. Brigit gently slaps his back, he splutters once, and again and more water comes out.

"He needs more breaths, not really breathing yet. Turn him over." Bob gives three more breaths. They turn him on his side, he coughs, and gasps in some air. He is breathing, opens his eyes and seems to be aware of the people around him, and starts to cry.

"Es bien, es bien." Crooked smiles and cracked laughter.

A woman runs up. She has a blanket and they wrap up the child. They can see that the side of his head is cut, and there is blood: some, not much. The man picks up the child, cradles him, put his cheek down to his nose and mouth. Yes. Still breathing and they carry him back to the bridge where the ambulance will come, or maybe a doctor first.

They are all gone. Bob sees Brigit is shivering. He too: shock, cold. He grabs her, she falls. Both crumple on the bank.

"What did you do? You nearly drowned. Do you know what you did, the risk you took?" Bob finds himself shaking. How could she take such a risk? "I was coming." Why had she not let him come and they could have done it together?

"I didn't have time. I knew he was in the water. I couldn't wait."

"You could've drowned. I could've lost you!"

"His head was stuck in the sluice gates and I couldn't push away and the water was so strong. It was awful. We were jammed there. I don't know how long. When I felt your hands on my leg I knew you would save us."

"Yes, thank God, but you could both have drowned!"

"I didn't know the water was so deep. I thought I could touch bottom, but I just sank in—it was so deep—I couldn't get a foothold. I just swam and dove down, but then I was stuck with nowhere to push us back. Oh Bob, it was terrible." They cling together, crying, more tears, still clinging, shivering in shock, in cold. "You rescued me. You saved us."

"You are reckless. It was like your feet and getting lost. You have to take care." Bob clings on to her even harder. "You are so brave. You saved him. I love you. I don't want to lose you—I can't lose you."

They just stay, clinging, rocking back and forth.

"I love you, Bob; I don't want to lose you."

"We must stay together. I can't stand all this."

"Yes, oh yes. Please, we must stay together."

"I'm sorry, Brigit. I'm sorry."

"Me too, so sorry."

"I know you are. You've told me, but now I am telling you too. Can we be together, properly, like always?"

"Yes we will. We are."

Chapter 32. El Niño

Did they sleep or just pass out there on the bank? A blanket was around their shoulders. Bob looks around. Their packs were next to them. He saw a man, the older man—he was sitting on a low wall—must have been watching, waiting. He came over; he still looked distressed, but he smiled at them.

¿"El niño?" Bob asked. He knew that is the word for a boy but it just sounded like a weather system. He gave his head a shake. How could his mind be so crazy to be all over the place like that, a weather system—now.

"Si si, hospital. Bien, bien," the man took exaggerated breaths to show the boy is breathing. Then he picked up one of the packs and beckons to them. "Vengan!"

"That's 'come', I think," said Brigit, "present tense, imperative voice."

Bob had to smile. She must be a bit better: out comes the grammar. The old man marched ahead carrying the pack. Bob picked up the other one and they stumbled along. He led them to a house and once inside they were greeted by the older woman. She fussed over Brigit, feeling her hands, exclaiming how cold they are. The table was ready for lunch, but first they must shower. She led them into a bedroom, gave them towels and showed Brigit the bathroom. As Bob waited his turn, the man came up to him holding out a glass with a brown liquid.

"¿Coñac?" Brandy, Bob got that, like the French cognac. Yes. That would be good.

"Si, gracias. ¿Y usted?" he said, gesturing to the man. So they both sat down and had a glass. Bob was worried he was going to get the chair wet with his still damp clothes, but the couple just laughed. And with this, and the brandy, the ice was broken.

Lunch was a big tureen of the green leafy veggie soup, lamb chops, new potatoes, spinach, and carrots. So tasty. Over lunch they learnt more details: two of the children were their grandchildren, the little boy and one of the girls. There had been a mistake over the school schedule that day. It was a half day, but the families had not been notified. The children had been left at the end of the morning by the school bus, but none of the parents knew. Instead of coming to the grandparents, the parents were all out working, the children decided to play outside. A toy car had fallen in the water.

After lunch, the woman, Anita—her husband was Joseph—said it was siesta time. What time was it? Three-thirty. So now they were on true Spanish time: late lunch and siesta. The bed was very comfortable. "Bob, I think they've given us their room."

"I think you might be right, but it's way beyond my Spanish and energy to protest. I'm sure that is what they want." And they crawled under the covers and leaning against each other fell asleep.

It was half past five when Bob came out of the bedroom. Anita had insisted on taking away their clothes to launder, so luckily Bob's shorts had been returned in his pack. Anita met him with their clothes in a neat pile. "Well it might be an older couple out in the country but they obviously have an excellent washer and dryer," Brigit concluded.

"Yes, I don't think they lack for anything around the house; it all looks very comfortable."

Once they were dressed, Anita and Joseph asked if they would like to go and see the boy, Pedro. He was in hospital, his parents were with him, and they wanted to meet Bob and Brigit.

"Sarria, andamos en coche – auto," explained Joseph: about twenty-five kilometres.

It was back to Triacastela, along a quiet road and into the city of Sarria. Joseph and Anita knew their way to the children's ward. Decorated in bright colours with movie and storybook animals and characters on the walls, the long ward had upward of twenty beds and cots. A nurse escorted them to the far end, to a corner bed with the curtains drawn. She looked in and said something, pulled the curtain aside, and motioned them in with a warm smile. The boy was sitting up in the bed, his parents on either side with one of the little girls from the stream. The mother looked up, saw them, exclaimed, and started to cry. She grasped Brigit and hugged her. "Gracias, gracias." Brigit hugged her back. "Es bien, todas bien." The father was shaking Bob's hand; Joseph was with them, and gave Bob a friendly pat on the shoulder. Then to the little boy—last time they had seen him he was a pathetic bundle in a blanket—now he looked quite stout and cheerful and they could see he was probably about six years old. Brigit and Bob both gave him a hug. This was Pedro, and with barely a reminder from his father, said a shy "gracias." The family insisted they sit on the two available chairs, though Bob finally managed to persuade the mother to take his. The curtain parted and a man and a woman entered in white coats: the doctors. More greetings, and then the man turned to Bob and Brigit.

"The family is very, very grateful to you," he said in fluent English. "They asked me to make sure you understood that." The family was nodding along like a Greek chorus. "Si, si."

"It was just common sense. Anyone would have done the same," said Brigit.

"No, it is exceptional that you managed to save him. We can see from his head…" and now he pointed to a bandage around the boy's forehead, "…that he must have been trapped under the water in the gate. Those streams are so dangerous when there is a flood, and you managed to free him."

"It was my wife who reached him first," said Bob.

"But I could not have got him out without my husband—I was stuck in the fast water."

"Yes, I can imagine that," said the other doctor. "But what is also excellent is giving him CPR. I understand you knew exactly what to do and you kept calm."

"We don't know how long he was without air; is he going to be all right?"

"Yes, no more than five minutes. It maybe seemed like a long time for you, but children are very resilient. We expect him to recover fully," she said. "This boy is very lucky that you were there. He would never have survived without your actions."

They both said they were happy to have been of help. The doctors wanted to know if they were all right. Bob did wonder about Brigit, but she said she was fine. The woman gave them her card and said not to hesitate to call; Brigit could have a delayed reaction.

When it was time to leave, word had apparently got out, and as they walked through the hospital, visitors, nurses, and orderlies were coming up and shaking their hands, smiling, giving thanks, and congratulations. Some "Buen Caminos."

The evening sun made long shadows as Joseph shepherded them back to the car: "¿Tourism?" he suggested and waved his hand around to show the district. "Samos." Bob nodded. "So, off to see Samos after all." They left the town by a road to the south, between avenues of trees, along stone walls and around meadows. Sheep were everywhere and cows and chickens. Houses, made of green-grey stone and slate roofs, dotted the countryside. Anita showed them that they were now travelling along the Camino trail. Uphill and then down again to the river valley and into the village of Samos. They could see an extensive stone building with an imposing church. The monastery seemed to take up the whole village. Joseph stopped the car at a large open double door that was part of the high outside wall of the monastery. This was the albergue. "¡Sello!" he said and made a motion with his hand of a stamp. "Credencial."

Bob understood: "He wants to get a stamp for our pilgrim's passport," he said to Brigit. This seemed all wrong, rolling up in a car and getting a stamp, but there was no stopping Joseph. Luckily they had their 'credencial' books with them and handed them over. They all got out of the car, but instead of going into the building, Joseph took off for a service garage across the street. Bob and Brigit looked at each other puzzled. "That's the albergue in there," said Brigit, "I'm going to check it out."

"Me too." They went in through the open doors to a long dormitory room with a round vaulted ceiling. There were rows of two-tier bunks constructed of grey metal railing. The walls were decorated with medieval-style paintings. There was Saint James with a great big scallop shell at his feet. He appeared to be blessing two pilgrims kneeling on either side of him with three others waiting their turn. And there was a coat of arms, and pictures of peasants working in the fields.

"It is striking, but I can feel the damp. I don't expect it ever warms up inside these great thick walls, and so close to the river," said Brigit. "And there is no sign of the monks."

Outside, Joseph came back with their pilgrim passports. Seems the garage was the check-in for the albergue. The drive out of Samos took them up a steep hill out of the valley. Joseph stopped the car and had them look back. From here was a magnificent view of the monastery, all laid out with the little village wrapped around it. Joseph pointed to the road they were on, "Camino," and they could see that this was the view pilgrims would have as they came up to this bluff of land.

Bob was concerned about presuming to stay the night. Taking Joseph aside, he managed to suggest that he and Brigit should go to a pension or albergue for the night. Exclamations of horror and calling out to Anita. She came over, and no, they were to stay the night. Brigit—la señora— was definitely to have a good night's rest in a proper bed!

Supper, which was supposed to be a light meal after the large late lunch, was a Spanish tortilla—the potato pancake—olives, a green salad and wine, but first a large glass of amber sherry. As they lingered over supper, two couples called in. They wanted to hear the news from the hospital, wish them well, and meet Bob and Brigit.

There was horror over the school schedule and the bus just leaving the children with no supervision. The police had come around while they were out. Before they went to bed, Joseph and Bob arranged that they would drive to Sarria in the morning and Brigit and Bob would pick up the Camino from there. "Works out well. They are going to see Pedro, and we won't miss a day that way, and we have seen the path," Bob pointed out.

At some point in the small hours, Bob woke up. It was deep darkness; he could hear the frogs from the river banks.

"Bridgy, you awake?" Bob whispered. He pulled her closer and began nudging his face around her neck, kissing her and down to her breasts; Brigit murmured and curled her legs around his thighs.

33. The Day after the Day

Joseph and Anita dropped them off at the bridge by the river in Sarria. It was nine o'clock and they were all anxious to get going: the grandparents to visit Pedro, Brigit and Bob to get walking again. Bob saw that the bridge had wrought iron railings in the shape of scallop shells. "Definitely back on the Camino." So with goodbye-hugs and handshakes and more thanks, they crossed the bridge and set off into town.

"It seems like an eternity since we were last walking properly," Brigit grumbled.

"What an amazing twenty-four hours. Father Juan had not even arrived with the backpack this time yesterday," said Bob.

They followed the yellow arrows up steps to ruà Maior and into the centre of the old city.

"We must get our credencials stamped here, this is the famous last hundred kilometre point to Santiago that qualifies you for your Compostela certificate," said Bob.

"Seems a bit unfair for the rest of us who have done the whole way. That must account for all these albergues."

"Three so far," said Bob. "That looks like a tourist information office ahead. Let's see if we can get a stamp."

Out of the town, over another river, and away from the railway, the footpath wove through woodlands. Soon they picked up a small country road that led into a village with low stone walls enclosing orchards and gardens.

"Look at those," said Bob. At each house was a delicate structure that looked like a miniature church: narrow, quite long, meter-high, with a peaked roof, some of wood, some in brick, but all elevated off the ground. "Maybe it's grain storage of some kind, and off the ground to keep mice out or maybe rats."

"I hope I get a bit more energy as we keep going," Brigit said softly. "I thought after that comfortable night I would be really rested."

"Do you want to stop? We could do a short day?" Bob looked at Brigit anxiously remembering the warning from the doctor of how she could suffer after-effects.

"No. I'll be fine. We've only walked four kilometres. I'll get a second wind."

"That was a lot of emotion yesterday saving Pedro, ourselves, and the rest of the day was intense too," said Bob. "Let's see if Barbadelo can come up with a coffee." In the end it was a woman at the albergue who invited them to make some coffee. Just instant, but that was fine. They sat on a bench outside the albergue looking out on village life.

"Bob, I still can't believe it was only yesterday that your backpack was returned."

"I have heard of something, I think it's called dilated time: when time just leaves our usual perception when

283

something dramatic or traumatic happens. You could be experiencing that, like the time under the water with Pedro," suggested Bob.

"But," continued Brigit, "it's been a bit like that these last weeks on the Camino. That time walking by myself; that was when I started to face things. There was one day near Navarrete in the rain. It was misery: not sharp agony, just grinding misery. I was starting to acknowledge to myself what I had done with Earl: the gravity of it all. I was so horrified I kept going into denial, but that day would not let me. Just plodding along through those endless rows of vines and the earth all clogged to my boots, I could not avoid it. It was an invasion. I can't believe, even though I had ended everything, I just pretended there was nothing there, for two years. When I suggested this Camino trip, I thought it was to be joyful together. But it has turned into this emotional storm—I'm trying not to cry—I don't have any reason to be sorry for myself."

"Brigit, just take a bit of time. I'll wander around and look at the church." Bob did not want to say anything; there was nothing he could say to comfort her. He agreed with Brigit. It was disgusting that it took her two years to wake up to her behaviour. But he understood because, until the last few days, he had not faced what his behaviour with the money had really meant to the family and most especially to Brigit. 'What is wrong with us that we have lived in this amoral bubble? It's horrifying and mortifying. What kind of people are we, and what values have we given our children?'

When he returned to the albergue, Brigit was inside putting the cups away and talking with the woman who was in charge. "Manuela was telling me that the albergue brings some business to the village. This used to be the village school building; they ask for an overnight donation, but quite often people don't bother. Can you imagine? So they are going to set a fixed fee, and are sad they have to do that."

****

Back on the trail, Brigit kept finding herself haunted by the previous day—in the village, hovering over the stream, under the dark water. Through all the memory of the shock and cold she knew that a great shift happened, but she struggled to piece together the chunks and follow the threads. The child, back together with Bob, Bob saying he's sorry, that he loved her. With the deep beauty of the Camino around her, she walked in silence. As an understanding of the emotions and terror came to her, she grew sad as she saw that, despite the euphoria of finding each other again, that there was still a lot to understand, accept, discuss.

As they walked further west, the weather was warmer. "I thought as we got closer to the Atlantic Ocean, it would be cooler," said Brigit.

"We are quite far south even though it's northern Spain and we have the sea on two sides now: north and west. It's temperate here.

"The plants are different too. We saw that palm tree in Barbadelo." A stream took over the path but on one side the bank was built up with large flat paving stones for walking.

"Let's dip our feet in," suggested Brigit. "We could take a lunch break." They took off their boots and socks and sat on the path with their feet dangling over the edge in the cool water. They were shaded by trees that seemed to grow out of a crumbling stone wall covered in gnarled ivy. Lunch was ham sandwiches and a container of olives. Anita had sent them off with a large packed lunch.

"What do you think is the most difficult part of our mess to accept, or maybe manage?" asked Bob.

"Not sure. Maybe the question of trust and I guess the secrecy too," ventured Brigit.

"Yes, the trust. How could we have broken that in such a bad way? You know it makes me scared. What kind of people are we? What about the children? What values have we shown them? Will they be able to have trusting relationships?"

"Bob, don't! I know we have screwed up here. But all those years when the kids were growing up we were steady and strong. And look how they have turned out. Heavens, Liz is a picture of moral values. Paul has a lovely relationship with Divya. I know you don't always agree with Don, but you could never fault him for his relationships. He's had a great set of friends for years. Maybe they are turning out so well in spite of us. We may not like it that Liz knows about my affair, but she took a strong stand. Believe me!"

"And she was on to me about the money. I did tell her to mind her own business, but that's not how she sees family."

"And being her parents' moral keeper."

"Yup. I guess in that department we have given her an overload these last few years. Oh dear," said Bob.

"It comes back to the trust. Trust is the basis of love and of a relationship built on that love," said Brigit. We broke that. How could we have done that?"

"Well, we did, and we must take responsibility for it," said Bob. "I think I took the strength of our relationship for granted. Even though we have forgiven each other, we still have to face not only what we each did, what I guess you would call the sin, but what it means, as in breaking the trust."

"I have to deal with what I have done to the one I love and those I love: how it affects the family—the sins of the mother."

"And father. We have been married thirty years and trust and fidelity were never an issue; we took them for granted. Then secrecy came along and our shame. Sounds like Adam and Eve in the garden—well that's it—we fell from grace when we sinned and then we kept it from one another," said Bob.

"But that's the nature of sin. If it had not been hurtful and harmful, we wouldn't have needed the secrecy. But the secrecy hurts because we had never kept, or needed to keep, secrets from each other. Well, nothing like this," said Brigit.

They packed away the lunch and dried their feet. The rustic track continued through a string of hamlets, each a few houses gathered together. Water still demanded space on the rough stone path. A line of stepping stones placed along an uphill kept them dry as the water flowed around them. They continued, pointing things out to each other, but mostly in silence.

They had been climbing steadily and now they looked down at a valley with a large lake that narrowed into a river.

"Portomarín," said Brigit. "That lake is a reservoir."

"They dammed the river and moved the town," said Bob. The main street had stone arches over the sidewalk with the merchants' signs jutting out over the road. Exploring around town they came to a square with a statue of a pilgrim and looking at it were some real pilgrims. Greetings and exchange of news. They were from Italy and had just checked into the albergue. At the head of the square was a church: an austere stone rectangular building with turrets along the square roof line. "We need Charles-Michel," said Bob. "Let's see. Yes, it was a fortress church of the order of the Knights of Saint John. They protected this part of the Camino which was a strategic because of the bridge."

"There are no windows on the side," Brigit was looking up at the sheer wall of stone. "The front portal is wonderful with those arches nestled one inside the other and decorated with those columns and flowers, and there's Christ in the middle in a medallion. A clever way of combining fortress and church."

"What do you think, Bridgy. Shall we stay here? The Italians said it was comfortable." They stood in front of the albergue which was a single-storey building set back from a wide flight of steps.

"I would like to keep going. Where's the next albergue?"

"We've done twenty three kilometres already. It is supposed to be a lighter day," said Bob.

"It's only four o'clock and I'm feeling fine. You know how I never really like it around areas that have been flooded for a reservoir. There is something sterile about it. Though they've done a beautiful job here of rebuilding the town. Could we go to a restaurant and have something to eat and then go on a bit more?"

"We still have sandwiches left."

"Yes, I know. But how about a salad. Then we could have the sandwiches when we get settled at an albergue."

"Gonzar is the next albergue," Bob was checking the guide. The meal was over.

"Gonzar, for the night. Good," Brigit agreed.

"Yes, it's about eight kilometres."

"I like that name. Gonzar. You know in Galacia, the name places are easier to manage. Mireille must be happy. I wonder how they are getting on. Any texts?"

"No, nothing. Well not surprising, I've had the phone turned off since siesta time at Joseph's and Anita. Anyway, I don't think the others can be that far ahead. We only missed a day, not even, thanks to Joseph giving us a ride to Sarria."

Pardon My Camino

Leaving Portomarín they had the path to themselves. They climbed out of the valley and through avenues of trees with views of the river and lake. The path meandered past fields then back to the road and into the village of Gonzar. The white albergue building stuck out next to the road. The dormitory was upstairs in a large room which went the length of the newly renovated building, another school house conversion. There were large windows catching a breeze and the ceiling was open with dark wood beams.

When Brigit took their washing out to hang it on the line she could see a woman tethering a donkey by a small ploughed patch of land. "Hola," she called out.

"Hi there!" she replied, "I'm guessing you're English speaking." And they introduced themselves. Karen was from northern California, "up north of Lake Tahoe." She had already reached Santiago, and was now walking back.

"When you've had your shower, we would love to chat. Have you had supper? We have a ton of sandwiches. Please help us eat them. I'll see if I Bob can track down a bottle of wine." There was no store in the village, but Bob, ever resourceful, went next door to the caretaker who sold him a bottle. "It's not local. Apparently there's not much wine produced in Galacia, but the village gets it in by the hecto-litre or something and bottles it up."

Of course they wanted to know about the donkey. "Dulcinea. She comes from the Meseta," explained Karen. "I started in Burgos, but I did find my pack a bit of a bore. Maybe I had too much. I met a couple from Holland who had a donkey and I fell in love with the idea. I guess I just put it out there into the universe as I was wandering around in a village on the Meseta and chatting with a farmer, and out of the blue, he offered to lend me a donkey to go to Santiago! The condition was that I bring her back. He introduced me to Dulcinea and gave me instructions about feeding and water. Then he helped me with a tether and pack saddle for my bag, and we set off. Of course, I am now totally in love with her."

After supper, they went out to see Dulcinea. As soon as she saw Karen, she started to bray and shake her head. 'That love goes both ways,' thought Brigit.

"She needs her evening walk," explained Karen, undoing the tether.

"But she walks all day!" exclaimed Bob.

"Yes, but with a pack and going the direction I need her to go. What she needs is time free of a load to just wander and mooch around as she pleases." So the four of them set off around the village, past the cemetery, the church, around houses and barns, by tractors and farm equipment parked in the road beside low stone walls. They greeted a few people as they went.

"Karen, you are fluent in Spanish!" said Brigit admiringly.

"I worked with an NGO in El Salvador, helping in villages with the vegetable gardens to broaden the crops and with programs for the women and children." They reached a farm yard and a couple were standing out in the evening sun. When they saw Dulcinea's St. James shell on her red bridle, they asked about the Camino which led to a lively conversation. Karen threw out some translations. She pointed to a tree. "That's a pear tree. When the pears are ripe, they take ladders and pick them, and the pears are shared around the village. The tree is quite ancient and it has been happening that way for decades. Have you ever seen such a massive fruit tree?"

On the way back to the albergue, Brigit asked about walking the Camino with a donkey.

"Well it's not for everyone. With a donkey, apparently, I am completely approachable. I have to make sure she has enough water; she needs lots and she gets tired and needs breaks. And for accommodation, many albergues don't work. She forages for most of her food, but she does need access to good grass. So, it becomes all about the donkey, but I have just embraced doing the Camino this way. And in Galacia they have such a natural relationship with animals."

"Yes it's wonderful," said Brigit. "Especially the older men. I see them out in the meadows. Sometimes they have a little lean-to and they just sit and hang out with their cows, keeping them company."

They left Karen to settle Dulcinea for the night and sat on the front steps watching the sun set.

"Brigit, if you had not felt guilty about having an affair, would you have just kept going with it?"

'Jesus Murphy,' thought Brigit. 'Where did this come from?'

"What do you mean?" she said.

"Well, generally, in our society, the norm is for people to be monogamous. But the perception of love has changed: I should say, legitimate love. Like inter-racial, and now same-sex love is broadly accepted, and all that has happened relatively quickly. And some people are, what's it called — polyamorous. I heard an interview on the radio with a woman explaining that she had a husband and a boyfriend-lover. Not just an occasional fling, but an established lover relationship."

"Bob, no! This not how I see a marriage relationship. It may sound ironic, but I believe in faithful monogamy."

"We never stopped to question our attitude to fidelity when we got married," said Bob.

"That's because we both understood what it meant. I know I violated that, but what I did, that is not what I consider to be normal, acceptable, or how I see marriage."

"I was just wondering. Let's go in."

'Well,' thought Bright. 'So much for my peaceful night. Really, screw Bob and his wondering! Is he suggesting he wants an open marriage now? And who's to blame for that!'

34. Love by Other Names

Brigit is jolting along on the donkey, looking around at the buildings lining the city streets. Charles-Michel is leading her and Emilio is with him. "I'm like the Virgin Mary. She wore blue—I'm in white—a white cloak and hood on a dusty donkey!" Up the wide shallow steps to the large church and the front doors are open and in they go, donkey and all. Emilio stops the donkey and Charles-Michel helps her down and they take off the white cloak and underneath is a wedding dress, low cut across her breasts, plunging back and—dear Lord—the skirt on one side is high up her thigh and full length on the other, all covered in sequins, white, silver, glittering. And how is she to walk on these open-toed, sky-high stiletto heels? And the hair. What is this buffoon beehive, stiff with hair lacquer, a big-hair up-do! The church is full of friends—Mireille, Colin, the family and up at the altar she can see Bob.

"Charles-Michel, what's going on?"

"Brigit, it's your wedding day of course." He smiles sweetly.

"But I'm already married." She takes his arm and best as she can, totters up the aisle to meet Bob—and then, who steps in from the side, but Earl. Then the priest says:

"Brigit, we are gathered here today to ask you what these men are in your life? Bob and Earl: who will be your husband, and who will be your lover?"

She came to and there it was, vivid in her mind, in the darkness. "Dear God, help me, I thought I was beyond this. Am I to be forever tortured?" Here she was in an upper bunk and all these other people—didn't they realize that she was in crisis? And Bob, she could hear him actually snoring. How dare he just sleep through all of this when he was the one who put those ideas in her head? She looked at her watch: four am. The pain of it all made her ache, and nowhere in the narrow bed could she possibly be comfortable. Why did he ask me that stupid question? What was it exactly? "If I did not have feelings of guilt could I—no, it was, would I—have continued with the affair?" But what he left out of the question was: "would I tell him about it."

Despite her indignation at Bob's question, after that dreadful dream, in the dark hours of the predawn, in a room full of sleeping strangers, she sunk into the situation that Bob had set before her. She thought back on the affair: the start of it, the adventure, the attention, the sexual thrill, her desire, feeling his desire for her, even the secrecy of this clandestine life. Just thinking about it, she felt herself becoming aroused. A fantasy flitted through her mind, of climbing down into Bob's bunk and seducing him while all the others slept. So that's how it went with those kids she had heard rumbling in the night. But what did she think?

What she knew was that all that flirting, the thrill of anticipating the next encounter, the intensity when they were together, the wondering and speculation: all that is magnified at the start of a new romantic relationship. Before Bob, she had not had any relationship that had gone as far as intercourse, but she had had erotic romances. And she remembered that heady, exciting, breathtaking time, even the feelings of secrecy and thrilling guilt. What if her parents knew what she was doing? Of course, since having teenagers of her own, she now knew that her parents would have had a pretty good idea of what was going on; it was just civilized to pretend on both sides, that the parents did not know. So if those raw intense sexual feelings she had conjured up, enough to arouse her, were the early days for a couple, what did that say for a sustained love-relationship? Well in the ordinary way, one would build on that. But she had a husband and did not want to build any other partner relationship of the lover kind. It was just the thrilling part she had wanted with Earl, none of the hard work. So juvenile.

When Brigit made it downstairs Bob was sitting at the table adding granola to a yogurt pot.

"Hi Bob. Hi Karen."

"I was thinking in the night," said Bob. "How do you find your way back along the Camino? The arrows and signs are all facing for coming from the east so you can't see them going back."

'Oh that's just great!' Brigit grumbled to herself. 'As I lay there agonizing over our future, he's wondering how to walk the Camino backwards!'

****

Walking out of Gonzar, through the mist Bob could see the ancient pear tree reaching high above the roofs. He had slept well, but that did not mean he was not thinking about their situation. His questions last evening had sprung up and rather surprised him. 'Don't know if thinking aloud is always a good thing.' But he felt it was a legitimate question and they both knew they had to work through all this. He had imagined a strange scenario: What if the timing had been reversed? What if Brigit had been having the affair and he knew or suspected, and then he had had the opportunity to make those investments in the exploration company. Would he have felt somehow that he had permission to borrow all that money without consulting her, behave badly, because she had hurt and betrayed him, and there was a moral deficit owing to him? Well that was crazy thinking, because he had sincerely thought he was going to do good for the family, whereas she was just being destructive. Except that now, he acknowledged there had been a lot of ego and pride on his part. How much did they need? But no, he had to justify some economic-cultural thing from his background about making it big, and getting serious money.

They were observing the quiet morning time. Bob broke the silence. "Why did you feel compelled to make up all the money that we owed?"

"I didn't do it all. You made some, I made some, we rented out the cottage, the kids got summer jobs. We did it together. Anyway, what was the choice?"

"There's always a choice: not a pleasant one. We could have declared bankruptcy and started again."

"Phew, I know, and we thought we might have to. It's when I saw what that meant, losing the house, the cottage, most everything; they just leave you enough for survival. It would have been far worse. Just think professionally what that would have done to us. I felt it was better to grind through a few really tough years and then get over it. I know people do lose everything and start again. You hear stories of people being transformed and facing their fears and coming out healed and redeemed. But I didn't think that way would work for us."

"But look where it did lead us. I mean we nearly lost our marriage, and our savings are gone. You did cling on and were in control, but at some point, you lost it and went into chaos."

"I've never seen my whole control thing like that before. Did I never really give you a choice?" asked Brigit. "I don't know if our marriage would have survived bankruptcy. I think I am too materialistic—apparently. But then I sabotaged the whole thing anyway. Was it me who gave you the idea we needed more, much more money?"

"No. That was all me," said Bob. "You have always said how fortunate we are in all things including money. How gratitude is one of your fundamental values and religious principles. I would say we both appreciate the value of money and were always careful with it. I hope not parsimonious, but responsible. It's another value we share that I broke. Like our attitude to marriage and fidelity that we share and you broke."

They kept walking through the morning mist.

"How come you slept badly?" Bob asked.

"Last night I had a crazy dream."

"Crazy dream. Tell me about it."

"Hmm, it involved us, and others. Are you sure you want to hear?"

"Absolutely. Dreams are very revealing. Could help us move forward."

They both had a good laugh over the donkey and wedding dress episode. The scene at the altar was not so amusing. She also told him about her thoughts when she woke up, which led her round to addressing his questions of the evening before and the polyamorous question.

"Thank you for telling me. If we had been in a pension, you could have lived out the fantasy," teased Bob.

They climbed up a wooded path to a hamlet: Ventas de Narón. By the side of the road was a tiny, weathered chapel built of large rough cut stones, and on the roof above the door was a bell hanging from small stone arch with a cross on top.

"This is just enchanting and looks so old. 'Capela de Magdalene.' I wonder what the history is?" said Brigit.

"The guide book says there was a battle here during the time of Charlemagne."

"We need Charles-Michel. We were going to text them."

Bob was not keen to turn on the cell phone. The others would not be far ahead and they probably could have joined up, but he did not want to end this time with Brigit. It was good to be alone with her, to reconnect properly. After so many years they were really talking again. And they were talking about their marriage, their relationship and that was vital. "And we're good at it," he thought. "We're a great couple."

"I've been thinking," said Bob. "There is so much we need to sort out, and it's raw and emotional. I think when we get home we should get some proper counselling. What do you think?"

"I think we are making some good progress."

"It is very good that we have this time together and we are doing well. But we're getting close to Santiago. When we get back to civilization it will not be so easy for us to continue at this level. That's what Father Estevan told me; the Camino gives you time and space, also people and events that can help heal."

"Was he the monk at Rabanal? So you did talk more with him."

"I admire these monks, at least from my vast experience of the two I have talked with. Anyway, why don't you think about us getting counselling?"

"I don't need to think any further. It makes perfect sense and it is what we should do. It would be very conceited of us to think we could work through this without help. We must do this properly. Otherwise it could come back to haunt us."

"Yes, it's like the trees: people cut down the tree completely or they prune it right back, but carefully and purposefully to let it grow back, like we've seen they do here. That's us. If we had given up on our marriage, it would be like cutting the tree down, but we are going the other way so it can—we can—grow back. We could call it the Spanish sweet chestnut way."

"Bob, I do love you."

"I love you too."

They reached the hamlet of Portos. At the café-bar they went in to see if they could have lunch.

"Si, si." They had pasta, veal scallop, green beans, and bread, but they decided to stick to water: too early to get sleepy.

"You know Bob, I would love to be able to give back to the Camino in some way. It's such a wonderful experience and it has helped me—us -save our marriage. It would be lovely to contribute in some way."

"What about volunteering at a hostel? Like Mary and Peter at Rabanal. Didn't they say they are always looking for volunteers?"

"Yes that's possible. Would you like to do that?"

'Not sure about that," said Bob. "But you could. You get more holiday than I do. Then I could join you and we could catch up on some of the sightseeing."

"I could do that anyway, but maybe there is something else out there too."

Bob nodded. "Anyway, we had better keep going."

As they prepared to leave, Bob asked Clara, the woman who ran the restaurant about the albergue in the town. She said it was very nice, right in the centre, but could get crowded. If they were looking for something quieter, her sister had a room she rented out for guests.

"Una habitacion, mey bonita, con baño."

"What do you say Bridgy? I really fancy a room of our own. Sounds good, and it may give us more Spanish practice."

"Si, queremos hablar español," said Brigit. Which Bob thought sounded like a rather strange things to say in Spain, but they met so many non-Spanish pilgrims, he did appreciate that Brigit was anxious to get into conversations with locals.

"Es perfecto. Podran hablar con mi hermana y su esposo." So whether her sister and brother-in-law actually wanted to talk with a couple of Canadian pilgrims, they were enlisted for the task. Clara phoned up and yes, the room was available. She drew them a map with the address and phone number and sent them on their way.

"I hope we are not being extravagant," said Brigit as they followed the footpath by the road that was now climbing again.

"Has it occurred to you that living on the Camino is actually cheaper than being day to day at home? We have our albergue donations and food. You don't do any gift or souvenir shopping because we don't want to carry it. We don't pay for transport. A night or two at a pension is not out of line. Anyway I want you to myself and of course you want to practice your Spanish!" He gave her a big grin.

35. Of the World, Of the Divine

It was four o'clock when Bob rang the bell at Clara's sister, Eva's house, in Palas de Rei. Eva showed them to their room. There were patio doors out to the garden and the room was cool and pleasant, plain and clean. She gave them towels and then brought some lemonade and said they must relax and pointed to the chairs on the patio.

After laundry and showers they somehow migrated to the bed. "Looks more relaxing than the chairs in the sun," said Bob. "I like these old fashioned narrow double beds," and they reached out for each other. They lay face to face, letting their whole body lengths touch, feeling the contact of their skin. Brigit could feel Bob hard against her. But neither of them moved; they held each other, letting the tension mount but not giving into the urge to go further. But eventually they let their bodies break together, now touching and pushing, finding every place they could connect until they allowed themselves the reward of Bob entering her eager body.

They snoozed, murmured, nudged. "Shall we get up?" Brigit asked. She knew he was awake, though he pretended to be asleep.

"Hmm, you see I was right."

"Well no doubt, but what about?" she quizzed.

"Getting a room of our own. You see it's brilliant,"

"Yes dear, you are right. Clever you! Let's get up and phone Liz and see what's going on at home." And she pulled the covers off him.

"And we must get our credencials stamped — the last hundred klicks. We don't want to be accused of hopping on a bus or something," said Bob.

When they passed through the house, Eva asked what time they wanted breakfast, "How lovely. Breakfast too; we are becoming so decadent"

They found a public phone, dialled the string of numbers, and got through to Liz.

"Hi Mum and Dad. I'm glad to hear from you. I was going to send you a text."

"Here we are darling. Is there a problem?"

"Not this end, but are you guys okay? Paul went to check on the house and the phone messages. There was one all in Spanish, very fast. Paul said there was a string of numbers so he thinks that could be a phone number. We did wonder why someone in Spain wanted to talk to you in Ottawa."

"Don't really know what that could be, unless it's someone from Sarria. We did give them our home number at the hospital. I gave them the cell number too but it's been turned off," said Bob.

"Why the hospital? Are you hurt?"

"No not us, but we saved a little boy who fell into a stream; then later his grandparents took us to see him in hospital. Anyway, the doctors asked for our contact details. But the little guy was doing fine so I don't think it's anything urgent."

"Well what about you? Are you all right?" asked Liz.

"Yes we are fine. In fact more than fine. And your mother and I are sorting through our issues and we are doing very well. Saving the little boy gave us a new perspective and a big wake-up. And Liz, one thing we know for sure, is that we want to stay together."

"Oh that is so good. You guys are great." And Liz's voice broke up as she struggled to talk. "I'm sorry but I'm so relieved to hear that. I have been so worried, for so long." And now they could hear her crying.

"Liz, we didn't mean to upset you."

"Upset me!" she choked. "What do you think I've been for the last years about you two, my darling parents?"

"We are so sorry, Liz. We know you've been very concerned, and it's been difficult for you. We are not out of the woods completely, but we know we want to stay together. When we get back we'll get help: counselling."

"Yes, yes, that's good. That's a good plan. Oh, I am so happy. You have no idea how worried I was."

"Yes. We can imagine. You are such a good family person; we are so lucky to have you as our daughter. How are you? How's the baby?"

By the time she had told them about her last check-up and her family news, she was composed again. "Following you on Google, you really are getting close to Santiago."

"Yes, it's three days of walking according to the guide. And we've gone all soft and are staying at a very nice bed and breakfast tonight."

"That's so sensible. You don't have to be hard-core pilgrims all the time, you know."

"The albergues are fun because of the people you meet, but the sleeping is a challenge."

"We all really miss you and we're excited to think you will be home again soon."

"Yes, we feel it's starting to be time."

"Please take care of yourselves. I love you."

A volunteer at the albergue stamped their credencials. It was bursting at the seams with a large group of school students from Germany. The volunteer said they had done well to get a room elsewhere for the night. She knew of Eva and said she was sure they would be comfortable. She recommended a bar-restaurant in the town that could give them some supper. After their large lunch they just needed an ensalada mixta. They sat on a patio outside and watched people out and about enjoying their Friday evening.

"How do you feel about Liz?" asked Bob.

"Sad and guilty about what we've put her through. She has been worried about us for so long. She saw us both going off the track. It really is role reversal. And there she is, as far as we know, she and David, steady as a rock. And they run the farm together. I wonder how we can make it up to her, and the others too," said Brigit.

"You can't go back. As much as we wish we had not done what we did, we can't undo it. But we can move forward, and learn from it and grow and be better. I am sure that is what the kids want and expect of us: to get back to being a functioning couple, behaving like adults and parents, supporting and encouraging them in difficult times, and rejoicing and playing together as a family."

"Yes Bob. That is well said. You are right."

****

Leaving Palas de Rei the next morning they came to an old statue of a sad pilgrim presiding over a water fountain and close by a modern statue with a pilgrim couple, rejoicing, with their arms in the air. A cockerel and his troop of hens were happily poking around on the Camino path; Bob and Brigit picked their way through them and onto a quiet trail that ran along the bank of a meadow.

At the next village, Mato-Casanova—"well how about that for a name!" exclaimed Brigit—they stopped and sat at a stone table in the church yard. All of a sudden, from nowhere, a flock of sheep rushed around them; they checked out the grass along the wall, seizing mouthfuls as they went, and then they were off. They didn't even notice Bob and Brigit, far too busy with the grass, and no one was with them.

"Well that was an extraordinary moment. We might as well have been church-yard statues!" marvelled Brigit.

"It's just more dumb pilgrims for them. There must be generations of their ancestors putting up with us crowding their space." said Bob. "I guess I had better turn on the cell phone. I forgot about it yesterday evening." And he dug around in his pack. "Hope we still have battery." The phone pinged and burped its way through start-up.

"There are some lovely wild flowers here. I'm amazed they have survived the sheep. Violets and this is some kind of lily." Brigit was checking out the church yard.

"Heavens, we have a whole slew of text messages. How come we are so popular all of a sudden? Mostly Charles-Michel, English and French. Must be important."

"What's it all about?"

"Doesn't say, just been trying to reach us. It's important, please call, text, but get in contact."

"Wow, that's a bit alarming. I hope there's no problem."

"Let's see if we have phone service here. "Allô, bonjour Charles-Michel, qu'est-ce qui se passe?"

"My God, where are you guys?"

"We just left Palas de Rei. We spent the night there."

"They didn't know about you at the albergue, and the night before you weren't in Portomarín. We've been trying to reach you."

"Are you alright? Is someone hurt?"

"No, we are fine. Did you leave the Camino?"

"No. We stayed in a very nice pension last night, comfy bed, and a tasty breakfast. Anyway, why did you want to know where we are? I'm touched!"

"Maudit, you guys! Emilio has been nagging me to reach you. Did you get your pack?"

"Yes that worked out fine. What's up with Emilio? Apart from another reason to get in touch with you!"

"This is nothing to do with me-us, but you two. The police are looking for a couple of pilgrims who saved a boy from drowning near Triacastela. Emilio thinks, from the description, that it could well be you two."

"How come Emilio is involved?"

"When he said he might know who they were, the police have been hounding him ever since. Is it you?"

"Yes, we did help this little kid. He had fallen into one of those irrigation channels and got stuck. Brigit jumped in to save him and then I came along and helped. The poor little guy was in a bad way. He needed CPR, we got him breathing again, and the family came and got him to the hospital."

"Oh, so it was you. The authorities want to talk to you."

"We aren't hiding. We stayed overnight with the grandparents, and we all went to the hospital to visit the boy, Pedro. We met the hospital staff, and the doctors asked our contact details which we gave them. They all said thank you and next day, we set off again."

"You must report in."

"Charles-Michel, I don't much like the sound of this. Brigit and I are getting along very well here. We are sorting

310

out our issues. Little Pedro was a blessing as we came to our senses. Sounds like the police are annoyed with us for just getting on with our Camino."

"You can't go around saving kids and then disappearing."

"Why not? Keep hearing stories like that. Anyway, we didn't disappear. So what should we do?"

"Not cause a diplomatic incident. Can you see the headlines?: 'Senior Canadian public official refuses to help Spanish police with their investigation over a drowning child.'"

"Okay, very funny. However, there is the language thing too. I would feel more comfortable if we could have someone with us. Is Emilio very busy? Is there any way he could help us with this? We would feel better if he was with us when we meet the police. I trust him."

"I expect he would be happy to. It's Saturday so he's busy at the hotel, but tomorrow evening he could probably drive down. Let me get in touch with him and he will work out how to do this. I think it's turning into a big deal because of the school and the kids being left on their own."

"You're right. We need to do this carefully. You don't want to get stuck on one side of a conflict. Charles-Michel we don't need this."

"We'll sort it out. Now for pity's sake leave your phone on. Was it off all that time? Really you guys!"

"Okay, glad to hear we are going to see you soon."

"Well, do you think I'm going to let Emilio have all the drama and glory? Anyway, you may need me as your adviser. Talk to you later, and I love you both."

They sat there looking at each other.

"Wow, I can't believe this. Here we are minding our own business and next thing we are part of a police alert. First the sheep visitation and now the manhunt!" said Brigit.

"You know what this means?" said Bob with a grin.

"Many things, but what?" said Brigit

"We are going to have to behave like adults!"

"Oh shit, because I guess saving a kid from drowning doesn't count."

Bob was glad they could make a joke about this news. He did not like the sound of this business at all.

The day grew into a precious dream to be cherished, not the nightmare dramas that Brigit had been enduring, but a wander through an enchanted land—except it was real. Suddenly, this cocoon, this precious time of revival for their love, their marriage was to come to an end. Not the fact, but the romance and clarity of it all. Not just life intruding but what now could be a threat. They savoured the trail through the woodlands, along the meadows, among the flowers. They met an ancient one out with his cows for a Saturday walk taking them down to the stream for a drink. And then the Eucalyptus trees began to line the path, tall, bare, mottled grey and olive green trunks, bark peeling. Into the village of Lobreiro.

"It means 'Fields of Rabbits.'" said Bob reading from the guide. "If Alice in Wonderland was to make an appearance along with the Cheshire Cat, I feel it would not be a surprise."

"Yes and we have the Mad Hatter and the Queen of Hearts waiting for us."

"Now don't be bitter!"

"I'm not, just being a smart aleck! Anyway you brought up Alice!"

"I know how you like literary references. We haven't seen those before." They looked over a low wall into an orchard at something that looked like a wide witch's hat made with thin twigs flaring out like a skirt or a broom: this on top of a woven willow cylinder.

"I wonder who lives in there."

"Maybe Alice's dormouse!"

"I thought he lived in a teapot."

A fork in the road left an open space wide enough for a narrow stone column with a cross on top. A green wooden gate led to the church built of grey stone. Above the door was a carved image of the Virgin and child with angels on each side. "Oh look, they're swinging censers with the incense." Brigit made out in the stone. "Preparing us for the enormous censer at the cathedral in Santiago." Brigit ran her hand over the rough stones then turned to look at Bob. "If that was the only thing waiting for us in Santiago— but Santiago also means this police business. I've been trying to not think about it. What can be the trouble? Has something gone horribly wrong, like with Pedro?"

"I know. It's infuriating and upsetting." Bob put his arms around Brigit. "I'm so sorry, darling, but I think this could be a bit rough. I don't like what I've heard so far. But we will sort it out. We've been through worse."

"But what on earth could they want us for so urgently? I know they have to do their reports. Do you think it's just that?"

"I don't think they just want to say thank you. But they will have questions. With such a serious event, they do have to sort out what happened. Let's try and not worry. We will see what they want when we meet them. And we will have Emilio with us, and Charles-Michel. He's pretty savvy."

"But I just want to rejoice for the end of our Camino and now it seems we've got all this shit to deal with and it's starting to nag away at me. How dare they?"

In Fuerlos the village street went up and along the high bank of the river. The houses, spotted around at random, were built in grey and ochre field stones. In front of one, next to a smart wooden varnished front door, was a white plastic chair, and placed upright on the chair—a bunch of leeks. Plump, white with the green tops shooting up way beyond the back of the chair. "Beautiful! That could be in an art gallery!"

"Hola, bienvenido ¡Entren!" The priest was standing at the door to his church—the elderly man was beckoning them in; they went up two deep steps straight into the church. He shook hands, told them to take off their packs, and started to gently walk them around showing them the statues and shrines. As their eyes accustomed to the dim light, they could make out the details. At a small desk at the back of the church he held up a stamp and asked for their credencials. 'Parroquia St.Juan' the parish of St. John, Brigit read the words on the rectangular stamp around a strange image of a crucifix. The priest led them back towards the door only to stop in front of a large wooden crucifix, the one on the stamp. They stood and gazed. A Jesus on the cross as they had never seen before: large, smooth, carved muscles and bones on the gaunt body, an elaborate loin cloth, the crown of thorns holding down flowing hair over a hollow Spanish face, a full beard. Knees bloodied, feet nailed one over the other. But his arms: one nailed to the cross, but the other free and pointing down to the ground. And the face, looking down towards the pointing arm, what was the expression? Inward and outward, compassion and awareness. They both stood, looking, the priest watching them. Brigit turned to him. He explained that no one knew what the artist had in mind, but he saw it two ways: the simple one was that Jesus was pointing to the Camino, to show the way to the thousands of pilgrims. But the priest also saw this Jesus as man and Christ the son of God: here, as our bridge to the Divine, reaching down and reaching up, showing the way. Brigit looked at the priest with tears in her eyes. He gave them a blessing and sent them back onto the Camino and on their way.

"Oh gracious, I think we should get a coffee," said Brigit taking a deep breath of fresh air.

"It's almost lunch time. Should we wait?"

"No, we can get lunch in Melide. I really need a coffee and bit of a break now."

They found a bar-café up the road.

"This has been quite a morning, ending up with that church. What a Camino moment."

And then their phone rang.

36. Deeply Camino

"Allô, Charles-Michel, comment ça va vous autres?" Bob answered the phone.

"We're fine. Where are you?"

"Perfect timing. We're having a coffee in Fuerlos, just before Melide. We just had a wonderful Camino moment talking with the priest here."

"Well, you lucky things; I'll want to hear all about it. I reached Emilio and he's happy to be on hand with the police. Anyway let's all just keep walking at the moment. You're aiming for Ribadiso and we should be at Arca de Pino this evening, which leaves us one day into Santiago. We've been talking and we would like to join up with you so we can all walk into Santiago together. We've told the police we will only meet them at a place along the Camino. I've told Emilio that is non-negotiable."

"Okay. We'll just keep walking. That would be so great to all walk into Santiago together. Can you all afford the time?"

"Of course. We've made good time overall; it works out well for Colin and Mireille, and my return ticket is open anyway. It just feels so right to get back together after all our adventures. I hope to have the police details by the end of the day. We don't want to be cloak and dagger, but we haven't told them where you are. We said you are delayed. We don't want them turning up at an albergue and talking with you before we get there. Okay then. Au revoir."

"Did you get that, Brigit?" asked Bob. They looked at each other and spluttered in laughter.

"Oh my God. What is this turning into?"

"I know," said Bob. "I can't make out where our situation begins and the Emilio-Charles-Michel team take over! I'm beginning to think they are perfect for one another. They both love organizing and a bit, maybe more than a bit, of power-play. Anyway they are dealing with the police and keeping them at bay—so far. "

It was Saturday and Melide was busy with shoppers as well as pilgrims.

"Ah bonjour, vous êtes les canadiens, n'est-ce-pas?" For a horrible moment, Bob thought that his nemesis François had found them again. But no, it was the poor fellow who was with François when they last met, when he was going on with all that crap about my losing everything. But where this man is, can François be far behind?

Brigit came to his rescue. "Bonjour. C'est René, n'est-ce-pas?"

'How on earth did Brigit remember his name?' She went straight to the point and asked him about François. "Where was it we had last met, a bit before O'Cebreiro?"

"Villafranca del Bierzo. Yes." After that, François met up with some other people and decided to walk with them. René explained. "It really was a relief as I wanted to go slower; I am with some very nice people from Luxembourg. Now I have time to see the sights. Like this beautiful town. You must visit the church."

They found a restaurant to give them a salad and a beer; they were too early for Spanish lunch. But the ensalada mixta turned out to be a plato mixto with fries, salad, fried egg, chicken, and crusty bread.

"I was not expecting so much, but most of the time on the Camino I seem to be able to eat whatever is put in front of me," said Brigit.

"Well we never know where the next meal might be coming from. It might be slim pickings for food this evening," said Bob breaking off some crusty bread.

"Yes, weekends are a rather strange time for being a tourist. You kind of don't fit in and often things are closed down, at least in Europe."

"Yeah, not like Vegas. Did you like the church? I thought the statues of all those monks were striking. Good for René to have shaken off François." said Bob.

"You know how I was talking about giving back to the Camino." said Brigit. Then I thought a bit wider, not just the Camino as a pilgrim path, but where the route goes as a community. And then with Pedro and the children and my work with the school, I was wondering if around Triacastela and Sarria I could set up school partnerships. Maybe I could use Emilio's talents and contacts to help me. I would love to do something with the little ones at Pedro's school; gracious, they might need a bit of loving with all this going down."

"Wow, Brigit, trust you to come up with a lovely idea like that. Clever you," and Bob gave her a kiss. "Nevertheless, first we have to deal with the Guardia Civil and get to Santiago."

When they reached the village of Boente, they caught up with the group of German students they had seen at Palas de Rei. They were taking a break and filling up their water bottles at a stone fountain. Bob and Brigit greeted the students, who were in their mid-teens, and were all very courteous: many spoke some English. As they got going again, Bob and Brigit fell in with the teacher, Wolfgang, and Ursula, a parent volunteer.

"They have to behave," explained Wolfgang. "There are thirty-six students and we are only five adults."

"How do you manage with food?" asked Brigit.

"We have a support vehicle with us. It has a gas cooking stove and kitchen ware."

"Finding albergues must be a challenge," said Bob.

"It is all arranged ahead of time. There are no spontaneous night stops for us," Wolfgang laughs.

Now they were crossing the River Iso and arrived directly into the albergue at Ribadiso. Many of the students were already waiting at the desk with the hospitalaria who was lining up the credencials to stamp them all at the same time. Brigit and Bob added theirs and put a donation in the box.

When Bob went out to hang the washing, he met Wolfgang.

"Yes we are all settled in." There is lots to eat and would Brigit and Bob please join them for supper? "We will have an adult table," Wolfgang assured Bob.

"We would love that. Thank you."

The adults were at a picnic table, some of the students were sitting at other tables, and some just on the grass with groups of friends. Two of the boys were using a laptop.

"Every day, two students have to write up the day, where we walked and what they noticed," explained Ursula. "For some it is quite an Aufgabe, how would you say? Chore?" She laughed.

"At the end of the evening, we all come together to sing the Ultreia song of the Camino Pilgrims. You know the French one"

Tous les matins nous prenons le chemin, tous les matins nous allons plus loin, jour après jour la route nous appelle c'est la voix de Compostelle!

Ultreia! Ultreia! Et sus eia! Deus adijuva nos!

As they sang in the evening light, the phone rang in the office. The volunteer answered. The voice on the other end was official.

"This is the National Police. We are trying to reach two Canadian pilgrims and they may be at Ribadiso this evening. Robert and Brigit Matthews. Have they checked into your alberge?"

"Canadienses. Today no. We often do have Canadian pilgrims, but not tonight. There are French, Italian, British, and Spanish of course. We have a large group from Germany: students. There are thirty-six youth and seven adults."

"Yes, I could call you if they come in, but most pilgrims have arrived by now. Buenas noches."

It was a pleasant cool night with the windows overlooking the river letting in a breeze

****

Bob and Brigit were ready early the next morning and decided not to have breakfast at the albergue but walk to Arzua, which was only three kilometres away.

"And we can call Charles-Michel." They said goodbye to Wolfgang and Ursula. "Tschüss, we will see you on the trail."

It was a lovely early morning misty walk. There was a tunnel under a main road and then back into woodlands and farms.

"Brigit, you know this is crazy."

"Oh you mean the police thing?"

"Well, that too, but you and me." They were looking out at a meadow with horses grazing in the mist. Bob took Brigit into his arms.

"I feel like we are on a second honeymoon these last few days, except we are sleeping in a dorm, and now with a whole crowd of kids. And, much as I love the others, I'm going to have to share you again."

"Yes, you are," said Brigit, returning his kiss.

They had coffee and a croissant at a cake shop in Arzúa.

"I feel sad this morning knowing we are near the end. But, as they say about the Camino, 'The Way is the goal.'"

Bob agreed. "But there are good things waiting for us at home. Let's call Charles-Michel."

"Bonjour." Charles-Michel was low-key: "We are just getting sorted out for the morning, still at the albergue. You're up early."

"Yes, we came into Arzúa for breakfast."

"Anyway, we have a plan. We are going to walk back along the trail today. The albergue here knows what is going on as we had the joy of the police coming to see us last evening. We can spend a second night here and leave our packs. So for the police, they want to see you this evening. The chief of Police is coming out from Santiago to meet with us here, in Arca. They wanted to collect you and drive you to Santiago. I said that would not look good for them: depriving pilgrims, who had walked from St-Jean-Pied-de-Port, from their last day of walking into Santiago. They're a bit twitchy and feel you are hiding."

"Why can't it wait until we get to Santiago," said Bob. "What's the rush?" Bob saw with this news that the Police Chief was coming out to meet them, and on a Sunday, the situation was becoming even more serious. Whatever it was, this was not good.

"Bob, I think we should contact the embassy in Madrid. Just to put them in the picture. What do you think?" said Charles-Michel.

"That seems a bit extreme, until we know what the problem actually is. However, if this is going to be complicated, they might appreciate a heads-up."

"I have their number. Do you want me to call?"

"I will. Just give me the number. So where are we likely to meet up? I guess you guys will be speeding along with no packs to carry."

"I am thinking around Calle. But just keep on the trail and no detours!"

"Thanks Charles-Michel—for everything."

"Brigit, did you get that, about the embassy."

"Yes, and he's probably right. I guess that's what they're there for. Will they be open on a Sunday?"

"There'll be a duty officer. I'll call and see."

The embassy was ahead of them as the National Police had already called.

"As though we keep track of all the Canadian pilgrims on the Camino—would be a full time job," said the officer. "But this is good that I have your cell number. And please contact us after your first meeting this evening. We can see from there. By the way, Mr. Matthews, we will let your office in Ottawa know."

"Is that really necessary?"

"Well you know how the minister would not like to be caught unaware of events: one of her senior staff rescuing a drowning child in Spain!"

"Well, it was my wife, actually."

"Really, Brigit, how many other people want to jump on this bandwagon? Poor little Pedro. He only wanted to rescue his car!"

"Exactly! And I don't see what difference twenty four hours can make? Is this the way they operate or—I really don't like this, and now I am getting scared as well as angry," said Brigit

"Let's just see what happens. We've done all we can at this point. And we have the embassy on standby, but I'm sure it won't come to that," said Bob.

"I would like to take a little time to go and sit in the church," said Brigit. 'It would help me and I want to give thanks for all the good stuff: especially us. That's what's most important."

"Of course, darling. We've got time; we'll make time. Let's find the church, and then I'll go and buy the food and I'm happy looking around."

****

Iglesia de Santiago was modern, but some of the stone and wood decorations in the church were older. There were some worshippers: two pilgrims and locals. Brigit found a quiet spot off to one side.

"Dear Lord, where to start with all the thank yous and my gratitude. Restoring my husband and saving my marriage, my life. Thank you for such love and grace. Help me to live my life worthy of these great gifts." And as Brigit prayed for her family, for Pedro and his family, and all the pilgrims along the Camino, an image came to her of Jesus walking on the water.

After some time, Brigit looked around. Bob was there, looking at a series of carved wooden panels behind the altar. He pointed to a medallion at the top of the carving. "That's St. James as Matamoros, the warrior. I think I'm just getting it sorted out: St James as pilgrim and then St James on a horse with a sword. It's confusing because some of the traditional statues of pilgrims are just that: pilgrims; and others are Santiago all dressed up as a pilgrim."

"I bought a local cheese," said Bob. "It's a regional speciality and I saw a statue of a cheese maker in the plaza. I got a bottle of red wine and I'm going to make the sacrifice of carrying it. We can celebrate when we meet the others with wine and cheese."

They worked their way out of the town then back to woodlands. The day was now quite warm: the vegetation appearing almost tropical with more palm trees and the ever present eucalyptus.

"Bob, when I was in the church, I had this vision. You know the story from the Gospel when Jesus sends His disciples in the boat across to the other side of the lake, while He goes up the mountain to pray? A storm blows up, and it's dark. The disciples are terrified and then they see this ghost walking on the water to them—it's Jesus. Peter, the know-all, wants to walk on the water too. 'If it is you Jesus, you can order me to walk to you on the water.' Jesus said, 'Come on!' and Peter does. Then he gets afraid and goes under. But Jesus saves him, chastises him for his lack of faith and helps him back into the boat. That's what I feel like. God has saved me from my drowning and helped me get back into the boat. Set me right. Am I back in the boat, Bob?"

"Brigit you know we are, both back in our boat, the same boat. I guess in the spirit of the story, we are still struggling with the sails and the oars. But you said they had been told to go across the lake to the other side. That is what we're trying to do. It's not plain sailing, but we have the boat and we want it to move forward, despite the storm. Oh darling, don't cry." And he took her in his arms. "We'll make it, you'll see. Look how well we are doing. And we are not taking any of it for granted, are we, especially not each other. Don't you see, darling?" And they clung together again, waiting for Brigit to calm down.

37. And From You No Secrets Are Hid

"Hola, los peregrinos." There they were, the three of them coming along the path "You did make good time!" said Bob: hugs, affection and greetings. They found a bank on the edge of a meadow with a view over the hills and settled down for lunch.

"Wine is good out of a tin cup when you are outside in Spain with friends," said Colin.

"So we want to hear all about your adventures. We've only been getting all this pestering from the police," said Mireille.

"Yes, it is amazing. One day out of our sight, and you are wanted by the police. And I don't want to dis the Spanish police," said Colin. "Here we are, guests in their fair land; but they haven't been able to find you, and they are taking this personally."

"What about Emilio? He was the one who told them about us." said Bob.

"Have no fear. He's on his way. He had to work late last night at the hotel."

So Bob and Brigit told the story. "From our point of view it's all straightforward. Obviously, the police don't think so.

But I do see there could be a stink about the school and the bus driver just leaving the kids in the village, unsupervised," said Brigit.

"That's the crunch. I think the different authorities are keen to blame anyone but themselves," surmised Charles-Michel.

"Well, we did miss you guys," said Brigit.

"Hang on. We didn't miss them that much," said Bob.

"Well what about Charles-Michel's history lessons?" said Brigit.

"Such a break not to have to deal with all those saints and sinners, kings, wars, pestilence, and famine. So, tell us about how you all fared since Triacastela?"

Mireille chimed in: "Compared to you, we were absolute dullsville. No burning houses, no drowning children. But we did do the walk to Samos, as true pilgrims. No car rides for us!"

"Did you get a stamp? Joseph insisted that we get one, I did feel a bit of a fraud as we had come by car," said Brigit.

"Oh, I think you guys earned it, and maybe you'll earn it even more by the time the police have finished with you," said Charles-Michel.

"Thanks for that," said Bob. "We did look in at the hostel at Samos and my conclusion to all this is, and I don't want to sound sexist but, the nuns have it together when it comes to Camino hospitality, and the monks like the general idea, but they don't care a fig about comfort."

They lazed in the sunshine, enjoying each other's company.

"We've got twelve kilometres to go. Better pack up. Great to be back with you two," said Colin. As they started out, a solitary person with a stick and hat came towards them.

"Emilio!" shouted Brigit. "You found us, and look you are all ready for the Camino." She gave him a hug.

"Of course I found you. Brigit and Bob need my help and it was time to see Charles-Michel, and Colin and Mireille; I have been missing everyone. Also, it was time for me to walk the Camino, only a short way, sadly. They all moved forward and the others carefully went ahead of Emilio and Charles-Michel. They strung out along the path, Colin and Bob in the lead and Mireille and Brigit together.

"How are you, Mireille? Any adventures for you?"

"Just the Camino. Glad you're back, as it was a bit strange with just the two guys, lovely as they are. But I can see you and Bob are so happy together. You said it was after you saved the little boy."

"It was being in danger like that. Bob just kept telling me he was not going to let me go and I just clung on saying 'yes, don't let me go.' Later, the grandfather took us to their house and looked after us. And Bob says, since then it is like being on a second honeymoon but staying in dormitories."

"Oh, that bit's no good."

"Not that bad. We stayed with the grandparents, and crafty Bob managed to get a pension room in Palas de Rei."

The albergue at Arca had two beds saved for them next to the others. Emilio said he would call the police. While Brigit was showering, Charles-Michel and Bob had time to talk.

"Bob, I can't say how happy I am to see you and Brigit back together."

"Thank you. Me too." Bob felt his throat catching. "She is such a darling. It took me this to realize what a jerk I had been about the money. You told me in León to take responsibility for that; you were right." He was silent for a moment. Charles-Michel just watched.

"I nearly lost her. I couldn't see anything in that water: her or the kid. It was so deep and fast. They were both pinned against the sluice gate. And then when we did get out — thank God, Brigit was managing, but this little kid was just limp, like a bundle of rags, not breathing, and his skin was grey. I started CPR." Bob closed his eyes, silent again. "We kept at it. We couldn't get him breathing. Then, at last, he choked. That was the most beautiful sound on earth."

"I had no idea it had been so dangerous. We saw those streams just racing along," said Charles-Michel.

"Yes, at the hospital the doctors showed us the injuries to his head."

"Bob, I don't want to put you through this again, but Emilio needs to hear this and maybe Colin too as a doctor. If they try and downplay what you have done, we want our facts straight." So Bob and Brigit told the whole story again. Colin looked serious. "Brigit, have you been checked out?"

"I'm fine. Just so happy we could save the lad. And you know it brought us back together, brought us to our senses!"

"I am so happy for you two. But Brigit, you did sustain acute physical and mental stress. Just be aware that it can catch up with you later."

The police meeting was for seven o'clock. Colin and Mireille were told to wait in the reception area. Emilio and Charles-Michel were emphatic; there would be no interview if they did not come in with Bob and Brigit. They were conducted to an interview room. Bob looked around. He had expected an office, but this was a bit harsh. However, the head of police was all charm, asked them about their Camino, was interested in Emilio's hotel and position on the rural council. He made sure he had their names and asked if he could see their passports and pilgrim credencials. His deputy took down details from their passports and the chief looked at the credencials.

"You have a stamp from Ribadiso, but you did not stay there."

"Yes, that is where we stayed last night."

"My office called. They said there were no Canadians. Why is that?"

"I don't know. We checked in at the front desk and got our stamps."

"Mr. and Mrs. Matthews, there are several things we do not understand about your time in Galicia. You seem to be, during this time—shall we say—hiding."

'Oh, here we go.' thought Bob. "Not at all. Let's look at our credencials and follow the route and places we stayed in Galicia." But the police chief was only interested in the Triacastela page.

"Samos. What happened there?" So Bob and Brigit carefully explained how they had visited Samos.

"And Portomarín, why did you not stay there?"

"We chose not to. We went on to Gonzar and stayed at the albergue there." Before the chief could ask, Bob said, "And at Palas de Rei, we stayed in a private room at a pension. As I have told you, the following night we were at Ribadiso."

The chief of police pursed his lips, smiled, and handed back the credencial book. "I see. You make that clear. But you did keep your cell phone closed at this time. Now let us talk about Pedro Valente. How do you know this family?"

"As you know, we saved Pedro. After he was taken to hospital and it calmed down, his grandparents invited us to stay at their house," explained Bob carefully.

"So you know this family," said the chief.

Bob looked at Charles-Michel and Emilio who were both looking grim and frustrated. Charles-Michel gently nodded his head as much as to say, "Keep your cool, we are here."

"Before my wife and I saved the child we did not know this family at all."

"But you saw the children in the village?"

"I think it would be helpful if I told you what happened that day when we came to that village," said Bob in a firm but calm voice. Once again Bob and Brigit told the story. But this time Bob made sure he added the details of the depth of the water, how muddy and dark it was, the speed of the current, and the steep banks. The Police chief cut him off: "Why did you stop in this village and why did senora Matthews walk away by herself?"

"I had to adjust my backpack. My pack was stolen in León. I had only got it back that morning and the straps had been changed.

"You did not tell me your bag had been stolen. Did you report that to the police?"

"Yes, most certainly. We reported to the police in León. It was the police who recovered it and contacted Sister Alicia at the Albergue Santa Maria to see if she could contact me, which she did."

"So where did you stop?"

"At a bench just before the bridge. We had walked there the day before when we were waiting for my pack."

The chief of police brought his head up and his shoulders back. "Oh hell," thought Bob. "What have I told him now? Too much. It's just the truth, but he's going to chew this up." Bob looked over at Charles-Michel.

"You were there the day before. Tell me about that."

They explained how they had walked there, sat on the bench, and walked back.

"Who did you meet in the village that day?"

"Nobody. It was very quiet. The only people besides ourselves were two other pilgrims on their way to Samos."

"But the school bus driver saw you that day," the chief said softly.

"There was no school bus. There were no children."

"I think you forget. The school bus driver saw you and when he came next day and saw you again, he understood you were from the village and would be there for the children."

"That is absolutely not the situation. We have told you the village was empty and there was certainly no school bus," said Bob.

"That is not how we understand things. When the children got off the bus, you, señora Matthews, went with them up the stream. The rest of you are free to leave but señora Matthews must stay while she answers the rest of my questions."

Everyone looked at Brigit in horror, and more horror as they now saw that she was pale and shivering.

"As you know, this is not the case at all. We will end the interview now. We will be contacting the embassy and get legal help," said Charles-Michel getting out his cell phone.

"You cannot use a cell phone here," the deputy told Charles-Michel. If the chief of police thought he was dealing with calm and polite Canadians, he was in for a shock. The room erupted.

"I have clear instructions to call the Canadian embassy."

Emilio was talking in very rapid Spanish to the chief.

Bob looked at Brigit who was now shivering quite violently.

"Brigit, what is it?"

"I don't know. I feel faint and sick."

"Emilio, get Colin." He would have gone himself but did not want to leave Brigit.

Emilio went to the door and shouted in the direction of the waiting room. Colin and Mireille both came running. Colin went straight to Brigit and knelt down by her chair and took her hands, talking to her gently. He turned to the chief and Emilio. "We need a blanket, quickly, and she needs a warm drink. Weak tea with sugar if possible. Quickly!"

He turned to Bob. "It's okay but she's in shock. Brigit, I think we should get you out of this room. The reception area is better. Could you manage that? We will help you."

"Yes, I can manage."

Someone brought a blanket and a policeman appeared with a mug with a tea bag and some sachets of sugar.

"Okay Brigit, you need the warmth and you need the sugar. It's a quick fix but you'll see it helps. Let me feel your pulse. How's your breathing?"

"But they want me to stay here for more questions and told the others to leave. They say the bus driver said I was looking after the children and that I took them for a walk along the stream. They just made it up and they want to arrest me. I'm really scared."

"Brigit, that's not going to happen. Did you hear the uproar? Charles-Michel phoning the embassy and I don't know what Emilio was telling them but this will end up in an enquiry the way he sounded. And Bob, can you imagine him letting you be kept here."

"But they are the police!"

"They may be, but they are just making it all up. It's disgusting!" said Mireille.

"Drink some of the tea, Brigit."

"It's too sweet."

"Supposed to be."

Bob joined them.

"Bob, I am so scared they're going to arrest me."

"No. Not over my dead body, but I it won't come to that," and he managed a smile. "Sorry not to be with you. I had to stay and talk to the embassy people. Thank you, Colin and Mireille. Charles-Michel is sorting out the details; basically someone will be here tomorrow and they are contacting a local lawyer."

"It was just awful. So much worse than I had expected."

"You are being brave. It was very nasty. He was all smooth and then he just came out with this whole fabricated story and then accused you."

"Those bullies. Imagine just picking on Brigit. It makes me sick!" said Mireille.

"Now where is Emilio? Let's hope he's not getting arrested," said Colin.

"As far as I can understand, which I am not sure I do, he was telling the chief what the people in the village had told him. You know they are all so grateful and are just furious with the school and bus people," said Charles-Michel. "I'll go and see."

He was gone a little while but when he and Emilio joined them, the chief came with them.

They agreed that when the lawyer was contacted, they would all meet again at the police station in Santiago. There was no more talk of detaining Brigit. There was no apology either.

"Let's get out of here." said Bob.

It was a quiet group that went back to the albergue. They all crowded on Brigit's and Mireille's bunks, and chatted and tried to make each other feel better as best they could.

"Heavens, are they sending someone down from the embassy?" asked Brigit.

"Coming to Santiago in June is rather pleasant," said Charles-Michel, downplaying what sounded rather serious. Then Bob's phone rang.

"Señor Matthews. Good evening. My name is Tabor Carrera-Ramos. I am an abogado, a lawyer, here in Santiago. Your embassy in Madrid has called me to help with a situation, for you and señora Matthews.

"Yes, thank you. Good to hear from you," said Bob.

"I am sorry to hear you have been having a difficult time. A misunderstanding with the police. It would be good if we could meet as soon as possible. You are in Arca for the night. Could we meet for breakfast? There is a restaurant close by: El Mirador. Nine o'clock? Does that work for you?"

"That's good. Thank you. Your name is señor Carrera-Ramos?"

"Please, Tabor."

"Fine, and I'm Bob. I'll see you tomorrow."

Bob stayed with Brigit, stretched out beside her, soothing her, and himself, but the bed was ridiculously narrow and eventually he had to climb up to his bunk.

38. Holy-Moly City

The next morning Brigit was brisk and emphatic. "This stupid business is not going to wreck our last day on the Camino and our walk into Santiago," she declared. But first we have breakfast with the lawyer. I know this delays you but I'm so glad we are all sticking together. Thank you."

"We didn't all join up again for Santiago to be split up by this ridiculous business," said Mireille.

Tabor was waiting for them at the restaurant and had arranged a table in a room off the main dining room.

'Oh my, he is rather charming,' thought Brigit as he graciously greeted the rather large group.

"Now, you must tell me of your adventure. May I call it that? What I would like to do first is for you to tell me about how you saved the child and other details I should know. Please tell me everything so I can be of most help."

Once again they told their story. 'The others must all be getting sick of hearing this. I know I am,' thought Brigit. But when it came to the details of the interview with the police chief, Charles-Michel and Emilio reminded them of points that she and Bob had missed. As he heard it all, Tabor looked more and more horrified.

"I see that is serious for the school. But to accuse you, who saved the child... it is a scandal."

He and Emilio went into Spanish—each getting more indignant than the other.

"This is what I would like to do," Tabor continued. "Mr. Brian Fraser is on the nine o'clock train from Madrid; he will be here a bit after two pm. I will meet him and talk about this. We will be lodging an official complaint with the police. You, dear pilgrims, must walk into Santiago. May I suggest you stay at the central albergue Seminario Menor? Can we then meet again at five pm? There is a lovely hotel next to the cathedral: Hostal de los Reyes Católicos. We will talk with Mr. Fraser and I will arrange to meet the chief of Police at seven. Does that make sense for you?" He shook hands with them all but held on to Brigit's hand. "Please, Brigit. I ask you to not worry today. This will all be well. It is horrible for you but by this evening it will be past. Promise me you will enjoy your arrival in Santiago and the cathedral."

"Okay, everyone" said Colin. "We don't have any extra time. Let's get going."

Emilio had some advice for them all: "There are many people who just come for the day to walk into Santiago, so don't get upset about this. It can be difficult when you have walked so far and through wild places, then here you are with people all excited because they have done a day on a bus to get here. So you must be tolerant: another Camino test for you."

The first part of the trail was through eucalyptus and pines. It was going to be a hot day, and the shade was pleasant.

"How did you sleep, Brigit?" Colin was with her.

"Not bad considering all this stupid drama. You know it pisses me off that they are doing their best to wreck the end of our Camino and for you all too, not just Bob and me. I tell myself that this is just another Camino lesson. It's amazing all the lessons and transformations I have been through on this walk. You remember how bitchy I was with Bob at the start—poor man?"

"Your Bob is just doing fine. We can see how happy he is to be with you. He's so proud of you."

"Bob is such a wonderful man. I am so lucky to have him as my husband and as the father of my children," and she smiled up at Colin.

"Gee, you guys are like an inspiration for married life. I would not have said that at the start of the Camino. I thought you would not even survive the path together and that would be your Camino lesson. But look at you both now."

"Thanks, Colin. We will go for counselling. I mean, it's a lot to deal with and we have both done some bad, bad stuff. And now we are under attack from strangers."

"That's all absolute rubbish. They have to take responsibility for their screw-up. You can't mess with kids like that."

"Colin, how are you feeling about your hostage situation at your hospital? Has the Camino has helped you?"

"Actually, I have come to feel proud of the way I behaved and handled the situation and myself. Yes, the Camino has shown me that. I hope you and Bob feel the same about saving that lad."

They passed an elaborate way-marker: a tall stone plinth with the word "Santiago" carved into a banner: a walking staff with the pilgrim's bag and a large scallop shell. People had placed little stones on the top.

"Is this the city limits?" asked Mireille.

"Not yet." said Emilio. "We have to climb Monte Gozo."

They were skirting around a tall wire fence along the end of an airport runway. They stopped at the village of Lavacolla and sat on a grass verge next to a large church.

"This was an important Camino stop in the day," said Charles-Michel. "Before heading into Santiago, the pilgrims were expected to wash themselves and their clothes in this little stream."

"All washing in this tiny stream. More misery for those poor pilgrims," said Colin.

"Emilio, what is Monte Gozo?" asked Mireille.

"It's the place where the pilgrims could get their first sight of the towers of the cathedral of Santiago de Compostela. Gozo means happy. Now it is rather different. Papa Juan-Pablo Two celebrated mass here for World Youth Day—and he called on all young Catholics and others, to make the pilgrimage. Since that time that it has become popular again. In the 1990s, the city decided to make it a place for music concerts and a hostel with eight-hundred beds. There are many critics of the project: to build everything, they had to flatten the top of the hill."

At Monte Gonzo they got their credencials stamped at the cafeteria. Brigit was glad to see that her pilgrims' passport only had three blank places left. She was anxious to get it filled up by the end of the trip and had been asking cafés as well as albergues in the last few days to stamp her book. She even insisted they go into a TV station they passed after Lavacolla, and success! The security person had a stamp and ink pad and there it was: "TV Galicia, Camino de Santiago." Emilio was amazed.

"Brigit, you are a pioneer. I have never seen that."

"That's our 'leave-no-stone-unturned-Brigit.' Drives the kids crazy!" joked Bob.

"I didn't come all this way not to have a nicely filled pilgrims' carnet."

"Thus speaks the school mistress."

Down the hill, and a short stairway, and they were in the city. Over a bridge, a bit more walking, and then, at last, they were among the elegant buildings of the old city.

"Albergue or cathedral first?" asked Bob.

"No question. The cathedral," said Colin.

Along the streets there were pilgrims everywhere. Around an ornate fountain a group was sitting on the steps, clapping and cheering the pilgrims as they arrived.

"Hallo there our friends!" It was Manfred and Leopold, the young men who had brought them their cell phone. "Welcome to Santiago and congratulations."

"And to you too," said Bob. "We didn't expect to see you."

"We are just back from Finisterre. We walked to the Atlantic coast and we have just got back."

They reached the cathedral. There they were, in the enormous open plaza, the Prazo Obradoiro with flags, banners, and crowds and a wonderful view of the west facade of the cathedral. It was massive: two tall towers and a smaller one and the building stretching each side along the front with colonnades and high windows. They joined the great crowd in the square and just took in the view and the excitement.

Brigit and Bob hugged each other. "We've made it, darling," said Bob.

"We have, we have. Well done us," said Brigit.

"Brigit, hallo." It was Ursula from the German student group.

"I just expect François to appear at any moment," said Bob. "But now we are here I think I could put up with him. We have to register with the Camino office to say we've arrived and get our last stamp. The Oficina is an important moment."

****

The Camino office was just around the corner from the Prazo. Their credencials were carefully inspected and approved. They each received their Compostela: a parchment-coloured certificate with a brown decorative edge and a medallion at the top of a pilgrim figure. They also got the stamp in the last square in their little books. Rather an unassuming one after all: a smudgy figure of a statue with an oval with "Oficina de la Peregrinación S.A.M.I. Catedral Santiago" and the date stamped at the bottom. But all the sweeter for its simplicity. They put their Compostelas away in the cardboard tubes kindly provided by the Oficina. The volunteer told them to make sure they attended noon mass at the cathedral next day as they would list the number of pilgrims who have arrived from each country.

"We have some serious visiting to do tomorrow," said Mireille

"Now the meeting at the hotel de los Reyes Católicos," said Emilio. "It is a Parador hotel; you know the ones Franco set up in beautiful buildings. This was an albergue built by Isabella and Ferdinand. Now you must pay many Euro to stay here."

Tabor and Brian Fraser were already at the hotel in a quiet area off the main bar. Tabor had prepared a report with their account of saving Pedro, which had been delivered to the Police station at noon. "Plenty of time for him to read it before our meeting."

'Tabor, not only charming, but he does not let the grass grow under his feet,' Brigit reflected.

Tabor continued. "It would have been good for you to review it, but time is important. I kept it straightforward for this first document."

The embassy had lodged an official protest on the nature of the questioning citing Emilio and Charles-Michel as witnesses. "This situation is really ridiculous," said Brian. "You are caught up in the local politics and rivalries. This will quite likely provoke questions beyond the regional level. The media are just getting wind of all this. Bound to get picked up by the national newspapers and networks. Too good a story for them to miss."

"This is so civilized," thought Brigit. "I could just stay here in this comfortable chair and have another glass of wine,"

"I am sorry, but it is time to go to the police," said Tabor.

Mireille and Colin were heading to the albergue. "Now the cavalry has arrived, you don't need us," said Colin giving Brigit a hug. He whispered in her ear: "You're going to be just fine. Chin up."

When they arrived at the police station, several reporters along with camera operators were waiting for them. They were just outside the police area, but as access was through a single gate, and they could not avoid them. A few questions came in Spanish and Tabor and Brian handled them. Now the attention turned to Bob and Brigit and the questions were in English; of course the assignment editors had made sure they sent out reporters who were fluent in English. "Señora Matthews, is it true you saved the child Pedro Valente from drowning?"

Brigit glanced at Brian who gave her a discreet nod. "My husband and I helped Pedro out of the water. He was playing and had fallen into an irrigation stream."

"Could he have got out by himself?"

"No. He was trapped under water."

The questions kept coming. "Why are you talking to the police here in Santiago? Why are they questioning you?"

"Thank you. That's all," said Brian.

Inside the police station there were terse good evenings and introductions for Brian. The chief was annoyed and held them totally responsible for the reporters being at his gates. "This was a bad thing to contact the media. You are just making your situation worse." However, Tabor, who obviously had had to deal with him before, and would in the future, calmed him down, and explained that they had nothing to do with the media. They were as put out by their presence as he was.

After that, things fizzled out. Bob and Brigit were ready for round two, but the police had got the report and were aware of the complaint that had been filed.

"I now understand better what you were trying to explain," the chief said.

"The bastard!" thought Brigit. "'Trying to explain'". "It would have helped if some listening had gone on."

"We will of course be consulting with our advisers and legal department and with the authorities in the Triacastela region, but at this time Señor and Señora Matthews are free to leave."

'And about time too,' thought Brigit but she felt her shoulders settle and as she moved her head, she was able to get rid of the crick in her neck. 'Such a pompous ass.'

Leaving the building, Brian said to Bob and Brigit: "How about letting Tabor and me deal with the media; they will want to know what happened with the police."

Further exchanges in Spanish with the reporters. After more questions, there was a pause and Tabor and Brian looked at each other and seemed to agree. Brian turned to Bob and Brigit. "They wish to know if you would like to give a message to the Valente family."

"Go for it, Brigit," said Bob.

"We send our very best wishes to the Valente family and our love to Pedro and hope he is feeling much better now. And we would like to thank the Valente family for their hospitality and kindness to us."

39. Santiago, My Heart

The evening sun slanted through the park as Emilio led them along a manicured path. "If you come on the Camino from Portugal, this is the way you arrive." They were walking back to the albergue.

"This is how to enter Santiago," said Bob as they stood overlooking the cathedral with the main west facade facing them.

"And when it is dark it is even more beautiful as there are the lights on the front of the cathedral," said Emilio. They sat on a bench and admired the view.

"I feel I have lived an eternity today," said Bob.

"I'm still getting used to the idea that we are free and I will not land up in a Spanish prison," said Brigit. Thank you so much, Charles-Michel and Emilio, for looking after us."

"I am embarrassed that this happened. This is not how I see my country."

"Emilio, don't feel bad." Brigit took his hand. "It could happen in Canada, or anywhere. The important thing is that it was put right. And your country is wonderful. People here are so welcoming and kind. We all come and tramp along the Camino, expecting to be looked after."

"Thank you, Brigit. I am so pleased I could help. I have made a reservation for dinner. It is now eight-thirty, and we need to be there in an hour."

They returned to the albergue to find that Wanda and Shirley had arrived and were happy to join them at dinner. "Really very late for us, but here we are in Santiago. We must do something special."

"Perfect that we meet up with you. And this is our friend Emilio," said Brigit.

"You are quite a hero," said Shirley. We have been hearing the story from Colin and Mireille. What a dreadful ordeal. So glad that is behind you!"

The restaurant was just outside the old city and, no surprise, one of the owners knew Emilio. Brigit felt a note of sadness: this was to be the last evening they would all be together. Colin was going to continue on to Finisterre to see the "end of the world" overlooking the Atlantic Ocean.

"I thought I would come to the mass with you at noon and then head out after that."

"Emilio and I will come to the cathedral, too. Then we can get a bus to Arca and collect the mini-van."

"I do not want to leave you, but I should be back at the hotel."

"Emilio, you have been more than a good friend," said Brigit. She heard her voice falter.

"Brigit, I will continue to be your friend. And when you come for your school programs, you will stay at the hotel as my friend. You can bring Bob too, if you wish."

351

'This man is so sweet,' she thought.

The chef came to the table carrying a large oval platter with a great big flat fish. He showed it to them with enthusiasm—they peered at it.

"Oh my, that is one ugly looking fish," said Bob.

The chef said something to Emilio and eventually, with help from Colin, they worked out that it was a John Dory.

"That's its name?" said Charles-Michel. "It sounds like a Canadien Voyageur in his canoe. Jean Doré, 'c'est l'aviron qui nous méne, qui nous méne'," he sang, and Brigit and Wanda joined in.

"You guys are après-Camino punch-drunk," said Colin. "Let's get back to the fish—John Dory are excellent."

The poor chef was looking a bit bemused by all this. There was the fish with a frill of spikes and quills around the edge and a big, flat eye peering up at them.

"This is special that we are offered this," explained Emilio. "This is a very large fish and we are a good group to eat it. He will cook it just for us." They all agreed on the fish.

"Mireille, what are your plans?" asked Bob.

"I'm meeting up with my friend who was volunteering at the albergue in Grañón. We are going to Bilbao to spend a few days. Then I will make my way to Paris to fly home."

"It's sad all over again," said Brigit. "Like when we said goodbye in Triacastela."

There was a general burst of laugher around the table.

"And look what happened then," said Charles-Michel. "We should deliver you home to your kids."

"Really, between you and the police, we are just the victims here," grumbled Bob.

While they relaxed waiting for their meal, Emilio told them some of the history of the city of Santiago. "It has always been a place of habitation—people settled in these hills and then of course came the Romans. In the ninth century, hermit Pelayo found the bones of Santiago. They built a church for them. Pilgrims came and a community grew here. During the Reconquista, Christians called on St. James for help, but with so much conflict, the Bishop became worried for the relics, so they were hidden. But pilgrims continued to come to Santiago. In the eighteen-hundreds, the French and British used this area as their battle ground in the Napoleonic Wars and much damage was done. Added to that, the monasteries lost their great power and much of their wealth, and the pilgrimage went into decline. Then Santiago's bones were rediscovered, the Pope recognized them and the church encouraged the pilgrimage. And now thousands come every year for so many reasons and here you are." Emilio smiled around the table.

The fish was delicious, as was the profusion of fresh vegetables and the red peppers stuffed with fragrant rice. They consumed quite a few bottles of wine. At one point Wanda was concerned about being locked out of the albergue for the night.

"Wanda, you are travelling with Emilio. All doors are opened for us. He may well have the key," said Colin.

"Well, I did mention we could be late," said Emilio with mock solemnity to more laughter.

As they lingered at the end of their meal, Bob stood and asked for their attention.

"This is our last night together, and all of you, at different times have been our companions along the way, for Brigit and me, together and apart. And I want to thank you all, for your loving support and patience. Sometimes I expect you were ready to tip us off the boat to get on with it. You all know that Brigit and I have been through a crisis. Though I expect it looked like it could be the end of the road for us, the Camino is not a road. It is The Way. This sacred path has given us the chance and the great gift to find ourselves again—keep the best, throw out the bad, and reinvent what we need to. We are still working on it all. But we are sincere and will be diligent. You lovely, worthy people have not only been our Camino companions and friends, but heavens above—therapists in your patient friendship. We give you our heartfelt thanks and gratitude."

It was a long, warm evening walk back to the albergue. They decided against a taxi. The walk was good after the meal. Brigit was walking with Charles-Michel.

"Can you come and visit us at the cottage later in the summer? It's not far when you visit your mother in Mont Laurier. Do bring her. We have room."

"That is a lovely invitation, and you make it all sound so easy, so maybe it will happen."

"You know, I do think it's great you are going to spend time with Emilio."

"Now, don't get carried away. These are very early days; we agree that we want to give ourselves some time to know each other better. I will have my own room. There has been no first kiss."

Brigit laughed, "Can you manage without your gang as chaperon?"

"Now don't mock me, Brigit. 'Once bitten twice shy' is one of my favourite English expressions."

"I'm not even going to worry. You know what you want and what suits you."

"But if we are to talk about you. I don't know if, in all this rubbish that has been going on, has anyone really said how brave you were to save that child?"

"I really was frightened last evening at the police station with el Jeff, the police boss, but not for long. I have felt protected all along. It seems to be all part of God's plan. And saving Pedro. Anyone in that situation would have tried to save a child."

"Don't downplay your actions, Brigit. You not only ventured, but you persisted and succeeded even though it was looking impossible and dangerous."

"It's what Bob and I had to go through for our reconciliation, and all this stuff with the police; it's just part of that. What we have been given is a great gift. We just had to deal with the Philistines."

At this point, Emilio caught up with them. "I have just been telling Charles-Michel how pleased I am that you are going to be spending time together."

"The first time I met him I invited him to dinner at my hotel, so it is about time, I think. You agree?"

"Oh, Charles-Michel knows when the time is right for him, and he had to finish his pilgrimage before he got fancy dinners at fancy hotels."

"Yes, he is wise and that is one of the things I love about him. And my hotel is very nice. But I don't know about this word 'fancy'. Brigit, I have not told you how happy I am that you and Bob are lovers again."

Brigit let out a low, sweet laugh. "Thank you, Emilio. That is it, exactly!"

****

They arrived at the cathedral and climbed up the ornate outer zigzag double steps. Brigit remembered what she had read about the Portico de Gloria, the masterpiece by Maestro Mateo from the twelfth century. And here she was. There were three great doors elaborately decorated with carved figures from the Old and New Testaments: the last Judgement, the redemption of Christian souls, the Kings, Apostles and Prophets, many angels, and musicians with instruments. On the main column of the central door was the Tree of Jesse—the tree of life. Here were the holes that had been worn in the marble by pilgrims over the centuries where they had placed their hands in gratitude. At the top of the column: Jesus, and beneath him, St. James, there to welcome them. Emilio led them around the back of the column to show them a carving of a kneeling pilgrim: Maestro Mateo himself. Inside, the building was vast: austere but ornate. They gazed at the columns that led their eyes to the high golden altar. Topping it all, St. James as the warrior and below that St. James again, seated and smiling, painted in vivid colours and gold. As Brigit took it all in, she was puzzled by the activity behind the seated Santiago.

"Come and meet the Saint," said Emilio, and he took them around the back of the high altar, up steps and to a walkway that led them behind the statue of the seated St. James. "You can embrace him. It is the pilgrim tradition." Emilio put his arms around St. James's neck and gave him a hug. 'So those were the hands around the statue, in gratitude and love, not giving him a dust!' Brigit realized. Down in the crypt, they saw the silver chest with the relics of Santiago and his two companions: Atanasio and Teodoro. It was sacred, but Brigit was more moved by the contact with the statue of St. James.

A crowd had gathered in the cathedral for the noon mass. A nun was up at a lectern giving them a rehearsal practice for the chants and responses for the mass: "Laudate omnes gentes, laudate Dominum": the Taizé chant. Brigit knew it, and the one before it. Not bad for an Anglican deep in Catholic Spain. They were seated in the central part where the transept and the nave meet. They could see hanging from the ceiling the famous Botafumeiro, the censer that was used for the incense. It was so large and heavy, it took a team of people to swing it above the crowd seated below. They would not see that as it was only used on a Sunday. One of its functions, apart from the incense carrying prayers to heaven, was to cover the smell of so many pilgrims. Now sitting waiting for the service, Brigit and Emilio were quietly talking.

"Emilio, it is so charming that pilgrims can touch the statue of Santiago."

"Yes, it is special. And it is not only pilgrims. For the people of Spain, there is such a love for Santiago, that in fact we call him Santi in affection. There used to be a crown on his head and people would put that on themselves. Then it was gone, so people put their own hats on Santi."

They all took communion. Colin turned out to be Anglican. "So you see Brigit, not such a lost soul after all."

"I never thought you were, but you do hide your church light under a bushel."

"It does not shine very bright, but it does please my Mum; when I'm home with my parents I go to church with them."

"Well, that's perfect. God works in many ways, as we know."

"That's what Father Estevan said in Rabanal," said Bob. "That it was comical that God used El Cid's horse and the chickens at Santo Domingo. I thought that was pretty funny."

358

Emilio was delighted: "He is such a gifted priest." And they realized that he was just up the road from Emilio's hotel and of course he would know him.

The reading of the list of pilgrims was a bit disappointing. It was all rather confusing where they were from and where they started. "But I am sure we were in there somewhere," said Mireille.

"I am loving this, but I must get going," said Colin.

"And me too," said Mireille. Emilio had helped her book her seat for the train to Bilbao.

"Oh my God, it's so sad to leave you all. But Brigit and Bob, I will come up to Ottawa for a visit," Mireille promised.

40. So Many Paths Along the Way

So it was just Emilio and Charles-Michel with Bob and Brigit, but not for long.

"It's a three-hour drive to the hotel from Arca," Charles-Michel explained. "So we should be home by late afternoon."

Brigit smiled to herself, despite him saying that being with Emilio was no big deal, Charles-Michel seemed to be settling in very well to the idea of his time at the hotel. At an outdoor café opposite the Parque Susana, they ordered a bottle of the clear white Ribeiro wine. That came with olives and slices of tortilla. They relaxed in the sun. Charles-Michel had brought a newspaper, and the three of them competed to translate as they read along. Emilio looked on and was rather pleased when they got stuck and needed to call on his help. It was a lovely afternoon with dear friends.

However, soon enough, Charles-Michel and Emilio had to leave. Brigit did not even try to stop the tears from streaming down her cheeks.

"They have been such dear sweet friends with all that has happened." Bob put his arm around her shoulder as they watched them walk away.

"Okay, darling. Let's plan. What shall we do? Here we are, no path to follow, no one else to please," said Bob.

"You were such an angel agreeing to come along on this trip. I think you should be rewarded with a trip to Bilbao and the Guggenheim," said Brigit.

"Yes. At last! We will enjoy that. Some modern architecture will get us back to this century. And as I suspect you don't want to walk there, we need to rent a car."

"There was that travel agent at the Camino office. And we must book a flight back for Paris."

"That probably means we won't have time to leave today," said Bob. "And I don't think we ought to drive after this wine. We are allowed to stay another night at the albergue, but I'm thinking hotel. Emilio pointed one out to me. Let's try there. But we've got to fetch our packs."

Another walk past the cathedral and to the albergue. Yesterday's people were back on duty now, and they asked how it had all gone with the police and seemed glad that all was well.

"Though it would be a lot more exciting for them if it had gone badly for us," said Brigit.

"Really Brigit, what happened to gratitude and grace?"

"Oh you are turning out so much more virtuous than me. In fact, you are becoming quite preachy."

"You think so, eh? Well who dragged me on the Camino? And I am getting the hang of it, chatting with monks and priests along the way?"

"I know. I'm a bit jealous of all your encounters and clerical conversations."

"Someone told me it was all there for the taking if I just looked. Now who could have said that?"

"You bastard," she said giving him a slap across his backpack.

The hotel was narrow and European: an architecturally sympathetic restoration of an old building. "Oh is that what they call it?" said Bob to Brigit's comment. The room too was slender, with lovely pale woodwork.

"Glad we only have our packs—there's no room here for suitcases."

Brigit took off her boots and stretched out on the bed. Bob decided his pack could just stay on the floor. His boots came off and he jumped onto the bed with Brigit. "Come here, woman."

****

"You know, Bridgy. I really like this daylight loving."

"I know, darling. So do I. It wouldn't be so urgent if we had a normal life. It's all delayed anticipation and titillation when we have a room to ourselves. How many nights was it in the albergues with the Camino troops?"

"Hmm, Ribadiso, Arca, and last night."

"Only three nights. Are you sure?"

"Yes, so who's lecturing about urgency now? Don't get too cozy. We should call the kids."

362

"Would it be awful if you did that without me? Those eight hundred klicks are catching up with me and it is exhausting being on the police's most-wanted list. This bed is so comfy. Tell them I love them."

****

Bob is in a bar, underground. The long zinc counter is lined with men: workers in their dusty dirty overalls and big boots, covered in white cement powder. The television is on, Spanish blaring, the bull-fighting channel. But the men are not looking at the TV. They are all looking to the end of the bar where Brigit is sitting. Sitting there, just gazing into the middle distance, pretending she doesn't know that all these men are looking at her, not just looking, but with lewd gazes and bawdy asides. Why did she just sit there and let them gloat? He could feel his anger mounting, he wanted to shout out to her but his voice was stuck. He wanted to go and grab her, hurt her, but he could not move; she just kept sitting there, smirking.

****

He woke up, sharply, full of burning anger. Which hostel? No it was a bed and with Brigit. Dark. Where? The hotel, Brigit is snoring. He pushes against her.

"Hmm, what is it?" she grunted.

"You're snoring. Are you awake?"

"Well now, sort of. What is it?"

"I had this awful dream. About you. Brigit. I was so furious. I could have been violent. I could have hurt you."

"What's this? That's nonsense. It was a dream."

"Oh Brigit, I'm so sorry. How can you forgive me?"

"Bob, now stop it. It was not you. It was a nightmare. You did nothing wrong."

But Bob could feel the dream, so real and overwhelming. "Brigit, what are we going to do? Will you ever trust me? And I lost all our money."

"Listen, we know we still have much to work out. I am so sorry. I am the one who has put you in this state: my stupid, stupid hurtful fault. Forgive me."

And they clung together and cried and eventually slept some more.

****

Brigit saw herself back at the river bank after saving Pedro, except this time it was bleak. The pain of the sin was still there, but not the ecstasy of finding each other again. It was the reality check. Gone were their friends, the police drama, even Tabor and Brian; it was just them now. They had done so well. What was this new despair? "Please, show us mercy," she prayed through her pain and sadness.

364

****

The noise of the city traffic through the open window woke them up.

"It's like I have a mighty hangover," said Bob. "It's not the wine, not like this. I feel miserable and exhausted. I want to make things better but don't know what to do."

Brigit took things in hand: "We are going to go out and get breakfast."

They found coffee, croissants, and some fruit.

"Bob, I've been thinking. When I was in Burgos, I saw a poster for Guernica. How about we go there? It's not far from Bilbao."

"You mean the place?"

"Yes, the town, the town of the painting. The painting's back in Spain now, in Madrid. You remember how we saw it when it was in New York at MoMa?"

"Of course, I do. I would never forget that time with you Brigit."

"Exactly, and I would like to go and see the town where it all happened - the bombing."

"It's sad and brutal. Are we up to that?" asked Bob.

"Yes, we can manage it darling We are woven into a dark side of our own. In fact I see now that this is so timely. I would say brilliant like the Brits say, except that it's dark and not bright. Robertson Davies says. 'One always learns one's mystery at the price of one's innocence.'"

"What do you think that means?"

"Well, for me it means that we need to explore and develop the whole aspect of our being, and that means going into our dark, sort of subterranean primal side. And that it is all part of us, and we need to understand it, and integrate it."

"Amen. That is quite a thesis. I see what you mean. We can either just get caught up in our bad stuff and get buffeted around or we can embrace it, see where it takes us, and what we can learn about ourselves and our potential—in the big picture."

"Yes, the great human and universal project," said Brigit. "And we've managed to put ourselves in the front row of our drama at this time. So we have to go from the innocence to the mystery."

Bob looked at her. "Well, it is brilliant, darling. It is a good idea to go to Guernica. I do love you so much. Here you are being brave and practical and spiritual. I don't deserve it."

"Bob, enough of that now. No more feeling guilty talk!"

The phone rang. It was Charles-Michel.

"Hi guys. You're on the news. We heard it this morning and its running all the time on TV. Clips of you both." They caught up on the news of the drive and the hotel—so good to get some decent sleep. "I envy you going to Guernica. Good trip back. We'll be in touch."

"Shall we get going?" said Bob. "I know we've not seen all we should in Santiago, but I think I've about had it for here. Let's pick up the car. We can follow the coast line. Lots to see and fish to eat."

366

Chapter 40

"Yes, time to go," said Brigit. "We have been hanging around here long enough. Let's go for it!"

EPILOGUE

Let Us Keep the Feast

As the train from Madrid train pulled into León, Bob knew that it would be a happier experience this time. It was not even a year since he and Brigit had been here for the Camino and the misadventure with his pack. On this return journey, their son Paul and his fiancée, Divya were with them. Out of the train and on the platform and there were Charles-Michel and Emilio to meet them.

"Emilio, I am so happy to see you," said Brigit as they hugged. Everyone climbed into the hotel minibus. "What would we do without it? We always seem to be a crowd," said Brigit.

"Paul and Divya, you are going to walk the Camino," said Charles-Michel looking back at them from the front seat.

"Yes, we will set out after the ceremony. We only have two and a half weeks, so it will be Camino Light for us. But we're totally inspired by Mum and Dad so we will come back and do the rest one day, I'm sure."

"Please have a bit less of an adventure than your parents. They should do another Camino without all the drama"

Charles-Michel had already been there a week and had helped with some of the preparations: checking names and some background details.

"Is this going to be a formal event?" Bob asked. "Beyond the invitation and the plane tickets, we don't know a great deal about what's happening."

"There will be a ceremony and then people want to meet you: the Valente family of course. And Tabor and his wife are coming for the day. And we have set up a couple of media things too. One with national television in the village. I have arranged all that for the day after tomorrow, to give you a day to get over the trip."

"You didn't mention the police," said Brigit.

"No. But they will send a representative to the ceremony," said Emilio. "They wanted to hold it all in Santiago, but we said no. For so many reasons, including that it may not have the best memories for you. It needs to be around Triacastela. It's a local event. The village would be too small and not practical, so it's going to be in Sarria. Shall we stop and let Paul and Divya see a bit of the city? The cathedral square, and the market." Emilio found a parking spot.

Pardon My Camino

"And for bravery and courage, we have the honour to present Brigit and Robert Matthews with the Spanish Award of Chivalry." The local band struck up while the governor of Galicia hung medals on blue ribbons around Bob and Brigit's necks. There were more speeches and applause. Pedro presented Brigit with flowers. Later in the town hall there was a reception. Local wines and cheeses and other delicacies. Bob and Brigit were surrounded — The Valente family of course, the doctors and nurses from the hospital, the local volunteers from the Triacastela albergue and from Barbadelo, Manuela, who had kindly let them make coffee at the albergue, even Eva from the pension in Palas de Rei and her sister Clara from the café. They were introduced to many officials. Emilio stood with them explaining who they all were and how they fit in. Brigit and Bob were amazed that all these people had remembered them and had come to meet them.

"This has been news for months now. And then the idea began that you should be recognized for your bravery and also to make amends for the way you were treated. You have truly become local heroes. So when they were organizing the event, people wanted to come: all those you had touched. And I did help, put pressure on the officials to make sure all these people could be invited. I knew you would wish for that and it is important."

"Thank you, Emilio. That is exactly how we would like it. So lovely and touching to see them all."

****

Later back at the hotel, they sat around the fireplace; it was a chilly spring evening up on the plateau.

"I feel this has renewed a wonderful dimension for the Camino with local people," Charles-Michel said as he put a log on the fire. "Of course it has always been important, but they can get tired of so many people traipsing through, and some pilgrims are not respectful of private property, not closing field gates and littering. But your story connects people back to the pilgrims as people."

"We keep hearing stories of how the locals reach out and help pilgrims — inviting them out of the rain, in for a cup of coffee, making sure they are on the right path and safe," said Paul.

"And giving you the Camino wishes and asking you to pray for them to the saint when we get to Santiago," said Brigit.

Paul and Divya went to bed. They were leaving early for their start the next morning. Charles-Michel would drive them to Astorga. Bob was going too as he wanted to rent a car so they could go and visit the Valentes. Brigit had appointments with schools to further her school twinning project.

"Well, my friends, this has really been an odyssey for your two, and somewhat for me too," said Charles-Michel. Emilio was looking after the last of the dining guests, so it was just the three of them in Emilio's private sitting room. "How are you doing as a couple? You know I feel I can ask this as I was such a witness and confidant."

"Yes, you were. We are so lucky to have you, and poor you, you did land in the middle of our chaos," said Bob. "Can you image we were friends at university? We barely had contact for thirty years, and then you are called upon as a friend like never before. We are doing well. Our true hope is to learn together through this and we have—we are. We sometimes feel like neurotic celebrity types or something; we each have a psychologist and we share a marriage counsellor. It is hard work and can be tough. However, we think they are ready to graduate us soon."

"You are both great. There are not many couples who could come through all that and be the stronger for it. You are quite an inspiration."

"Charles-Michel, are you saying there is coupledom in your life now?" Brigit inquired.

"Yes. I can say that Emilio and I are looking seriously at that eventuality. He came and stayed with me for a while this past winter."

"Charles-Michel, you never told us. We could have got together," said Brigit.

"We kept it all very low-key. It was February, so winter. I was working most of the time. But we did have Carnival in Quebec, and we went to visit my mother."

"Mont Laurier in the winter. Beautiful," said Bob.

"Yes, and on the way back we stayed over in Montreal. But he loved it all and Mum loved him. Emilio charmed her and her friends. I just took a back seat. And he enjoyed Mont Laurier, said the community reminded him of this village."

"That's perfect!" said Brigit. "How are you going to organize in the future?"

"Until either of us retires, we will just manage: me visiting a couple of times when he can't get away and then he closes the hotel in the deep winter and he will come to me. We'll see how that works. After retirement, we will see again. I enjoy helping around the hotel. I am training at the bar. It's really great for my Spanish. You know how people like to chat over a drink."

"Are you getting married?"

"Really, Brigit!" protested Bob. Charles-Michel smiled at Bob.

"We are looking at that. It does make certain things easier in the long run if we are just being pragmatic — health care, residency. Not automatically. You have to show it is not a marriage of convenience, but we have time."

"And there is the romance and the beauty of the commitment when you truly love each other and want to spend the rest of your lives together."

"Now don't get carried away, Brigit. But I do like your sentiment." Emilio came in at that point and Brigit and Charles-Michel caught him up on their conversation.

"I knew Brigit would approve of our plans. She is not only a romantic but practical too, dear Brigit."

"Emilio, have you thought where you would get married? Spain or Quebec?"

"I think as we have Charles-Michel's mother, maybe in Mont Laurier. What do you think, Brigit?"

"That could be so good. We could do a party at the lake. It would be wonderful."

"Okay, you two, this is getting out of hand," said Charles-Michel. And he looked at Emilio, and Brigit could see the love in his eyes.

"Yes!" she thought. "If he had not had to nurse us along through our misery and dysfunction, who knows? He might have never met Emilio."

Disclaimer

Pardon my Camino is a work of fiction. While most of the places along the Camino de Santiago in the book are real, some details and places have been imagined to serve the story and are used fictitiously. All characters and conversations are drawn from the author's imagination. Though some of the incidents have been inspired by events experienced by the author on her travels along the Camino, they only served as an inspiration. All the other events and incidents are fiction and drawn from the author's imagination.

About Julia

After a career in broadcast production, Julia retired and made plans to walk the Camino. It took her three visits to northern Spain before she made it to her destination, the city of Santiago de Compostela. Undaunted, Julia kept plodding along, and as a romantic and a bit of a Pollyanna, she had thoughts such as, "What if this or that happened?" and with the magic of the trail, a story emerged.

Here it is!

Julia lives in Edmonton, Canada and is blessed with a husband, kids and grandchildren.

And Many Thanks To...

My walking companions along the trail: from St-Jean-Pied-de-Port to Logrono: Krysia Jarmicka. Logrono to Castrojeriz: Claire Day. For the rest of the Camino, I set out alone but met Jessica Brown who became a supportive and fun fellow-pilgrim. For encouraging me with the writing and for their reading, suggestions and corrections: Lois and Rudy Copper, Krysia Jarmicka, Sophia Stauffer, Ray Rideout, Anthea Sargeaunt & Catherine Samson. For his ongoing and persistent encouragement as an author and a pilgrim: Ronald Tremblay.

My two main references books: *A pilgrim's Guide to the Camino de Santiago* by John Brierley and for historical content (the book Charles-Michel carried with him): *The Pilgrimage road to Santiago – the complete cultural handbook* by David M. Gitlitz and Linda Kay Davidson.

For their online advice on publishing, first, Arthur Slade who pointed me in the direction of the amazing and generous online resources of David Gaughran. Thanks to Kimmy Beach for her editing and to Lorna Stuber for formatting and advice.

Gratitude to my family for encouragement and lack of nagging about how this project was dragging out and for their patient digital help.

And for all those who kept asking and assuring me that I should and really could write this book, such as Denis Collette: "Alors Julia, ce livre? Quand est-ce qu'on va pouvoir le lire?"

Thank you for reading my book.

Please visit my website and blog and sign up for my newsletter:

Juliawriting.ca

or

Juliasargeaunt.ca

Quote Credits

Chapter 36. *Ultreia. 'Chant des pèlerins de Compostelle'*. Written by J.C. Benazet.

Chapter 6, 22 and 27: *Don Quixote* by Miguel de Cervantes. Translation by John Ormsby (1829-1895)

0300 1210175

Printed in Great Britain
by Amazon